I0451915

LA MISERIA di BIANCO

a paranormal thriller by

Stephen Woods

MUDDY BOOTS PRESS

This is a work of fiction. Names, characters, places and incidents are the product of the author's imagination or are used fictitiously. Any resemblance to actual events, locales, or persons, living or dead, is purely coincidental.

La Miseria di Bianco

Copyright © 2015 by Stephen Woods
All rights reserved. Published by Muddy Boots Press.
www.MuddyBootsPress.com
Edited by Karmin Dahl
Cover art designed by Nicole Anderson
www.anobrainart.com

This book is protected under the copyright laws of the United States of America. Any reproduction or other unauthorized use of the material or artwork herein is prohibited without the express written permission of the author.

Available from Muddy Boots Press

La Miseria di Bianco by Stephen Woods

A Path of Ashes, **Book 1** by Brian Parker

Origins of the Outbreak by Brian Parker

The Collective Protocol by Brian Parker

Battle Damage Assessment by Brian Parker

Upcoming Novels from Muddy Boots Press

A Cursed Earth by Stephen Woods

Fireside, **Path of Ashes Book 2** by Brian Parker

Dark Embers, **Path of Ashes Book 3** by Brian Parker

ONE

Let me set the stage for you, I'm dead. This wouldn't normally concern me, but it's the fourth time this week. This time, it's particularly gruesome with four jagged slashes running from my left shoulder diagonally down to my right hip. Loops of intestines protrude, pink and glistening, where the incisions penetrated the muscle wall of my abdomen. My right arm rests between my legs where one of the coroner's assistants placed it when they loaded me into the body bag. Tattered flesh and bits of tissue are all that remain at the joint where it used to be attached. I'm fairly certain my neck's broken, and the white vinyl bag I'm lying in holds a soup of blood and body fluids that slosh and squish around me from the movement of the gurney. And the wonderful thing about all this—I'm totally aware.

Being immortal is not always the blast you'd expect.

Alonso Jones, the night shift attendant at the Fulton County Medical Examiner's Office, whistles a tune as he wheels me down the ramp to the receiving room. One of the gurney's wheels squeaks annoyingly in time to Alonso's whistling. If I could speak, I'd beg him to shut up. I'm trying to think and the whistle-squeak rhythm is distracting. I'm trying to figure out how I came to be in this predicament and what I can do about it.

I know how I was killed, slashed with razor-sharp claws then flung through a fourth floor window by my arm to land on the sidewalk. Hence the broken neck and incredible amount of goo that leaked from various points on my body. I know what killed me. A demon, one more powerful than anything I've ever encountered before. I just can't figure out why. Sure, it was pissed because I tried to kill it, but that doesn't explain why it was there to begin with.

I'm jolted from my thoughts by the impact of the gurney with the double swinging doors that lead from the ramp to the receiving room.

Alonso parks my gurney by the wall and finally stops

whistling. "Here we are," he says.

The slop in my bag finally stills its back and forth rippling and settles down to baste my backside. I listen to Alonso's sneakers squeak on the tile floor as he walks away, then the screech of the tortured chair as he sits at his desk. Alonso is a big man, almost four hundred pounds, and anything that has to support his bulk qualifies as being tortured. He immediately begins to whistle the same tune. I've heard it before, but can't put a name to it. Healing was going to take time and me being stressed about it won't speed anything up. So I relax, concentrate on the melody, and drift back to the beginning.

*****

I was born in 1827 in the Austrian Kingdom of Illyria, now north eastern Italy. Christened at birth as Antonio Bianco, I go by the Americanized version now of Anthony or Tony White. I grew up outside the village of Repen near Trieste and am the youngest of three sons in a family that eked out their survival by farming the steep, rocky hillsides around our home. A stone and mortar hut with a thatched roof, a few goats and sheep, and what we coaxed to grow from the tough dirt was the sum of the Bianco family fortune.

My father, mother, brothers, and younger sister all seemed satisfied with their lives. The thatch roof overhead and a full belly was the measure of a good life to them. Never mind the back breaking labor necessary to keep the roof above and their bellies full. I remember my father when he was in his forties and he looked seventy. All my memories of my mother are of a bent and wrinkled old woman and she was younger than my father. I decided at an early age I didn't want to be a farmer. The very mention of wanting to leave home would drive my father into a blind rage. After enduring countless beatings for simply stating my opinion about a different life, I finally ran away at the age of fifteen.

Trieste is a port city and that was my first destination. If I intended to see the world and all it held, I couldn't think of a better way than by ship. Even though I'd grown up a day's walk from the sea, I had never seen it, but its scent had tempted me year after year, blowing across my family's land. Before he died, my grandfather, who had been born near Venice, told me stories of the blue Adriatic and I dreamed of its beauty using the salty smell I longed for to guide my thoughts.

I fairly flew through the winding streets of the old city down to the harbor where dozens of twin mast coastal cargo ships lined the wharves. Men and animal carts moved everywhere. Cranes worked loading and unloading cargo. The shouts of fish mongers advertising their catches competed with the bleating of goats and the whole place smelled of fish and horse manure. But the water, the water I had so dreamed of seeing was finally before my eyes.

It's hard to describe the disappointment I felt. Not the brilliant blue of my grandfather's stories, but a muddy gray with debris from years of commerce and garbage from the fish stalls floated in the harbor. I stood on the edge of the dock, staring in stunned silence, ashamed and scared of the choice I had made to run away from the only home I knew.

*****

The sound of a zipper being pulled brought me back to the present. As I look up, black hands pull the sides of the body bag open and a large face peers down at me.

Alonso smiles and exclaims, "Yo, Tony! You gonna stay dead all night?"

I still couldn't speak, but my eyes worked so I shifted them to the right. Because of my broken neck, my head had lolled over onto my left shoulder and I need help getting it straightened back up. I kept repeating the movement with my eyes. I look straight into Alonso's eyes and then shift them to the right.

After what feels like ten minutes, he finally catches on and says, "Oh, your head. Got it."

Alonso moves to the top of the gurney and grips both sides of my face in his ham-sized hands. He wrenches my head roughly into an approximation of straight. It's all I need. I immediately feel the healing begin. I hear the grinding of the broken bones as my muscles pull things back into place and that itchy sensation as nerves once again transmit signals. The dull ache as my vertebra fuse back together is something I should be used to, but it is still irritating. It isn't long before the ability to speak returns and I ask Alonso to help me sit up, which he does by grabbing my shoulders and hoisting me upright. The sides of the bag splay open and a good portion of the liquid I'd been soaking in spills out onto the floor and my detached right arm flops out and lands with a splash right in the middle of the puddle.

Alonso jumps back to keep from getting it on his shoes. Looking down with a sour expression he says, "You're cleaning that shit up."

As I swing my legs over the side of the gurney into a more comfortable sitting I position, I mutter, "My arm?"

"Yeah, don't worry I'll get it," Alonso replies sarcastically.

"You left me in that bag for what felt like hours, then, when you finally do check on me, you try to finish tearing off my head! The least you can do is hand me my arm." He doesn't reply, he just steps as close to the puddle as he can without getting anything on his new Pumas and bends over, gingerly plucking my arm from the goo. He holds it out like he is holding a snake and I snatch it away from him. As I try to fit it back into its place on my shoulder, I say, "Thanks."

"Don't mention it," he replies, then watches as I struggle to get the arm lined up properly with the socket. I know instantly when I get it right. I let go of my arm and it stays in place as the healing spurs to life. Once I am sure the arm isn't going to fall off, I look up at my friend and he gazes back at me with a disapproving look.

"Dude, you are funky."

"Thanks," I repeat. "Can you help me up?"

"Nope." When I scowl he continues, "These shoes cost me over a hundred bucks and I'm not getting your juice on them."

I can understand his point, so instead of arguing, I slowly slide off the gurney until my feet connect with the floor then pull myself upright. As I straighten, a knot of intestines pops out of one of the not-quite-healed holes in my abdomen. I grab it and push it back in, keeping my hand over it so it doesn't happen again.

"That's just nasty," Alonso says with a shake of his head and a curl of his lip.

"Instead of standing there, can you go get me some clean clothes?" I don't wait for a reply and start toward the emergency shower located in the corner of the receiving room. I don't bother to undress, instead I pull the lever as soon as I step in and let the water wash over me.

I hear Alonso call from behind me, "You left a trail. That's fucking gross, Tony, seriously man."

I don't acknowledge his comment and simply say, "Clothes, Alonso," then go back to showering the piss and blood away. I ignore Alonso's continued bitching about the mess and let the steamy water wash over me. As the water loosens the grime, I start to peel my old clothes off until I finally stand naked under the spray. The healing is almost complete and, as has happened countless times in the past, no sign of the recent injuries remains. My skin is as perfect and clear as the day I became Immortal.

As the hot water runs over my body, I lean against the wall of the shower and think once again about my current problem. I don't normally take jobs to help other people. It's not that I don't like people. I think they're okay, if a little naive. The simple fact is a person in my particular situation can't afford relationships. You draw attention and there have to be explanations. I like to stay below the radar, but this job was different. I was trying to help somebody and the job had been nothing but trouble since I took it. Like all the other times I've been in trouble, this one started with red hair, green eyes, and a great body.

*****

I rented a small, two room furnished apartment on the lower west side of Atlanta called The Magnolia House. It's designed to look like an old southern plantation, but it was actually built in the fifties and has seen better days. The landlady is a woman named Mrs. Betty, who is in her seventies and smokes like a steam engine. Betty doesn't tolerate any shenanigans from her renters or their guests and keeps the place clean and quiet. But the best thing about Betty is I pay my rent on time and she leaves me alone.

Around the corner on Sycamore Street was my favorite coffee shop, The Cup and Bean. I went in every morning for a cappuccino and a pastry, I'm still Italian after all, and that's where my current problem started. It was about two weeks ago on a typical Atlanta summer day, hot and humid. I was leaving The Cup and Bean around ten in the morning and had my sunglasses propped on top of my head with a to-go cup in one hand. As I stepped out the door, the transition from the dimly lighted interior to the bright sunlight outside temporarily blinded me. I stopped squarely in front of another person and we collided. I heard a soft female grunt and the contents of the bag she was carrying spilled onto the concrete. Still half-blind, I apologized for being so clumsy and bent over to pick up the items she'd dropped. I failed to notice that she'd already bent over and I smashed my nose into the back of her skull.

The pain in my nose was sharp and immediate and I swore as I stood back up. The woman rubbed the back of her head, wincing, the spilled items momentarily forgotten. When I finally looked at her through my watering eyes, her beauty staggered me. Her coppery red hair was pinned up in a style I'd not seen since the forties. Brilliant green eyes set in a gorgeous face with flawless pale skin that was accentuated by bright red lipstick made it almost impossible for me to look away. The snug fitting, cream-colored blouse emphasized her ample bosom and led down to a trim waist. The gray pencil skirt flared over her full hips and tapered to an end just below her knees where smoky stockings clung to shapely calves. Her feet were encased in black patent leather pumps with stiletto heels. The effect was stunning and left me speechless. One word kept repeating in my clouded mind: Goddess.

I'm not a bad looking guy and women have always found me attractive, at least that's what I'm told. I was twenty-two years old on that day in 1849 when I was transformed and I haven't changed a bit in the one hundred and sixty-four years since. I'm still trim and fit, a little taller than average during the time of my birth, but average now at five feet, nine inches with dark wavy hair. I am and will always be just as I was on the day I became immortal. I love women and, since learning the facts of life, have spent a great deal of time jumping in and out of their beds. This has probably led to the many problems I've encountered over the years from my liaisons. No, not probably, it has, I should just admit that straight up.

Still stunned, I tried to find my voice but she spoke first, "I'm so sorry, I didn't see you."

"No problem. My fault," I said, my voice muffled by the hand pinching my nose.

"Are you bleeding?" Before I could respond she continued, "No? Well good, no worse for wear then. Can you help me with my things?"

"Sure," I mumbled and bent to collect the scattered contents of her bag. Turpentine, black candles, and two clear plastic bags that held what looked like herbs. An alarm bell rang once in my foggy brain, but was immediately ignored and forgotten. I straightened and placed the items in the canvas shopping bag she held open for me.

"Thank you," she said smiling sweetly.

Then with no further delay, she stepped around me and continued down the sidewalk. I stood and watched admiringly as she walked away. She had taken maybe fifteen steps when she paused, half-turned and looked over her left shoulder. Seeing that I still stood watching her, she smiled, turned back, and quickly disappeared around the corner leaving me bewildered in front of the coffee shop.

I shook my head to gather my thoughts and walked back toward my apartment, conveniently in the same direction the woman had gone. When I turned the corner onto my street, I was surprised to find she was no longer visible anywhere. I paused and scanned the area for any sign of her and found nothing. I shrugged and continued on my way. She must have had a car parked along the street to have disappeared so fast. No matter, just a random meeting. As I reached the steps leading up to the front of Magnolia House, I smiled recalling her image to mind.

"You'll never see her again," I muttered out loud as I started up the steps. Sometimes, it's amazing how wrong I can be.

*****

Alonso's voice brings me out of my reverie. "Your clothes and a towel are on the back of the chair. I don't know what you're going to do about shoes."

"What? You're not going to give me your Pumas?" The look on his face is priceless and I bark a laugh. "Relax, Alonso, these will work for now. I'll wear them till I can get back to my apartment," I state while picking up my favorite hiking shoes and pouring bloody water out of them.

As I step out of the shower and reached for the towel, he asks, "What are you going to do?"

"Think I'll catch a cab back to my apartment and then I'm going to drink a whole bottle of tequila." I prefer Patron, Anejo, but right now anything will do.

"That's not what I meant."

I hesitate for a second as I finish toweling off then answer, "I know."

Alonso and I have been friends for as long as I've lived in Atlanta. I moved here two years ago and landed in the morgue almost immediately. I'd followed a vampire here from Nashville and was determined to kill him quickly and get back. Overconfident, I let him get the upper hand and instead he killed me. That night, when I woke up in the morgue healed, I'd nearly given Alonso a heart attack. After he calmed down, he started asking questions and I realized he was an extremely intelligent man. He figured out pretty quick I was different and I decided he might be helpful to me so I came clean and told him the truth.

He took it better than I expected and we've been friends ever since. He's helped on more than one cleansing by following my targets and reporting on the occasional oddity that came into the morgue. I hadn't brought him in on this case, but I'd confided to him that I wasn't comfortable with the situation. Which of course he was kind enough to remind me of now.

"This is the fourth time you've come in here this week. Each time is worse than the last. Maybe you need to take a vacation, get out of town for a while," he says, real concern showing on his face.

As I finish getting dressed, the sopping shoes last, I nod and answer, "I'll think about it." I look over at the mess I'd made around the gurney and Alonso knows what I'm thinking.

"Don't worry 'bout that shit. I'll take care of it."

I thank him and pat him on the back as I start up the ramp to street level. I have to walk a couple of blocks before I can catch a cab, then it takes around thirty minutes to get back to my apartment. I pay the driver and go straight up the steps to my little flat, grab a bottle of Patron off the kitchen counter and fall onto my sofa. I don't bother with a glass and drink straight from the bottle.

I kick the wet hikers off and sit back, thinking about what Alonso said. A long out-of-town vacation. Maybe he's right, but there is no way to make that happen. Either way, I have to do something. I have no intention of winding up back in the morgue for a fifth time.

TWO

Vampires, werewolves, demons, witches, they all exist. There are hundreds of lesser creatures from myth and legend that also exist, but pose no threat to humans, unless you venture into their lairs. Most are forest dwellers and shun the company of man, so contact rarely occurs. It's the big four that pose the problem and are a constant threat as humans are their main source of food and fun. I've heard these creatures referred to as supernatural, but the Catholic Church has a more appropriate name for them: unnaturals.

These fiends are not what books and movies have portrayed them to be. For example, vampires are not gentlemen and ladies, dignified and proper, or even human in appearance. They are nothing more than ravenous beasts with only one desire, to feed. They do live solely on human blood and, unlike the myths, once turned they become very unhuman-like in appearance. Their skin is paler than death and their facial features resemble a giant bat with a flat, convoluted snout with rows of sharp teeth instead of dainty little fangs. These will rip a person's throat out in one bite. I've encountered few that choose to wear clothes and their hands and feet are claws.

And despite what anyone thinks, they always prefer small children and are experts at breaking into homes and stealing kids away. Hundreds of children disappear daily and the parents are most often blamed by police and the public. I'll admit there are those parents, but in more than fifty percent of cases, vampires are to blame.

Werewolves are another species that, once turned, never look quite human again. They also endeavor to remain hidden and only reveal themselves to their victims. A scared victim will flee and the chase is what the werewolf craves. Of course, the flesh available at the end of the chase is a nice bonus. They feed mainly on the homeless and street people. That portion of our society that won't be missed by friends and family if they vanish. Male werewolves prefer female victims, mating with them during the kill. Female werewolves however are not so picky and will take a man or woman with equal savagery. Both sexes love to play with their food.

Demons are the vilest of the unnaturals and the only ones that don't start as normal humans. They're spawned from the gates of Hell and are said to be the children of Satan himself. As far as I know, there's no proof to support or deny this theory. What I *do* know is that they're the hardest to kill and require significant religious weapons that have been blessed. Demons can't come into the realm of men unless summoned by a human. Ordinarily, this human enters into a pact with Satan and summons the demon for a specific purpose.

Most are used as a tool of revenge to exact retribution for perceived wrongs against the one doing the summoning. They're controlled to an extent and aimed by this person. Once they've fulfilled their task, the demon returns to Hell. Once in a while, one will break from its master's control, kill them and then rampage through our world wreaking havoc until they're eventually cleansed.

The last of these major four are the witches. While not usually cannibalistic, they will at times consume human flesh, and man, and they do love to torture their victims. The trouble with a witch is that they look normal. Maybe one in a hundred will have warts and appear as the typical crone from Halloween and myth, but the majority look like the average everyday human. Most are quite fetching, using spells and incantations to improve their beauty and extend their lives. A witch, a young and very beautiful witch, was responsible for my living so long. She cursed me with immortality to be her mate for all time and I killed her for it.

Pity her death didn't lift the curse and her murder still haunts me.

All the unnaturals, because of their conditions, have extremely long life spans and while difficult to kill, are not truly immortal. They're capable of death because there is no true immortality. Even I can be killed with enough effort. Just like a witch, if my head and heart were removed and burned, there would be no way for me to regenerate. I suppose if I were to be eaten by a lion, that might put a permanent end to me, but the thought of regenerating from a pile of lion shit keeps me cautious around zoos. Besides, I'm not the suicidal type, a least not yet.

As far as I know, I'm unique. A true human turned unnatural against his will, I have never met another like me. I have all the frailties of any other human with a few exceptions. I can't get sick ever. I don't grow any older and though I've been killed many times, I always come back. Other than that, I'm human in every way. I still feel pain. Every time I get injured it hurts, sometimes terribly. I get hungry and thirsty, and I feel love and anger.

You might think, "Where's the down side?"

I can never have children because the curse won't allow it. We live, really live because our time is finite. I've lost my sense of time because I just go on and on. I have no one to share my life with and I envy the couples I see, especially the older ones who've spent their lives together. I can never have someone to grow old with because I will never grow old.

I am alone.

*****

I wake up the next morning groggy and hung over. The sun streams in my large living room windows and I realize that it is actually closer to noon. The half-empty bottle of tequila sits on the floor beside the couch where I left it when I finally fell asleep. With no desire to even look at the bottle, I climb shakily to my feet and stagger to my tiny bathroom for another, more thorough shower.

Once undress, I turn the water full-on hot so that I'm nearly scalded when I step into the cascade. I painstakingly scrub all my nooks and crannies to remove the last of the blood and body fluids. I feel considerably better after showering and once toweled dry, go to my bedroom to dress. I choose the same style clothes I always wear. Loose, comfortable jeans, a dark blue vintage T-shirt that advertises the British rock band the Birds and this time I went with a pair of Adidas running shoes instead of my normal hikers.

As soon as I finish dressing, I walk towards the door, grabbing my keys and phone on the way out. Eventually, I need to find my car. A dark green '67 Jaguar E-type. It's not mint with a few scuffs on the interior and some rust showing here and there, but it runs great. I'd parked it around the corner from the apartment building where I'd been killed last night. I hope it's still there. First things first, a stop at The Cup and Bean is mandatory no matter what time of day I wake up.

An uneventful short walk later and I am ensconced at my favorite table. In a corner, close to the front window so I can watch both the door and the sidewalk. Few of the creatures I hunt would voluntarily reveal themselves to the bright light of day. I'm fairly safe during day light hours, but they have been known to use humans, willingly or unwillingly, for the errands they don't want to expose themselves to.

That and I really don't like surprises, ever. Blame that on the damn witch that cursed me.

Once seated, I call Alonso. I need help to get my car and it was either him or a cab. He answered on the fourth ring, "This better not be a telemarketer."

"Hey, buddy. Feel like giving me a ride to pick up my car?" I ask as pleasantly as I can.

"Tony?" Before I could answer he goes on. "Oh yeah, no problem It's not like I sleep or nothing. I sit here all day waiting for you to call so I can haul your sorry ass all over the ATL. Not like I haven't been helping you already. Besides cleaning your slop up last night, I've had 'bout a hundred phone calls already this morning wanting to know what happened to your body."

I stop him there by breaking in with, "Slow down. What about my body?"

"Don't worry, I took care of it. You came in as a John Doe, so nobody knew your name and I crammed your body bag with what was left of you into one of the drawers and logged you in for a late post mortem. They didn't know you were gone until ten a.m. when this detective came in for the results of your post."

"What happened?"

"Dude calls me right away wanting to know 'Where his body is?'. I told him I got no clue, it was in the freezer last time I saw it." Alonso laughs. "He wasn't real happy, but he ain't called back. My boss on the other hand has called every fifteen minutes to ask one stupid question after another. Did you put it in the drawer? Yes, you found the bag right. Are you sure it was there? Yes, it was there when I clocked out. Ask your day shift crew." He keeps on chuckling and I can picture him wiping a comical tear from the corner of his eye. "You sure do keep things entertaining, Tony."

"As long as you aren't in trouble."

"Don't worry 'bout me, I'm good. I do suspect a video surveillance system is in my future, though. Might make it tough to sneak you out so it'd be good if you tried not to get killed again for a while."

It's my turn to laugh as I respond, "I'll try. Can you come and get me or not?"

"Sure, sure. You at that nasty coffee place you like so much?"

I try my best Alonso impression and say, "Man, there some fine bitches up in this place."

Alonso breaks in immediately, "Stop, stop, stop white boy. It sounds bad when I say it. It sounds downright stupid when you do it. Sit tight, I'll be right there."

As I wait for Alonso, I think back to the beginning of this job.

*****

It was about a week after my initial meeting with the redhead outside The Cup and Bean. All through that week, my sleeping hours were filled with dreams of the two of us and she invaded my waking hours as well. I didn't seem to be able to get her off my mind even though it had been a chance meeting and I would probably never see her again.

On the evening all that changed, I was spending some time watching television and drinking tequila in an attempt to keep my mind off the beautiful stranger. I had just decided to go to bed when there was a knock at the door. Without really thinking about it, completely out of character for me, I opened the door unarmed.

There she stood, as much a goddess as the first time I saw her. This night she dressed in a simple black form-fitting dress with red heels. Her hair was pulled back in an almost severe way and held in place with chop sticks. The same blood red lipstick coated her lips and highlighted her pale complexion. Her neckline plunged to mid-chest, revealing the upper swells of her breasts and caused my heart to skip a beat.

I knew I was staring, but couldn't force myself to stop. Her appearance was so delicious and it had been a long time since I had felt such desire. A nagging voice started in the back of my mind, but I pushed it aside, not caring right now about what it might mean.

A small half-smile crossed her lips for just a second before she said, "Aren't you going to invite me in?"

I finally got my mind and body in gear and stepped aside. "Ah, sure, yeah, please come in."

As she walked past me, I couldn't take my eyes off the seams running up the back of her stockings and her perfect bottom. I couldn't believe this woman was actually in my apartment.

As I closed the door, she turned and said, "I've thought a lot about you since we bumped into each other last week." I nodded, not admitting that I'd thought a lot about her as well. She would probably slap me if she knew what I was thinking at that moment. "I'm in trouble and I think you're the only person that can help."

Ah, a damsel in distress. That got my brain working again. "What makes you think I can help?" I asked, trying to get my mind out of the gutter and back onto business.

"You believe in the occult." That alarm bell rang in my mind again, but I dismissed it as she went on. "I know you do. I felt it when we touched. Please, I have nowhere else to turn."

How did she know that? I should have been more worried about that, but for some reason or other, the panic

I usually felt when someone called me out didn't rise up at all. My eyes kept sliding from hers to her breasts and that was pretty much what occupied my thoughts.

"Can we please not play games? I don't have time, I'm being hunted so either admit that or I'll leave and my blood can be on your hands when the monsters get me."

Okay, I admit it, she had me at that moment, but I tried to play it cool. "I'm not sure I know what you're talking about." I stared at her seriously and motioned toward the seating area of my small living room. "Why don't you have a seat and tell me what this trouble is. You can start by telling me your name."

She moved sensuously to the sofa and sat, her knees angled away from where I sat in the only other chair in the room. Folding her hands in her lap and taking a moment to collect her thoughts, she said, "My name is Erin. About three weeks ago, I started to notice strange things happening around me. There are strange marks on the sidewalk outside my home written in blood. At night, I feel like I'm being watched and I think someone or something's following me. And... and I've seen things." She turned away after that last part, almost ashamed.

She had my full interest now and not just because of her looks anymore. The watching and following were typical of a werewolf. She may have come to the attention of one of the beasts and it stalked her to increase the fear level. The marks on the sidewalk in blood were vampire signs and used by the creatures to warn others of their kind away from an intended victim. Was it possible she was being stalked by two separate species of unnaturals? There had to be more to the story and I had a feeling it had to do with what she said about knowing I believed in the occult.

"What did you mean earlier when you said you felt I believe in the occult?"

She looked back at me and said very quietly, "I wasn't sure what you were until I actually bumped into you, but I could sense it... I'm a Wiccan."

I couldn't help it. I jumped up, startling her, and yelled, "You're a witch!" The alarm bell rang like mad now and I tried to decide whether to throw her out or kill her.

"No, no. I'm not a witch. I'm Wiccan, a forest spirit," she pleaded holding her hands up innocently. "I only do white magic to help others. Readings and herbal medicine. I would never do black magic! Please believe me."

*****

My table shakes and I look up as Alonso sits down across from me. He looks at me for a second then asks, "You okay buddy? You looked like you were a million miles away."

"Just thinking," I reply.

"About Red?"

I know he means Erin. I'd told him about her when we discussed the case and he was convinced she was bad news. I've found it harder and harder to disagree. Although I'd met a tragic end several times during my long life, I've never been killed four times in one week. It had to be some kind of record.

I constantly remind myself it was the case and not her fault. She is the victim here. It just happens to be me that keeps winding up in the morgue. That's why I answer, "About the case. Trying to decide what my next step should be."

"Well, if you're ready, we can start by going to get your car. Where'd you leave it?"

"On Dunbar. Let's go."

We amble out to Alonso's car. He'd parked by the curb, a late eighties gold Honda Civic with a perpetual lean toward the driver's side. It always appears to be preparing to make a sharp left hand turn. I can't help laughing every time I watch Alonso squeezing his enormous bulk into such a tiny car.

I still have the smile on my face as I sit in the passenger's seat and close the door. Alonso looks over at me and, noticing the smile, asks, "What?"

"Oh, nothing, thought of something funny. That's all."

"Is it private or would you like to share with the rest of the class?" He already knows the answer. This is a ritual we repeat every time I ride with him. At six feet, three inches and four hundred pounds, Alonso knows he is a big man. He just doesn't like being reminded of it. He is great to have watching your back in a fight and pretty light on his feet for a big guy, but he will never be mistaken for dainty.

"Well, if you're done snickering, can we go?"

I nod and reply, "By all means, let us proceed my dear Watson."

I laughed out loud as he mumbles, "Watson my ass," and pulls away from the curb.

The heavy Atlanta traffic reduces our progress to a crawl and the sickly wheezing of Alonso's air conditioner makes the sultry August air barely tolerable, but the trip is pleasant nonetheless. Alonso and I like each other's company and our easy banter allows us to say whatever we want without fear of offending the other. It's been a long time since I've had a friend and I enjoy Alonso's companionship very much. I spent so much time alone, I'd forgotten how it felt.

Eventually, we make it to Dunbar Street and turn south toward Drake Apartments. I'd tracked the werewolf to the building and went in last night with the intention of killing it. That's when I ran into the demon and landed in the morgue. I'd been armed with a custom made twelve gauge double barrel pistol that fired silver double aught buckshot. Perfect for cleansing a werewolf, but unfortunately it didn't even slow the demon down. My pistol is probably still lying in the apartment where it was knocked from my hand when the demon threw me through the window. I hope to recover it, too.

Staring out the window thinking, I'm not paying attention where we were going until I hear Alonso exclaim, "Shit!"

I turn to him and ask, "What is it?"

He points out in front of the car. "Cops!"

THREE

Cops, that's not good. I have nothing against the police personally, but they ask questions I don't like to answer. It's simply easier to do my job if I can avoid legal entanglements. As a Cleanser, my job is somewhat similar to law enforcement with a couple of major exceptions. I deal only with unnaturals, I can only kill a human if they're an agent of an unnatural and there is no arrest, no prosecution. I find them and I kill them. It's been this way for me since 1882 when I volunteered for the job. One hundred and thirty-one years I've been tracking, killing, and cleansing the world of these monstrous beings.

Cleansers have been around for centuries. They started out as priests assigned by the church to rid villages of the horrors that stalked the forests at night. Later, others joined their ranks, people that had suffered the loss of family members or had survived a near-fatal attack and were looking for revenge. As time passed, whole families became Cleansers and the task was handed down one generation to the next.

When I started, it had been thirty-six years since I'd become immortal and I'd gone through several emotional periods. Denial, then elation at the prospect of unlimited time, and then anger at what had been done to me. I was unaware of the existence of the Cleansers, but had begun my own form of cleansing by finding and killing every witch I could. It was during this dark time of my life that I met a Cleanser and learned about their holy ordained mission.

She was a young woman I met in a tavern in the small village of Dernbach near Dierdorf in Bavaria. I chatted her up and thought I was doing pretty well because she hadn't told me to take a hike or ran screaming from the place. I considered asking her to visit my room over the bar when the door burst open and a shaggy, hunched, mountain of a man entered.

His hair and beard ran together so only his eyes and

mouth were visible. In the firelight those eyes burned a dull red. I hadn't even noticed the long claws that showed below the sleeves of his heavy coat. He looked around the large open room of the tavern and when his gaze landed on the table where I sat with the pretty little thing I intended to have warming my bed, he snarled. I had no trouble seeing the large fangs that were exposed as his lips pulled back.

He immediately started toward my table and I reached for the cap and ball pistol tucked in my belt when my pretty little thing leapt onto the table and sprang straight at the beast. I had a split second to notice the wicked-looking silver dagger held high in her right hand before they collided and crashed to the floor. The patrons scattered and cries of alarm sprang up around the room as chairs and tables flew in every direction. I stood too stunned to move and watched as the beast's claws shredded the girl's clothes and skin beneath. All the while, her right hand raised and fell, plunging the dagger into his massive body over and over.

Finally, the beast stopped moving and, with a grunt, the girl pushed the creature off, rolling him onto his back. It lay on the bar room floor, a growing puddle of blood expanding around its misshapen form. The young girl extended her arm to me and numbly I helped her up. She ignored the blood seeping from her own wounds and quickly examined the beast.

Satisfied that it was in fact dead, she looked at me and asked, "What the hell? You've been trying to get me into your bed for over an hour and you can't help me kill one werewolf?"

Without waiting for me to respond, she ordered the innkeeper who was cowering behind the bar to get the village priest. After he left, she turned back to me. "That was a werewolf?" I asked. "I didn't think they were real."

She pointed at the thing lying on the floor and said, "Looks pretty real to me. If he'd got those teeth into you, you'd think he was pretty real, too. Course then I'd be putting you down along with him."

The priest arrived quickly and the girl identified herself to the old man as a Vatican Cleanser. He may have been old, but he obviously knew what she was talking about because he deferred to her wishes and jumped to accomplish everything she ordered him to do. Under her direction, the priest gave last rights to the creature and anointed it with holy oil. Then the body was removed by a couple of strong young lads who carried it to the village square, where it was covered with wood and set alight. The fire was tended all night to ensure the complete cremation of the remains.

I, on the other hand, spent the night in a comfortable goose down bed with Elspeth, the pretty little thing who'd killed the werewolf. I treated her injuries and then we treated each other's needs. We talked into the night and she filled me in on the life of a Cleanser. The next morning, I left Dernbach accompanying her en route to Rome where I intended to join the ranks of the Cleansers.

Elspeth was my recruiter and my lover. She was destined to become my mentor as a Cleanser. Even though she was much younger than me, she had been a Cleanser ever since her entire family was wiped out by a vampire. Seven long years in her mind, long enough to teach me the ropes. She vouched for me at the Vatican so I could enlist in the Swiss Guard. Cleansers were no longer priests, so it became mandatory to enlist as a Swiss mercenary. She taught me about all the unnatural creatures and I accompanied her on several cleansings before I went solo. Elspeth and I would still get together to share our experiences and a bed. Sadly, she died two years later, the victim of a drunken brawl between two men she had nothing to do with.

She had survived untold attacks by creatures stronger and more powerful and she died because one of the drunk bastards couldn't aim his pistol straight. I still miss her.

*****

I tell Alonso to pull over and he slows, easing against the curb, the hamsters under his hood thankful for the break. I study the scene before me, yellow crime scene tape stretches around the front side of the building with uniformed police standing along the perimeter to keep any spectators from getting in the way. The broken window four floors up near the southern most corner is clearly visible and the broken glass and part of the frame on the sidewalk below. I can barely make out the rusty red stain that marks the landing spot from my undignified exit. Several plain clothes guys, probably detectives or crime scene techs can be seen moving around inside the taped off area. Shit, that probably means they have my weapon.

I'd hoped it was late enough that the scene would've been finished up, but apparently my death deserved more attention than I thought. This is why I hate dying in public areas. Makes it a pain the ass to get anything done right. I just hope none of these guys were here last night to collect my body and recognize me walking around alive and well.

"What now?"

I shrug. "When all else fails, play dumb." I pop my seat belt and open the door to get out.

"Well, you should be good at it by now," Alonso mutters.

I pause and regard him for a second. He smiles back at me innocently, causing me to laugh and shake my head, because I know that any comment I make will bounce off him as harmlessly as a foam rubber ball. I step out, shutting the door behind me.

Alonso leans across the seat saying, "If you need me, call me." Without waiting for a reply, he revs the engine once then executes a U-turn and speeds back the way we came.

I watch him disappear north on Dunbar, then turn and start in the direction of the apartments and the contingent of police. I walk casually trying not to attract attention, just a guy out for a stroll. I stay on the opposite side of the street away from the building and walk all the way past so I can get a look at where I parked my car. As I get beyond the corner, I can see my car where it sits close to the rear of the apartment building. It appears untouched, exactly as I left it. Unfortunately, it was inside the yellow taped-off perimeter.

I swear quietly under my breath and start across the street. The nearest cop to me appears to be an older guy and would probably be more understanding, I hope, so I angle toward him.

As I approach, he calls out, "Finally decided to come over, huh?" I point at myself and he nods, "Yeah, you. I saw you get out of the gold Honda and saunter down here. Figured you'd come over eventually."

I try to appear as nonthreatening as possible, making sure to keep my hands in full view. "Sorry, I was hoping to be able to get to my car." I say pointing in the direction of the Jaguar.

He indicates with his thumb back over his shoulder and asks, "The Jag is yours?"

"Yes sir, it is."

"What's it doing here, with you getting dropped off way up the block?"

"Well, you see, officer, I met this lady and she didn't want my car seen anywhere around her place last night," I answer, trying to sound like a typical young man who'd been doing the wild thing with a hot cougar. "So I parked here and we left in her car. That was her dropping me off a few minutes ago."

He looks at me the way I would expect a micro biologist to look at a particularly interesting germ and states, "Your lady friend looked suspiciously like a big black guy."

Damn, should've had Alonso stop farther back. "Ah, no officer. She was a little blonde, I swear."

"Sure she was." Turning so he could shout over his shoulder, but never taking his eyes off me he calls, "Detective!"

I try not to jump when he yells and notice a tall, rail-thin man in a rumpled gray suit turn and look in our direction. After studying us a couple of seconds, he starts over.

The tall detective stops about ten feet behind the uniformed cop and asks in a slow, deep voice, "What is it,

John?"

The uniformed cop points at my feet and orders, "Don't move. Stay right there." Then he moves back to have a private conversation with the detective. The latter watches me like a hawk as John fills him in on what I said. I try to look as not guilty as I can manage.

The detective nods once then together they come over to where I stand. He doesn't smile or offer his hand as he introduces himself, "I'm Detective David George. What's your name, kid?"

I try not to smirk at the term 'kid' as I take in this man. Detective George has a taciturn expression and reminds me of the cartoon dog Droopy, with slightly fleshy jowls and soulful brown eyes. He's probably mid-forties and I have the feeling he doesn't smile much. Those eyes, though, I can see intelligence there. I will have to be careful talking to this man. If my lie gets too complicated or I lose my place, I know he'd catch it. It is his eyes that cause me to think back to a man I knew many years ago. A man with those same eyes.

*****

I had been in Trieste three months, living on bread crusts and a few salted fish when I could afford or steal them. I slept wherever I could find a place where I wasn't afraid of being raped or murdered. As a street urchin, I knew both possibilities existed. I stayed close to the docks and what money I made came from the odd jobs I did around the water front. I hauled fish guts and manure, swept up the fish stalls, anything to make a copper or two.

I'd seen the man around the docks on occasion and knew he was a sailor. I had no idea he was the master of his own ship, a twin mast, fifty ton, Caravela Latina. He was one of the very few people that spoke to me other than a curse word when they ran me off. He told me later that he saw something of himself in me, that's why he took an interest. Whatever the reason, he probably saved my life.

I was caught stealing a fish and the monger and his son had beaten me badly. I was bruised, bloody, and barely able to move. In an effort to get away from them, I had hidden in a stack of cargo nets and that's where Captain Stefano Caprisi found me. He carried me onto his ship and over the next several weeks, nursed me back to health. By the time I was able to leave his cabin, we had been at sea for over a week. I couldn't stand up straight and had to drag my left foot because the leg wouldn't work. I was also still pissing blood, but when I got my first look at the sea, all of my pain was forgotten. It was beautiful, just as my grandfather had said and I had dreamed.

We were in the Adriatic sailing for Greece with a load of Egyptian cotton cloth and papyrus. Captain Caprisi intended to sell the cargo and load up with whatever he could for a run to Turkey before taking on another cargo and returning to Italy. When he saw me, he had me come up to the wheel and we had our first real talk about the sea and what he expected from me.

"You're fifteen years old and a big strong lad. Once you're healthy again, you will start to work. You'll start in the bilge, which is the lowest point of the ship and you will finish here at the helm. You will learn every job on this ship by doing it for one month and then move to the next job. By the time we see Italy again, you should know almost as much about her as I do."

When I asked him why he was doing this he said, "I don't have a son. When I die, my wife will sell my ship and everything else I own to buy a big house and wine. I'd like to leave it to someone instead of her pissing it away." I told him I was honored and I would do my best. All he said was, "I know you will, because if you don't, I'll throw you over the side and let you swim back to Italy."

I don't know if he was serious, but I decided I'd better act like he was until I knew for sure. After a few minutes of standing beside him at the wheel, I wondered out loud, "What's her name?"

"Huh, who's name?"

I swept my hand around me and said, "The ship."

"Oh! *The Puttana.* She's called *The Puttana.* I named her after my wife." With that, he began to cackle and I joined in. It felt good to laugh and, for the first time since I ran away from home, I wasn't scared. I would live, work, and learn on *The Whore* and one day *The Whore* would be mine.

*****

The detective stands looking at me, waiting for my answer. I try to hide the fact my mind had wandered and answer his question quickly, "Tony White."

"Do you have an ID, Mr. White?"

"Sure," I reply, fishing my wallet out of my back pocket. I pull my Tennessee driver's license out of its slot and hand it to him. Detective George hands it straight to the uniformed cop standing beside him without even glancing at it. The uniform takes a couple of steps back and softly speaks into his shoulder mic.

George, however, never takes his eyes off me. "Now, what can I do for you Mr. White?"

I smile and point in the direction of the two-seater. "I'd like to get my car."

"Yes, the Officer said as much. But you don't live here?"

"No, I don't." I know where this is going and I don't like the direction. I need to think of something quick, so I go on the offensive, "It was just a convenient place to park. What's this all about? Did something happen to my car?"

"Relax, your car's fine, but I'm investigating a death that occurred here last night and your car is inside my crime scene." I notice he said 'death', not homicide or suicide. Maybe they aren't sure what happened. It's a safe bet they are unaware a demon had been involved and I'm positive he'd be surprised to learn I was his victim.

I pretend shock as I respond to his statement, "Wow, sorry to hear it. That's awful, but it has nothing to do with me." Regardless of my actual age, I still look like a twenty-two year old guy, so it's easy to act self-involved and disinterested in the events happening around me. In reality, I'm actually dying to ask Detective George a hundred questions. Primarily about Harry Crowe.

Harry Crowe was the occupant of the apartment that I had been ejected from. I'd tracked the werewolf stalking Erin to an old, blue Chevy pickup. With some help from

Alonso and a lady friend of his that works at the Atlanta PD headquarters, I obtained Crowe's name and address from the vehicle's plates. I set up surveillance on the apartment figuring if this was a werewolf lair, he'd have to come back eventually. As luck would have it, last night he did.

I stood behind a big Maple tree across the street from the Drake Apartments, away from any streetlights and watched the front entrance. Around nine p.m., the blue truck came down Dunbar and parked. The lighting is terrible around this place at night, but was good enough for me to see the hunched, shambling gait of the driver as he made his way into the building. That was all the proof I needed. Crowe was my werewolf, now all I had to do was kill him.

My plan had been simple. I look like a nice young man, nonthreatening. I'd knock on the door and when he opened it, blast him with the silver buckshot, cut off his head, stuff it in a bag and get the hell out. Then, I'd take it to a private location where I could anoint it with holy oil and burn the damn thing, destroying another werewolf forever. I had everything ready: gun, silver knife, and a bag for the head. But nothing could ever be that simple.

I'd made my way across the street and into the building without being seen. I already knew which apartment I needed and eased up the stairs toward it. Once I reached his floor, I hugged the left wall and made my way toward his door. As I neared, I noticed the door was already open with no light showing. I drew the big shotgun pistol and, holding it in front of me, eased inside the apartment. As soon as I crossed the threshold, the demon stepped out of the shadows to my left and the fight was on.

Movement in my peripheral vision alerted me to its presence and I managed to get off one shot, which did nothing to the hellspawn. I was dumbfounded, I came in expecting a werewolf and now I was confronted by a demon. I couldn't react fast enough before it knocked the gun from my hand and grabbed my right wrist. I remember being flung around the room several times before eventually my arm tore loose at the shoulder and I sailed out through the window. Falling's the last true memory I have before waking up in the body bag being wheeled into the morgue.

"Did you hear me, Mr. White?"

I look at the detective realizing he said something I hadn't caught. "Sorry, guess I zoned out for a second."

"Are you all right?"

"Yes, I'm just thinking about the poor man that died. It's terrible," I reply, trying to recover.

"Uh huh." George looks at me intently. "I asked you where you lived."

"Sorry, why do you need my address?" I ask innocently.

"I'm going to let you have your car, but you look a little shaken up. I'd like to stop by later to make sure you're alright," he says as he hands my driver's license back to me.

"That's not necessary. I'm fine." I wonder if I said something to make him suspicious.

His expression never changes as he said, "Just the same, I'd feel better knowing you're okay. It's not a problem is it?"

"No, no problem." I give him the address. The uniformed cop, John writes my information in his notebook. Detective George's eyes never leave me. Those eyes bore into me as if they can see my very soul and wring any untruths straight from it.

As soon as the cop finishes writing, George raises the yellow tape and motions for me to follow him. We walk to my car. As I unlock it and sit inside, he says, "Nice car. You have a good day, Mr. White." I thank him and start the engine. I put the transmission in gear, preparing to pull away and he asks, "You aren't planning to take any trips in the next couple of days are you?"

When I tell him no, he smiles for the first time and says, "Good, I'll catch you later, Mr. White."

I pull away and the other cop holds the tape up so I can drive under it. As I accelerate up Dunbar Street, I look in my rearview mirror. Detective George stands in the street watching me drive away. I have a strong feeling I'll be seeing him again very soon.

FOUR

I stop around the corner, out of sight of the cops, long enough to put the top down on the Jag. The car doesn't have air conditioning and even with the windows down, the air was stifling. As I start out again, the rush of air through the cockpit feels better and helps to clear my mind. I don't bother with the radio, needing to think instead. This case has become complicated beyond any other I've experienced. Usually things were simpler. It usually went something like find monster, kill monster, and move on to next monster. For the first time on a hunt, someone was trying to hinder me from destroying these monsters and possibly hoping to kill me in the process.

The last twenty-four hours have been exceptionally bad. I lost Harry Crowe. His truck had been nowhere in sight outside his apartment building. It was probably gone last night before my body was discovered on the sidewalk, which means he was in the wind and I'd have to track him down again. I lost my favorite weapon, the double barrel hand cannon, and I faced a third predator, the demon. On top of that, I now have this detective breathing down my neck. Oh, and I managed to get myself killed, again. Not my best day. But then again, not my worst either. I chuckle darkly as I remember that day, but I don't have time to think about it now.

I drive easily toward my apartment, the little green car slithering through the heavy traffic the way only a sports car can. The wind through the open top and the purr of the engine help to calm my nerves. By the time I reach Magnolia House, I feel better. My situation has not improved, but I'm as worried as when I first left the Drake. I park, put the top up, and lock the car, then jogged up the steps to my apartment.

The more I think about it, the more convinced I become that I've been set up. It explains so much of the past week that I had written off as bad luck, or me being over confident. Although the latest incident with the demon has been the most violent, I've landed in the morgue three other times this week. Those three times had all been at the hands, or rather the teeth, of vampires. When I took this case to help the Wiccan Erin, I determined the vampire to be the greatest threat. While the werewolf would most surely kill her if given the chance, it would want to play with her for a while first. He would want her as terrified as possible before the final chase.

The vampire, on the other hand, didn't care. As soon as he could find a way into her home or catch her alone on a dark street, he would move on her. So he was to be my first target. I gave Erin strict instructions not to be out at night. If it was unavoidable, she was to call me first and I would accompany her wherever she needed to go. I also gave her a few wards I knew worked against the creatures and would keep them from entering her home while she slept.

Many of the old legends are true or partially true. As I walk upstairs, I pull the small pocket journal of notes out of my pocket and flip through it, hoping it will help clear my mind and give me some semblance of a plan. My fingers find the pages on werewolves and absently I glance down at my scribbled handwriting. Werewolves hate wolfs bane and a few sprigs of it around doors and windows will keep them from getting in. Vampires hate fresh garlic and roses. It's the smell and, while not fatal, they can fight through it if they're really desperate to get to their prey. One thing they can't fight through and is fatal in large enough doses is ultra violet light. A simple UV light above a door or window will keep even the most determined vampire out of a house.

All of these were things I had Erin do and still it seemed the creatures were persistent in trying to get to her. Either I was missing something, or someone really wanted Erin dead. I flip another few pages and find my sarcastically written notes about idiots using crucifixes against vampires. Yeah, that was a joke.

Holy water and crosses do not work on anything but demons, for future reference. Silver is the only way to kill a werewolf and a wooden stake through the heart will paralyze a vampire long enough to chop its neck. Removing the head and burning it ensures no chance of regeneration, thus bringing true death to whatever creature I kill. Anointing the head with holy oil's a Vatican directive to all Cleansers and I suppose it's the church's way of trying to bring peace to the souls of the cursed. I don't know if it works, but it can't hurt. After the things I've seen, I can't really deny God's existence. If there's a Hell, there has to be a Heaven. I'm just not sure he cares.

I skim through the next few pages until I come across everything I know about Vampires and sigh. They really are a pain in the ass to deal with. They are sneaky and capable of developing intricate plans in order to get what they want.

It was for this reason I went after them first and it was them that caused my first three trips to the morgue this week. If anything's capable of setting me up, the vampires are a likely suspect. I went after the Werewolf Harry Crowe because I needed a break from hunting the vampires' nest. That might have been a mistake. I decide I will go back after the vampire and I will do it tonight.

After entering my apartment, I go to my weapons stash to gather the tools I'll need for this hunt. I modified the back wall of the closet in the bedroom after I moved in to provide a safe and hidden storage for all the paraphernalia of a Cleanser. I told the landlady Mrs. Betty that my closet stunk to high heaven and that I would pay to install cedar planking to help. She told me as long as every penny came out of my pocket, she couldn't have cared less what I did to the back of a closet. Now the stud space held my weapons and ammo perfectly and, as a bonus, I didn't get moths.

After removing the false wall at the back of the closet, I select a new Barnett, Zombie 350 crossbow with an Eotech 512.Xbow holographic sight. The state-of-the-art weapon is compact and can fire an arrow at three hundred and fifty feet per second with substantial knockdown power. The arrows, however, are not new. They are over one hundred and fifty years old and a gift from a priest I knew in the years just after I became a Cleanser. They are made from olive wood with a heavy iron tip and sharp as a needle. The iron tip ensures the arrow makes it through whatever covered the target like thick clothing or bone and the wood did the work of paralyzing the vampire.

I also select a long, curved blade knife for defense and removing the head, along with a leak-proof bag for transporting it. All this I stuff into a kit bag for easy carrying and prepare to close the false wall up when I noticed my alternate werewolf gun. A sawed-off Browning twelve gauge double barrel with shortened stock. I figure what the hell so I grab it and load a couple of the silver double aught shells in the breech.

Loaded up with weapons and the hiding place secured, I carry everything into the living room and dump it in the chair. I have a few hours before nightfall, so I decide to grab a bite to eat and a quick nap before venturing out to cleanse the vampire menacing Erin.

I eat a quick meal of leftovers from my fridge and stretch out on the sofa, setting the alarm on my phone to wake me just after sunset. The bottle of tequila sits where I left it the night before, but I won't touch it again until after the cleansing is finished. Hopefully I can celebrate a successful hunt in the morning with a touch of the strong amber liquid. I'm still smiling at the thought as I drift off.

*****

The dream opened as it all ways did, with a rush of wind, rain and the crashing of waves. Captain Caprisi was steering *The Puttana* hard trying to make port. We were still several hours out of Civitavecchia, the major port city that serviced Rome when the storm came on us fast out of the west. Wind driven waves and rain slammed into *The Puttana* trying to force her onto the beach as we struggled north toward the port.

I'd been on *The Puttana* for six years and had earned the first mate's position by virtue of my work. It didn't hurt having Caprisi as my guardian and destined to be his heir where *The Puttana* was concerned. I'd met his wife and daughters several times over the intervening time since I came on board. They were a rather unpleasant bunch and seemed to be much happier when the captain was away. They complained a great deal and spent every coin he brought them on clothes or entertaining the many guests, mostly men, that frequented the little villa in the hills overlooking Trieste.

I understood his choice of name for his ship better after meeting his family. I would never say it to his face, but it was obvious he was surrounded by whores. I think he knew and was the reason he stayed at sea so much. It's also why he chose me to be the inheritor of his ship.

It was mid-November and storms were common this time of year, but most came out of the east. This one surprised us and the sea had already begun to get wild by the time the sun came up. By noon, it was a full-blown gale and we were in trouble. I tried to convince Caprisi to drop the sail and throw out the anchor. I believed we could simply ride out the storm, but the captain refused.

"We're already too close inshore. There's no rocks here, only sand. If we drop anchor now boy, it won't bite and will drag through the sand until she breaks apart in the surf. How will that do for your inheritance?"

I relented and the crew fought valiantly throughout the afternoon until just before sunset. I could see the light house that marked the entrance to the harbor of Civitavecchia. We were preparing to make a windward tack to set up for a down wind entrance to the harbor when the lines supporting the mast tore loose and separated. The crew raced to make repairs, but it was too late. In seconds, the sail was free in the swirling wind and the mast slammed down across the rail and quarter deck, killing Captain Caprisi instantly.

My friend and guardian was gone and it appeared we were very near to losing the ship.

The second mate, a Frenchman named Dumas, ran up and, seeing the captain dead, grabbed me by the front of my shirt and screamed we had to abandon *The Puttana.*

I yelled back at him, "Get back down to the main deck and let's try to get this mess over the side. Maybe the drag will slow us down until we can drop the anchor. We have to keep her off the beach."

Near panic, he screamed back, "It's hopeless, she is lost. We have to get off or we'll be lost as well."

Without waiting for my call, he ran back down to the deck and he and the crew tried to put the single lifeboat over the side. The heaving deck made it virtually impossible and they had it sideways across the deck when a huge wave broke over the port bow and carried the lifeboat and the five crewmen away. Just like that, I was alone on the doomed ship.

Terrified and alone, I strained to see through the stinging rain and wind. *The Puttana* was being forced rapidly toward the beach and it wouldn't be long before she grounded. I had become a strong swimmer in my years spent at sea and I hoped if the ship didn't ground too far off shore, I'd be able to make the swim to safety.

I had to time it just right. Too far out and the strong surf would exhaust me before I could reach shore. Wait too long and she might ground before I jumped over the side. If that happened, she would roll in the surf and I'd likely be trapped, or crushed as debris tore loose and crashed around the deck. I waited as long as I thought prudent then jumped into the roiling sea and swam as hard as I could toward the beach barely visible through the rain-shrouded dark.

I swam hard for what felt like hours and drank several gallons of sea water before I felt the brush of sand on my bare feet. Standing up, I staggered onto the sand above the surf line where I collapsed. My stomach heaved and retched until there was nothing left. I rolled over onto my back and thanked God for allowing me to survive then passed out.

*****

The beeping of my cell phone brings me awake and back to the present. Rising up, I look out the living room window to see the sun had set. Glancing at my phone I see the time is eight-thirty p.m. It will be dark soon and I need to be on my way. A quick trip to the bathroom to relieve myself and splash some water on my face has me ready for

LA MISERIA di BIANCO 39

a busy night.

On the way back through the living room, I grab the kit bag holding my weapons and leave the apartment. At the bottom of the stairs, I'd just pushed the front door open when I hear another door open and a coarse female voice call my name. I pause and look over to my left to see Mrs. Betty standing in her door in her flowered house coat, cigarette clamped between her fingers, and a stream of smoke escaping from her nostrils.

"Yes, Mrs. Betty?"

"On your way out again I see," she declares. "Having any more problems with that closet of yours?"

I smile and reply, "No ma'am. That was almost two years ago. It's fine now, no problems."

"Good. You're a nice boy, Tony, you be careful out there, you hear?"

Her words make me curious, but I smile and nod anyway. "Sure thing. Thanks, Mrs. Betty. I have to go," I say as I start out the door.

As I go down the front steps to where my car is parked, I hear her yell, "And don't forget to clean that crap off your door. I didn't agree to any redecorating your door."

Confused concerning what she was talking about, I pause again. My door? What crap on my door? I haven't done anything to it, as far as I know. I'd have to remember to check it out later. I wave at her and shrugging to myself, go around to the trunk and drop the kit bag in.

With the weapons in the trunk, I climb in behind the wheel, start the engine and pull away, my landlady's crazy comment forgotten. I turn onto Sycamore Street and speed toward Erin's house. I need to check on her and start my search for the vampire there.

A short ten minute drive later and I pull up in front of a stylish two-story home with a wraparound front porch. Unlike all of its neighbors, this house is stucco and painted an earth tone. This, along with the clay tile roof, lends the home a Spanish look and reminds me of many of the homes in my native Italy. The tree-lined street and shallow front yards give the area a warm and inviting feel. There is no driveway, so I park on the street and quickly make my way to the front door.

It's almost completely dark as I ring the bell and wait for Erin to answer. I don't have to wait long as the door opens and she stands looking at me, a bright smile on her lovely face. As happens every time I see her, my heart flutters. Her beauty still astonishes me no matter how many times I see her. Dressed in loose white pants made of a gauzy material with drawstring waist and a white T-shirt that contrasts with the bright red lipstick and polish on the toes of her bare feet, she looks every inch my beautiful red haired goddess. The fact she isn't wearing a bra is evident and I have to swallow several times before I can speak.

I finally blurt out, "Are you okay?"

"I'm fine," she answers. I can't help it, it came unbidden into my mind and I think 'Yes, you are'. She continues before I can embarrass myself. "Would you like to come in?"

Her invitation takes me right back to the first meeting in my apartment.

*****

She had just admitted to being Wiccan and I had a little freak-out about her being a witch. She pleaded with me to believe her about not being a witch. She stood and stepped very close to me that night, so close I could smell her perfume. Lavender, soothing, I calmed down as soon as I smelled it. She reached out and touched my shoulder and the contact sent fire racing through me. After the initial jolt of her touch, the intimacy of her closeness further added to the calming effect.

She was speaking, but I couldn't hear a word she said. I could only think about how beautiful she was and how much I wanted her. At that moment, there was nothing I wouldn't have done for her. Need someone killed? I have a gun right here. Need to be worshipped forever? I'm your guy.

She'd withdrawn the touch and turned, stepping back over to the sofa. Once again she sat, looking up at me with those green, so green, eyes, waiting for me to respond. I felt calmer and I wanted to believe she wasn't a witch.

I could still feel the tingle from her touch as I sat across from her and said, "I believe you."

The smile returned to her lips as she exclaimed, "Good. So it's settled, you'll take my case." Before I could respond, she extended her arm holding a slip of paper, "This is my address. Come by tomorrow afternoon and I'll show you the signs." I nodded as I took the proffered paper and she said, "Great, I'll see you tomorrow."

She stood and made her way to the door. I continued to stand, looking at the paper she'd given me. As she opened the door, she turned toward me and said, "Thank you."

With that, she was gone.

I'd managed a "You're welcome," to the empty room…

*****

Remembering that meeting as I stand on her porch tonight, I know what the resulting proximity to her would do to me. I barely maintain control and reply, "Sorry, I can't. I just wanted to make sure you were alright. I intend to find one of your stalkers tonight."

A little pout replaces the smile on her lips. "Oh, okay. Some other time then?"

"Sure. Please stay inside," I state flatly, feeling I disappointed her. She graces me with one final smile as she closes the door. I turn and make my way back to the car, '*Idiot*' playing on a continuous loop inside my brain.

FIVE

When I get back to my car, I open the trunk to access my gear. As I arrange my weapons across the floor of the trunk, I feel more composed. Seeing Erin affects me more than I like to admit and I need to get my head back in the game, focus on the damn job in front of me like I always do.

I leave the weapons in the trunk until I need them. In today's America, in a community like this where there is an abundance of kids, child molesters are a real concern. Any single male lurking in the shadows wearing a trench coat's a likely candidate for having the police dispatched to check him out by a concerned neighbor. Sadly, that's why I don't wear one. It would be just as hard to stand around with a loaded crossbow in plain view, so I leave the weapons safe out of sight.

It's not the most conducive way when in a rushed situation, but it'd be even harder to try and explain my presence to a suspicious cop when I don't live in the area and have no good excuse for being there. I can see exactly how that would go. "No, Officer, I don't live around here. No, Officer, I'm not visiting anyone in particular. Of course, Officer, I have a perfectly good reason for holding this loaded crossbow. Yes sir, Officer, I'll turn around and put my hands behind my back."

Not the way I want to spend the evening, especially if I want to catch and kill a particularly dangerous vampire. I say particularly dangerous only because this one has gotten the jump on me three times already. He seems to be able to predict my moves and is ready for me no matter what I do. It's frustrating, considering up until now I've always believed I was good at what I do. The senses of unnaturals are much more enhanced than humans. A vampire can see, hear, and smell ten times better than I could ever hope to. Trying to hide or remain undetected is virtually impossible.

My years of experience have taught me where a vampire or other monster will hide and watch from, how he will make his approach to the victim. I keep saying 'he', but it's just as likely that a vampire will be female. It just happens in this case that it is a 'he'. I don't stay stationary when hunting a vampire. They're masters of shadows and sneaking about. Trying to do what they do will just get a Cleanser killed. I'll walk up and down the street like I belong there and search for the little signs I know that will lead me to where the loathsome thing's hiding.

Although, that is exactly how it got the upper hand the first time I took a trip to the morgue this week. I'd made about ten trips around the couple block square encompassing Erin's house when I saw the vampire on her roof. I nonchalantly made my way down the block to my car in order to retrieve my weapons and as I closed the trunk lid, I felt the hairs on the back of my neck raise. Before I could even curse, the vampire pulled me around and lashed out with its clawed hand, opening my throat. It didn't attempt to feed, it simply vanished. I was left standing there with blood spraying out onto the asphalt. I knew I was in trouble and had to get away from the car or it would be included in the incident. I don't carry any identification when I'm hunting in case something like this happens. I always try to go to the morgue as a John Doe. It just makes things easier.

I hoped my ability to heal would save me and managed to get several blocks away from my car before the blood loss finally became too much. I tried to make it to a more secluded area so that if I died, I could remain out of sight. It wasn't meant to be as I stumbled into an even busier area where I dropped dead in plain view of several people. I woke up a couple hours later to Alonso's smiling face and chalked it up to bad luck.

The second trip to the morgue happened much the same way, except I'd learned from the first encounter and did a better job placing my car with the weapons in it. This time, I managed to get an arrow into the creature before it realized I was there. While my arrow wasn't fatal, it did slow the vampire down and I pursued it to an area of flat roofed businesses. As I chased it over the roof tops, he turned and confronted me. You never want to go hand to hand with a vampire if you can avoid it. They're much faster and stronger and you have to be exceptionally lucky to win. I was not, again. Instead of fighting me, he simply pushed me. One little shove and off the roof I went. I could still see the smile on his distorted face as I fell to my second death in as many days.

The third incident was still a mystery to me. It was already late in the evening when I took up the hunt and I parked in a well secluded alley. As I exited my car, I remember being grabbed from behind and felt the tearing of flesh at the side of my neck. That's my last recollection until I awoke several hours later with Alonso looking at me. According to the report he related to me, my body was found quite a distance from where I parked. I can only assume the vampire carried me and dumped me at the location I was found. I have no idea why it would do that unless I was close to its actual lair.

One thing is sure though, this creature has my scent. It will be impossible to sneak up on and I'm sure it will be looking for me as hard as I'm looking for it.

*****

My plan for the evening is a little more complicated than I usually like. I don't intend to wait for the vampire to make an appearance. I will begin at Erin's house and hunt for it, tracking it backward by the signs they left. Undetectable unless you know to look for scratches left by claws and the smell of their bloody piss where they marked their territory. If I can find the trail, I'll track it back to where it held up during the day. As long as Erin did what I asked and stayed inside, I feel that she is safe. I'll wait for the blood sucker to return and kill it in its own nest.

It's a very time consuming process to hunt for a sign. I have to repeatedly jog back to my vehicle, move it along a few blocks, park, and repeat. With nothing but a flashlight, I start looking for anything that screams vampire in the alley behind Erin's house. It doesn't take long to find, but what I find isn't what I expected. Scratches on the wooden fence that mark the back side of her yard and the trees adjacent to it show the vampire has been using this approach for weeks. They are so numerous, I have a strong feeling there is actually more than one of the parasites staking out her house. The only good thing I find is the scratches indicate their movement came from one direction.

The trail leads up the side of a building and I have no trouble scaling a power pole and vaulting a small gap to reach the roof. Once there, the trail flows from roof top to roof top back in the direction of an industrial area barely visible to the south east. This is the same direction I'd pursued the vampire a few nights ago. That partially deserted industrial park would be the ultimate location for any vampire nest. I decide to test my theory and descend back to street level, retrieve my car and drive to the area to see if I can pick up the trail again.

I hop in the Jag and race toward where I believe the vampire's daytime hide out to be. It takes several minutes to make the drive and the closer I draw, the more convinced I become that I will find what I seek amongst the decrepit warehouses and plants. The area is quite large and will take all night to search properly. I consider calling Alonso and asking him to help me, but I'd never brought him in on an actual cleansing before. I've only used him to follow and stake out locations. He'd never been in for the kill and I don't think this was the one to start him with.

A chain link fence surrounds the site with the gate sitting wide open. I figure this to be the most likely point of entry, so I'll start my search there. I park and go to the trunk to get my kit. I tuck the heavy, curved knife into my belt and pull the crossbow from the bag, and drag the string back, cocking it. After fitting an arrow into the groove, I sling the remaining items still in the kit bag over my shoulder and ease the trunk lid down, trying to be quiet when my cell phone rings. The jangle of the phone sounds so loud in the still night, it made me jump. I quickly yank the offending object from my pocket and mute it to stop the noise. Glancing at the screen, I see Alonso. He must have felt me thinking about him.

I think about not answering, then decide maybe I need to hear a friendly voice before walking into the valley of the shadow of death. I might be immortal, but dying usually hurts, a lot, and it isn't something I relish doing tonight. I hit the answer button and bring the phone to my ear, whispering, "Hello?"

"You working?" he asks.

"Yes. Do you need something or did you just call to chat?"

"I'm not the chatty type," he states. "I'm following your girl."

"What?" I blurt out loud before thinking about it. I know he meant Erin and that brings two questions to mind. "Why are you following her and what the hell is she doing out? I told her to stay in the house."

"Figured," he says. "I'm off tonight and thought I'd drive by her place. I know how she's gotten under your skin and was curious if you were there. As it happens, I was just in time to see her come out and get in a car."

More questions flood my mind, if she is out, she is vulnerable and who's she with? I mean, we aren't dating or anything, but I don't like her not following my advice when it's me risking my ass for her.

"Is she alone?"

"Nope. She's with a dude. Nice car, too. Big Mercedes, dark blue. Real slick." I know he threw that last part in to make me jealous. It worked.

"Did you get a look at him?"

"Sure did. He opened her door for her. Real gentleman. Six-three, maybe four, thin, long black hair in a ponytail. Sharp dresser, too."

"Where are you?"

"Euclid, driving east," he answers.

I have no idea where she could be going, although I'm not that familiar with Euclid Avenue. "Do they know you're behind them?" I ask, trying to think of a plan.

"Hey man, that's insulting." Alonso snaps. "No, they don't know I'm back here. Traffic's heavy tonight and I'm keeping four or five cars between us."

"Good," I respond, ignoring his perceived insult. I don't have time to deal with it now, "Stay with them. Figure out where they're going, but don't call me. I'm close to a vampire nest. I'll call you when I get out of here."

"Where are you, in case you don't call or show up tomorrow?" That's my Alonso, all concern.

"Industrial area at the end of Baxter," I answer.

"Got it. You be careful," he adds then clicks off.

I turn the phone off and stick it back in my pocket. I don't like this development, but there isn't anything I can do about it now. She sure as hell will hear about it tomorrow, though. I heft the crossbow and start into the industrial park, thoughts of Erin pushed to the back of my mind.

*****

Focused is how I like to think of myself when I'm on a cleansing. I have no special abilities and none of my senses are any better than other humans, but my years of experience have attuned them to seek out the subtle signs left by unnaturals. It's like that tonight. I know I am close to the vampire and all of my nerves tingle with anticipation.

I want to verify this is in fact the location, so I intend to set out around the fence line to find where he crossed. When I first step to the gate and the large post supporting it, this plan became unnecessary. Right on the gate post, about a foot up from the bottom, a large, blackish stain runs down and spreads out on the ground. I bend over for a confirming smell and the odor of rotten blood and ammonia make me gag. Vampire piss, left as a warning so others would know this area belongs to him.

I smirk as I keep walking, keeping my eyes and ears as open as possible. Unlike the stories that people like to believe, vampires have no such thing as class or grace and do not live as gentlemen of high society. They are abhorrent animals that live in holes and sewers, wherever they can find a place away from humans and the sun. They're not dead during daylight hours, either. They rest and sleep during the day for sure, but they're just as dangerous and capable of killing during the day as they are at night. If a human is bitten and lives, which is rare, they will become a vampire. The turning process can take weeks to accomplish, but once bitten, the new vampire will immediately shun day light and thirst for human blood. The physical change is what takes time and leaves the person a grotesque monster that is twisted and hideous.

They are incredibly strong and fast. They have eyesight and hearing that far exceeds even that of predatory cats. This one has already shown me just how fast they could become. I walk from the gate down the garbage and debris strewn drive toward a line of four, long two-story brick buildings. Very few of the street lights remain and even fewer work, so there isn't much light. I risk using my flash light to avoid the noise of tripping over something and breaking my neck, again.

It's a good bet that wherever this thing lives, it will be below ground, so, as I enter the first building, I look for doors that might lead below the main ground level. The first building is more like a warehouse and has a completely open floor with support columns in rows along its length. I shine my light around the large empty structure and up into the rafters above. My light disturbs a few pigeons, but beyond them the place is empty. Other than the two, large roll up doors at either end and several broken windows, no openings are visible.

Having found nothing in the first, I move on to the second building. It turns out to be the twin of the first, open and vacant. Moving on, I visit the third and fourth buildings finding them to be exact copies of the first two. These had to be designed for storing something as there had been no machinery or places for it to be mounted. There was no place to hide and no way to get below ground in any of them. I know I am on the right track and the vampire's hiding place has to be close, I can feel it, just can't see it yet. I walk outside the fourth building and stand in the weed-choked parking lot.

Shinning my light around, I consider my options when the light plays across another structure. This one sits off to the side of the former parking lot and with the overgrowth of weeds, had been nearly impossible to see. It is single story, same brick construction with a pitched roof that has partially fallen in on the side closest to me. I quickly check the rest of the fenced in area to see if there are any other buildings I missed and find there is only the one. This has to be it.

Turning my light off, I cautiously make my way toward the low dilapidated structure. As I draw closer, I can see the door is missing and the opening yawns uninvitingly to the decaying ruin. I ease up to the door and, holding the crossbow up at the ready, I flash my light quickly around the first room. A few items of moldering furniture, a desk, and rotten carpet are the only things visible, but the smell of decomposition is unmistakable.

"Honey, I'm home," I breathe quietly with a satisfied grin at knowing my prey is near.

Noticing a door opposite of where I stand, I make my way across the wet, moldy carpet to where it led to another room with another door. The second room turns out to be much like the first, so I cross it without delaying. The third door opens easily and reveals a set of stairs going down through the concrete floor. The foul stench wafting up nearly overwhelms me. Fighting my gag reflex, I cross to the top of the stairs and shine my light down into the pit of hell and jump.

A leering skull stares back at me and I almost fire an arrow before realizing what it is. Looking closely, I can see the small skull sitting on the damp floor set in a way that anyone looking down would be staring straight into its empty eye sockets. Its size, along with its softer rounded features, tell me it belonged to a child. This is a taunt made by the creature specifically for me. It knows what I am and probably suspected I would eventually track it and find its nest. That means I was expected, not good news.

SIX

Steeling my nerves and gritting my teeth, I prepare to descend into the foul smelling home of the vampire. If he expects me, there is no reason to attempt stealth. I keep my light on and use it to illuminate the little hidey holes where he might lie in wait. I hold the crossbow up in front of me, ready to use as soon as I can get a glimpse of the creature and step down onto the first step.

I've found that first step is the hardest. Once made, all the others that follow are a little easier and it takes only seconds before I find myself at the bottom of the stairwell. I step over the skull of the long dead child and an immediate right leads into a long corridor made from poured concrete. The walls are damp and water trickles down here and there, leaving the floor wet with small puddles where the uneven floor allows the water to collect. Cobwebs run from wall to wall and hang from the ceiling in streamers. Old and rusted wire cages enclose light fixtures spaced along the roof of the corridor with a light switch set on the wall beside the door. I know it will be useless, but figure what the hell. I flip the switch up and down several times, not surprised when nothing flickers to life.

There seems to be no sense in hesitating, so I step into the corridor, shinning the light behind me as well as in front. Behind me, the corridor runs about ten feet to a dead end—I hate that term. The only direction seems to be forward so forward I go, slowly. The corridor runs for an indefinite length. My light can't penetrate the stygian darkness of the other end. It runs generally in the direction toward the front gate, so I know the overgrown parking lot is above me.

After about thirty paces, I come to a closed door on my right and a quick check of the knob finds it to be unlocked. I click the light off, push the door open, and step inside and to my right with my back against the wall. I then click the light back on and flash it around the room with the crossbow held high against my shoulder ready to fire. Nothing, the room, about fifteen feet by fifteen feet square, is empty.

Stepping back into the corridor and closing the door, I continue in my previous direction. I come to a door on my left a short time later and, repeating my tactic for entry, find it to be empty as well. This goes on for several minutes, a door will appear out of the gloom on either my right or left and I will enter to find it empty. The only smell is the ever-present odor of decomposition and for one fearful moment, I think I will be trapped in this never ending corridor, searching for a vampire that will eventually find and tear me to pieces.

But judging by how far I've walked, I have to be reaching the area under the front gate soon and, low and behold, there it is. I stand staring at the blank wall for a few seconds, perplexed. I shine the light back the way I came and nothing new seems in evidence. I know I did not miss any doors, so here I am, at the end of the tunnel, and I find absolutely zip. The odor of decomp seems stronger here and feels almost palpable. As I shine the light around, it glints off something metal on the floor. I glance down to find a rusted metal grate about twenty inches square. I kneel to inspect it and the cloying smell of rotten meat wafts up from the depths of the hole. I know that what I seek will be down there.

I slip my fingers through the rusted grating and pull up. The grate lifts away easily with little noise and I set it on the floor. Shinning the light into the hole, I can see a trickle of water running along the bottom of a tunnel, round this time, about four feet below me. Getting down flat on my stomach, I slip the arm holding the light and my head into the drain, holding my breath against the stench and praying that neither will get ripped off by the vampire I'm hunting. In one direction, the tunnel angles away into black nothingness. As I turn to check the other direction, I find myself staring into the empty eye sockets of another child's skull.

I nearly drop the flashlight, startled by the grisly gift left by my soon-to-be host. The skull hangs suspended by a string tied to a protruding bolt in the rim of the grate's frame. I can see the tunnel is about three and a half feet in diameter and I'll be able move along it on my knees if I bend at the waist.

Pulling back from the hole, I check to make sure the crossbow will fit through the opening and once it is in, I lower it to the bottom, quickly following it. I pull the kit bag in behind me and on hands and knees, push my gear before me and duck walk in the direction the skull pointed. The tunnel, which turns out to be a huge drainage pipe, is old and rust icicles hang down above me, scraping the skin when I rise up too much. Murky water runs in a small stream along the curved bottom of the pipe in the same direction I travel.

The pipe seems to slope down gently in this direction and I estimate I am about thirty feet underground. That's a lot of dirt to try and make my way through if I become stuck down here. After about a hundred yards of this, my light shines into a larger space and I see the pipe ends in a large sump chamber. About twenty feet square and ten feet deep, several pipes like mine empty into this sump. Water splashes and gurgles its way out of them into the sump where a drain at the bottom carries it away.

Years of storm debris and garbage, sticks and leaves lay in clumps along the perimeter of the sump. The rotten odor of decomposition is overwhelming here and the reason rests in little piles scattered over the bottom of the chamber. Dozens of child sized corpses, some only half rotten, others deteriorated all the way to bones, litter the place. Anger floods me as I look at the helpless victims of this foul creature. So many dead that I couldn't save, but at least now I can avenge them.

Sitting down in the mouth of the pipe, I ease over the edge and make the three foot drop to the floor with ease. I adjust my gear and pick my way through the detritus on the floor to the center of the chamber, being sure to not step on the sad remains of the child victims. They'd suffered enough and I don't want to add insult to it. Once in the center, I shine my light around checking every corner.

Closing my eyes for a second, I recite a small prayer for the children's sake and for mine, then taking a deep breath, I shout, "Alright you bastard, you've gotten me here! Now show yourself!"

Several seconds pass with no response, and then behind me, from one of the pipes, a hiss like escaping steam tells me where my prey hides. I spin to meet my foe and shinning the light on the opening, watch as the sickly, pale-skinned face of a vampire with pointed ears, flat snout, and needle sharp teeth emerge into the sump. As I watch, the thing crawls out until it squats in the mouth of the pipe, glaring at me with killer eyes.

From the sagging, deflated teats hanging against her chest, I realize this was a female vampire, not the male I thought I'd been hunting. She hisses at me again and prepares to spring. I react instinctually, bringing the crossbow up and swinging it in the direction I expect her to move. She obliges and I let fly with the arrow just as she springs to my right. My arrow and her body make contact in mid-flight. The heavy iron point punches through bone and cartilage, pierces the heart, and protrudes six inches out of her back. The olive wood does its job and she crashes to the floor of the sump, paralyzed.

I lower the crossbow and reach into the kit bag for the flask of holy oil, intending to perform the ritual and remove her head. I never hear a thing as a large weight lands on my back and shoulders from behind, driving me to the floor. It smashes my face into the concrete, breaking my nose and several teeth. Before I can react, a strong hand grabs the top of my head and wrenches it over, exposing the left side of my neck.

The fetid odor of rot is breathed into my face as a coarse voice rasps, "Now, I feed. Then rip you apart. You lay here for eternity."

With that, the needle teeth bite into my neck, tearing until the jugular and carotid artery are both torn and spurting blood into the creature's maw. I know I have to do something quick. Struggling with my left arm, I finally pull the knife at my belt and blindly jam it into the thing on my back. Over and over, I strike with the blade until finally, with a howl, the vampire releases its hold on me. With all my remaining strength, I surge upward, throwing the thing off my back. I scramble for the crossbow where it had been thrown by the impact. I jerk the string back, locking it, and dig another arrow out of the kit bag. My vision is failing and things are getting dark as I fit the arrow to the bow. I know I have only one chance or he would have me.

I don't relish the thought of lying in this stinking cistern, dismembered for all time, so I struggle to keep it together to make this shot. As my vision tunnels down to nothing, the image of the vampire swells in front of me. With the last remaining strength I possess, I bring the bow up and fire. I never see the impact as the lights finally go out for good and I drop dead amongst the remains of the children.

*****

The smell was the first thing I become aware of as consciousness returns to me. I lay face down on the moldering corpse of a little girl. Her long, golden hair greets my sight as I open my eyes. Unsure if I'd won the contest or if I had been dismembered and scattered across the floor of the sump, I will my body to roll over. I am rewarded with movement and the feeling returns to my arms and legs as I push myself over onto my back.

I take a quick inventory and find I still have all my fingers and toes so I sit up and look around the sump. The weak, diffused light from my flashlight shows I've finally had a streak of good luck. The male vampire lays in a heap about four feet away, paralyzed, the arrow point sticking through the skin of his back. The female is right where I remember her falling. The batteries in my light are failing and I know I don't have much time to finish my task, so I stand and start searching for my tools.

The crossbow and flashlight I find close to hand where they fell when I keeled over. The kit bag is still slung around my neck, but my knife I can't see anywhere. It takes a couple of minutes to find it. I can't help but grin that it is still embedded in the side of the male vampire. I roll him onto his back and pull the flask of holy oil from the kit. Anointing his brow, I make the sign of the cross and speak the Latin phrases I learned so long ago. With the ritual complete, I set to cutting the head from the body. I place it in the leak-proof bag and only then do I withdraw the arrow from the body.

Once the head is cremated, the body will decompose away, just like the victims lying around it. Now that the male has been dispatched, I move to the female and complete her ritual and decapitation with no delay. The flashlight is dimmer and I still have a long crawl and walk to make it back to the surface. I'm still not completely healed, either, but can't waste time just yet. I still feel weak and my face and neck hurt like they are on fire.

Everything happened so fast once it kicked off that I hadn't had time to think about the fact that it had been a pair of vampires and not the solo that I'd thought. After I cram everything into the kit bag along with the two heads, I decide to take a quick look around before leaving. Every pipe I look into with the exception of the one I used to enter shows signs of having been lived in. This isn't good. If true, there are at least three more of the things living in this nest and with a dying flashlight, I have no desire to be trapped down here any longer.

I go to the pipe I'd used for entry and toss my gear into it. Climbing in after and pushing the bag in front of me, I make my way as quickly as I can to the drain grate and climb back into the large storage corridor. As I place the grate back into the frame, I listen as hissing and scrabbling of claws come from the direction of the sump. I pause and concentrate, trying to determine how many voices I can hear. The fact they found their dead and decapitated brother and sister was easy to determine from the angry shrieks that reach me a few moments later. I decide it is time to get the hell out of there and fit the grate back in place over the drain.

A loud metallic screech sounds as the rusty metal settles into place. The shrieking and hissing from the sump stop and then the clawing at metal starts and grows louder as the fiends make their way along the pipe toward me. Now is the time to move and I struggle to my feet and stagger down the corridor toward the stairs. I almost reach the stairwell when I hear the grate forced from its frame with so much force it bangs and clangs against the walls.

I don't have much time. I pull on my last reserves of speed to reach the surface before the pissed off vampires can reach me. As I make the top step of the stairs, a shriek comes from below and it sounds so loud, they have to be right behind me. I'm not sure how I do it, but I push through the doors and stagger into the sunlight outside the crumbling building.

Just as I exit the last door, a clawed hand slashes out at my back, slicing through the kit bag straps, my shirt and the skin underneath it. I lurch forward, knowing I have made it by the narrowest of margins. One more second and the thing would have had me. I turn and look back at the door, knowing I'm safe in the sunlight. A pair of malevolent eyes stare back at me from the shadows, and then it hisses and is gone.

I finally take a breath, accepting the fact I'd nearly screwed up again. I should have believed my eyes when I found all the signs behind Erin's. I suspected more than one vampire had been involved, and yet I went down there as if I expected only one. It could have been much worse than fatal. My one true fear is that I will become dismembered in a place where I have neither help nor ability to reattach my severed limbs. If that were to happen, I would lay there for a very long time, a prisoner not because of bars or a cell, but because my own body would not function. I'd be awake and able to experience all of the fun it entailed. A not at all pleasant thought.

After taking a few minutes to compose myself, I start back toward my car. The sun is fairly high and I figure the time around eight a.m. I decide the parking lot to be as good a place as any and drop the kit bag and gather wood and other flammable material to build a pyre for the two remains. With wood on the ground, I place the heads on top and then pile more wood on top of them. I use the remainder of the holy oil in the flask as an accelerant and douse the wood. Fishing out a box of wooden matches, I strike one and let it fall onto the soaked wood. The fire flashes up with a wave of heat and I take a few steps back to watch it burn.

I stay there for over an hour until all that is left are two blackened and charred skulls. These I smash into powder with a piece of fence post, ensuring there will be no way they can ever regenerate. Satisfied that they were truly cleansed, I finally make my way to my car. I drop the rip and torn bag containing my weapons into the trunk and close the lid. Unlocking the driver's door, I gratefully drop into the soft leather seat, forcing myself to not just pass out there. I dig my cell phone from my pocket and hit the button to turn it on. After hearing the tone advising that I have a signal, I select Alonso's number and press dial. His phone never rings, but goes straight to voice mail. I suspect he'd been out late following Erin and switched it off to get some undisturbed sleep, so I leave a message.

"I'm out and on my way home. Killed two vamps. I'm going to get some sleep. I'll call later," I say then hit the disconnect button.

Dropping the phone in the console, I start the Jag's engine and pull out of the industrial area. On the road back to my apartment, I consider what my next move should be. I need to find out what Erin has been up to and I need to cleanse three more vampires besides the werewolf Harry Crowe. Not to mention there is a still a demon that needs to be dealt with.

First, I need to get some sleep. I'd be able to think clearer after that and I plan to ask Alonso for help with the rest of this cleansing. It seems to be getting out of control. With my plan conceived, I settle in for the rest of the drive to my apartment, looking forward to a long, hot shower and a set of clean sheets.

SEVEN

I smell bad and what's more, I know I smell bad. The odor of decomposition from the sewer and the vampire nest permeate my very skin. I don't think there is any help for my clothes, but I hope a shower will take care of the stench on me at least. The clothes will have to go in a garbage bag and out of the apartment as soon as possible. If this keeps up, I'll be out of anything to wear soon.

When I arrive back at my apartment, I go straight upstairs and strip in the kitchen and dump everything in the garbage. Hopping in the shower, I spend plenty of time soaping up until I can only smell that wonderful, clean scent. I think I scrubbed a couple of layers of skin off in the process. I exit the shower bright red and a lot fresher smelling than I went in. I towel off and slip on a pair of gym shorts and a T-shirt for the quick trip to the dumpster behind The Magnolia House. I don't run into any of the other residents or my landlady, thankfully. It would have been hard to explain the extraordinary stink coming from the bag I'm carried.

Back in my apartment, I eat a hearty breakfast of bacon, scrambled eggs, toast, and drink an entire quart of orange juice. One thing I've always found amusing, death usually turns a person's stomach and any thought of food will cause them to retch. With me, as soon as it's over, I'm starving. Now, I might find it hard to tear into a big plate of ribs after seeing a burnt and decomposing body, but generally nothing affects my appetite.

After eating and placing my dishes in the sink, I crawl into bed for a well-deserved sleep and am out almost as soon as my head hits the pillow. It feels as if the dream commences immediately and I find myself transported back to the wind and rain swept beach south of Civitavecchia on the night *The Puttana* sank...

*****

I awoke the next morning still lying on my back above the high tide line. As I opened my eyes, I stared up at a beautiful Mediterranean sky, clear and bright. The storm of last evening had blown itself out, leaving calm seas and the azure skies I so loved. I sat up looking for the wreck of *The Puttana*, but all that remained was some floating debris in the edge of the surf. Of the ship herself, nothing could be seen.

My home for the last six years and all the people I knew were gone.

I was alone again. I stood with bare feet and bare chest, dressed only in a pair of sail cloth pants and brushed the dried sand from my body. What would I do now? I remembered that the light house marking the port had been visible just before we ran aground, so I started north along the beach toward Civitavecchia. I had no clue what I would do once I reached the city. I would relate my story and hope to sign on with another crew. Maybe work my way back to Trieste and home, if my father didn't kill me on sight that is.

It turned out, I was still several miles to south and it took all day to walk. By the time I reached the outskirts of the city, it was late afternoon and I was tired, thirsty, and my feet were raw from the sand. I trudged wearily through the streets, people gawking at me, as I tried to find a tavern. This part of the city turned out to be mostly homes with a few market stalls here and there. The food on display looked good and my stomach growled with hunger, but I had no money so I continued on.

Around dusk, I finally reached the port and found what I searched for. Just like any other port city, the taverns were concentrated around the actual harbor and the Roman port was no different. By this time, I was near to exhaustion, with fighting the storm all day yesterday and being unconscious all night, I hadn't eaten or drank anything since evening before last. At the end of the street on which I walked, I saw a tavern, a sign above the door proclaimed it The Cat's Head and the lights were on and the door open.

I stumbled inside and fell into the first chair I saw, relieved to rest for a minute. I barely took notice of the several patrons who stared at me and my undignified entry.

I hadn't been there long when a stout woman with a scowl on her face approached and asked what I wanted. I told her I was the sole survivor of *The Puttana* and we had gone down south of the port in yesterday's storm. Her expression immediately softened and she said she would bring me some water. I thanked her as she turned to leave and she smiled.

As she left, several of the men who sat drinking gathered around me and began to ask questions. I tried answering, but I was still too parched to easily talk. A large older man came over and told the others to leave me be. Obviously a sailor by the way he was dressed he told one of the other men to go fetch the Harbor Master and sat down at my table.

This new man sat across the table looking intently at me for several seconds, then said, "I know your captain. What happened to him?"

"Captain Caprisi was killed when the mast broke loose and fell across the wheel deck. I wanted to save the ship, but the rest of the crew became scared and tried to abandon her. They and the skiff were lost in a wave," I said, still numb in disbelief that everything I'd known was gone.

He seemed satisfied with my answer. "What position did you hold?"

"I'm First Mate and have been for three years. The captain was my guardian," I replied as strongly as I could manage.

The woman returned with a large pitcher of water and a cup. Setting them in front of me, she said, "Leave him be 'til he's gotten some water in him."

I thanked her again and slopped some of the water into the cup, spilling most of it. She grabbed the pitcher and my hand holding the cup, steadying them and poured the water for me. I managed to down three cups before the Harbor Master arrived carrying a large ledger book. He sat down at the table, opened the book and had me relate the entire story while he recorded the events. He ended by having me name all the crewmen lost. Finished, he closed the book, a grave expression on his face and told me his office would pay for a meal and put me up for the night, but I would have to make other arrangements tomorrow.

The Harbor Master and the stout woman nodded to each other and he patted me once on the shoulder in a soothing manner. Then, he tucked the ledger of lost ships under his arm and left The Cat's Head. The woman introduced herself as Maria, the owner and proprietor of the tavern and the inn located above. She told me she would feed me and there was a room available if I wanted it. I told her yes and thanked her again. She smiled at me and went to prepare my dinner. The others who had gathered around to hear the story moved back to their tables, leaving me with the older man.

He introduced himself as Vincenti and asked, "What's your name, boy?"

"Antonio Bianco, from Trieste," I answered.

He told me he'd been First Mate on a ship until recently, but had quit and was looking for a new ship. Vincenti asked what I planned to do and I told him I would try and find another ship as well, seeing as I really didn't have any other skills.

He laughed and said, "Good luck with that. I've been here for a month and can't find anything. I've used up almost all my earnings and I'm going down to Rome tomorrow. Got to find some work if I don't want to starve." He paused for a second, and then asked, "You have any money?"

"No," I said. "I'll have to find something tomorrow or I'll be out in the street. I was a beggar once and don't fancy doing it again."

Vincenti nodded knowingly and said, "Why don't you come south to Rome with me? You look strong. We could probably find work together."

He told me he also had a room above the tavern and we could leave together in the morning if I wanted. I had no other prospects and if a seasoned sailor couldn't find work, then I would surely have difficulty, so I agreed. Besides, I wanted to see Rome and this seemed as good a time as any.

He laughed again and said, "That's the spirit. Now stop drinking that water and let's have some wine."

I went to bed that night with my belly full and very drunk. The next morning, when I awoke I had a bad hangover, but I forced myself to wash and get dressed. I felt moderately better when I went downstairs to meet Vincenti. He waited at a table nibbling at a crust of bread and sipping a cup of wine. When I sat down, he watched me, a slight smile on his lips.

I grew tired of his silence and asked, "What are you grinning at?"

"Nothing, I'm just curious," he answered.

Annoyed now, I snapped, "Curious about what?"

He sat his wine cup on the table and said, "I wonder if you intend to walk all the way to Rome with no pants on."

I looked down and was shocked to find I wasn't wearing my pants. I had been given a pair of shoes a little too big, socks a bit too small, a shirt about right, and a bag to carry a few belongings all from Maria. She said they had been left at the inn by her various lovers over time and she had no use for them. Somehow that morning, I had managed to put on the shoes, socks, and shirt and even had the bag slung over my shoulder, but I had forgotten the pants. I sat there naked from waist to ankles.

I was still trying to figure out how this had happened when Maria came to the table with a cup and some bread and cheese for me. Noticing my nakedness, she leaned over giving me a kiss on the cheek and said, "It's a nice one dear, but you already showed it to me last night."

Vincenti blew bread crumbs and wine all over the table and started coughing trying to catch his breath. Maria simply walked back toward the kitchen, a satisfied smile on her face. I jumped up, embarrassed beyond belief, and ran back up the stairs to retrieve my pants. As I reached the top landing, Vincenti had recovered his breath and his loud guffaws could be heard throughout the tavern.

It wasn't how I had planned to start my day.

Dressed completely now, I went back downstairs. Vincenti still sat at the table, the same silly grin on his unshaven face. I sat once again and immediately set about eating the bread and cheese Maria had brought, not looking up. Vincenti poured wine into my cup and I took a long pull, feeling better as the strong liquid rinsed my dry mouth.

We sat in silence for a while, both eating and drinking, when finally he said, "As you should be feeling quite good this morning, maybe we should get started toward Rome."

"I'm ready, anytime," I agreed. "I should probably say goodbye to Maria before we leave."

"Yes, probably," Vincenti said in a mock serious tone.

As I stood, I looked at him and his face was bright red. I could tell he was about to explode into laughter again. Without another word, I went to the kitchen to find Maria. I told her we were leaving and she came to me and wrapped me in her arms, squishing me into her huge bosom. She kissed me several times and made me promise to come see her again soon. I promised and, finally breaking free of her embrace, went back into the tavern. My traveling partner was standing by the door, a rolled up blanket tied across his shoulder and as I came out of the kitchen, he stepped out. I hurried to catch up and together we marched south out of Civitavecchia and toward Rome.

The trip south took us two days. It's only about thirty-five miles and we walked and hitch hiked on ox carts until we finally arrived in the city. I had never seen anything like it. Wide cobbled streets, buildings taller than even the tallest mast on the big three mast ships I'd seen, and the people. I thought that the entire world must be in Rome for I had never seen so many people.

With the last of Vincenti's coins, we paid for two nights at a small inn and immediately looked for work. We still had some of the bread and cheese given to us by Maria, but it wouldn't last long. On the evening of the second night, I sat in our room resting after trudging all over looking for work, when Vincenti came in excited. He told me he had found us a job that paid two silver coins each. I grinned at his words. Four silvers would easily buy us food and lodging for a month if we were careful. When I questioned him about the job, he lost his enthusiasm and said it was rough work, a bit of bullying.

I asked him to explain. "It's simple," he said. "The man that hired us is owed some money by another man that doesn't want to pay his debt. We're to go round to this other man and get the money."

I asked how we'd get the money. Vincenti said, "I'll hit him over the head with a stick and go through his pockets while you keep watch." He could see that I didn't like the idea much, so he tried to soothe my worries. "I know it's not what we talked about, but we need money. Four silvers will keep us fed and a roof above us long enough to find a real job. It's just this once, I promise."

I finally agreed and Vincenti led the way through the streets to a small alley. He told me we were to wait here and the man we were supposed to get the money from would come this way on his way home. We would accost him in the alley and then take the money back to our employer, who would then pay us for our services. We took up position on either side of the alley, hiding back in the shadows and waited.

An hour or so went by before a man, older than Vincenti, but taller and not as fat, wearing nice clothes, came walking toward us. I looked to where I knew Vincenti hid and saw him bring the stick he'd brought out from behind his back. This must be the man, so I tried to get ready to help my friend. I was scared, more scared than I had ever been and my heart was pounding so loud I was sure our victim must be able to hear it. He paid us no attention though and passed into the alley without a glance to either right or left. Vincenti came out of his hiding place and motioned me to follow.

I fell in behind him and we ran forward to catch up to the tall man. We lost sight of him around a slight corner and Vincenti told me to hurry so he didn't get away. Vincenti rounded the corner, his stick held high in preparation for clubbing the tall man and I ran a couple of steps behind. I heard Vincenti grunt as he came to a stop and I barely avoided colliding with him as I slid on the wet cobbles of the alley. The tall man stood facing Vincenti and my friend's club clattered to the ground. It was then I noticed the foot of shiny metal blade extending out of Vincenti's back. The blade pulled back, disappeared, and my partner in crime collapsed to the ground.

The tall man looked at me as he bent and wiped Vincenti's blood from the blade onto the back of his shirt. He straightened and slid the sword back into its scabbard then said to me, "Go home, boy, I've no wish to kill you." Without another word, he turned and continued on his way.

I went to my friend and rolled him over. A large pool of blood had already leaked onto the cobbles and Vincenti was dead. Shocked and scared, the only thing I could think to do was run, so I ran. I had not paid enough attention to the route we had taken to get here and I soon found myself lost. I went this way and that, never seeing anyplace that looked familiar. I wanted to get back to the inn, but had no idea of how to get there and I was far too scared to stop someone to ask.

Eventually, I came to the Tiber River and crossed the Ponte Sant'Angelo Bridge. The Vatican was up the hill several blocks and I knew how to get back to our inn from Piazza Pio XII, outside St. Peter's Square. I hurried through the streets toward the most powerful church in the world. My single minded wish to escape this night caused me to be blind to everything but my desire to reach the Vatican and caused me to rush straight into a man carrying several trays stacked with bread. He had been carrying them from his bakery out to a cart parked on the street. We collided and the loaves of bread went flying all over the sidewalk.

"Damn, damn, *damn*," he shouted looking at the ruined loaves all over the sidewalk. He turned and glared at me. "You should have been watching where you were going. I hope to hell you can pay for this."

I sat up from where I had landed, looking around me at the crushed bread, the wonderful aroma still hung in the air. I stood and apologized, "I'm sorry, sir. It's my fault. I was in a hurry and didn't see you."

Still angry he said, "Damn right it's your fault. How do you plan to pay for this?"

"I've no money sir. I'm looking for a job, that's why I was in such a hurry," I said still seeing my dead partner in crime on the cobbles, his blood all over everything.

He looked at me a second longer, then asked, "You were coming here looking for work?" He pointed behind himself toward his bakery. It was then that I noticed the help wanted sign posted in the front window of the shop.

A faint glimmer of hope appeared. "Yes sir, a friend told me you were looking for help and I wanted to get here before you closed," I lied.

"Well you didn't have to be in such a damn hurry. I live above the place. You could have come by anytime," he said, still angry, but cooling down some.

"Sorry sir," I said. "I didn't know that, but if you hire me, I will be glad to pay you what I owe. You can deduct it from my wages."

He inspected me for a few seconds then nodded, coming to a decision. "You're damn right I'll deduct it from your wages. Now go inside and ask my daughter Lilith for an apron and broom. Then get your ass back out here and clean up this mess."

"Yes sir," I said and ran for the door.

As I pulled it open he asked, "What's your name, boy?"

"Antonio, sir," I answered and rushed inside the shop.

EIGHT

It's just before dusk when I finally wake up. I slept all day and yet I don't feel rested. My twisted sheets are proof I tossed and turned because of the dream. I drag myself out of bed and into the tiny bathroom for another shower. Feeling better afterward, I dress and then go about straightening the apartment.

Around full dark, while I'm washing my breakfast dishes, someone knocks on my door. While I hadn't thought of Erin all day, she immediately pops into my mind. I feel a surge of excitement at possibly seeing her, and the thought of the two of us wrecking my newly-made bed had me hot and my body responds to the stimulus. I remember I'd been angry with her about something, but it doesn't matter at the moment. All that matters is seeing her. A nagging voice in the back of my mind informs me that something is wrong with this picture, but I ignore it. What could she possibly do to me?

I dry my hands and rush to the door, trying to think of something clever to say to her. The big smile on my face instantly falls away when I jerk the door open and see who's actually standing there. Detective David George, Atlanta PD, stands on the landing, his hound dog face unsmiling and those brown eyes boring into me.

Noticing the instant change in my facial expression, he asks, "Expecting someone else?"

"No. But I'm hoping that someone will drop by," I reply. "What can I do for you, detective?"

"I remember telling you that I would come by to check on you. I've dropped by a couple of times and spoke to your landlady. Guess we've just missed each other," he states, raising one eyebrow as if he's waiting for me to give him an answer to some great question.

I nod. "Yeah, I've been busy. As you can see, I'm fine. Thanks for coming by." I smile at the slight disappointment on his face as I try to shut the door, but George steps forward and places his hand flat against it, keeping it from shutting. My options are limited at this point. I could engage in a test of strength and try to slam the door on him, probably pissing him off, or I could reopen it and see what else he wants.

I choose the latter option and ask, "Is there something else?"

"Well, now that you mention it, I have a couple of questions if you have a minute or two," he answers. He takes another step forward, crossing the threshold into my apartment before asking, "May I come in?"

Trying to hide my annoyance, I step aside so he can enter and reply, "Very well."

Looking at the door as he walks fully into the apartment, the detective comments, "Nice door. You do the work yourself?"

I glance at the door seeing nothing but my old oak door in need of a new stain. "No, it's the way it was when I moved in." Without turning, he nods and continues toward the seating area. I vaguely remember Mrs. Betty had mentioned something about my door recently, but there's nothing on it. It was odd that two people asked about the door, but I have more pressing issues to deal with than a door. Like the detective currently making himself at home in my place.

Without waiting to be asked, George selects my chair and sits down, forcing me to sit on the sofa. I recognize this as a tactic to make me uncomfortable and put him in a better position to ask his questions. It works, too. I feel silly sitting in the middle of the sofa like a small child. I quickly shift to the end farthest away from him and relax against the arm. This brings a slight, fleeting smile to his lips as he silently watches.

After several uncomfortable seconds, I break the silence. "You have something you want to ask me about?"

"Yes," he sits forward slightly. "Tell me again why your car was parked at the Drake."

Letting my annoyance show, I say, "I've already explained I met a woman who didn't want her neighbors seeing a strange vehicle in her driveway. I parked there because it was convenient and rode with her. She brought me back to my car and I found you guys all over the place. I don't see what the problem is."

George looks thoughtful for a moment and then states, "There wouldn't be a problem if your alibi wasn't a lie."

I stand, pretending to be angry. "Are you calling me a liar?"

His expression never changes. He continues to look relaxed and in charge as he replies, "Yes, Mr. White, that's exactly what I'm saying. Please sit back down. We both know you aren't nearly as outraged as you're pretending to be."

Shocked by his candor, I sit back down. Once again, I had tried to play the self-centered, typical young male. I like this act because it's what most people expect when they see me and it's easy, but it isn't working with Detective George. Over the years, I'd been in contact with many different people and learned how to interrogate them, how to read their body language and judge their character. I could even tell when most of them were lying. I did what I had to do to find my prey and this detective is no different. Time to switch tactics.

Keeping my voice even and calm, I say, "Well, if you don't believe my story, why don't you tell me what *you* think I was doing there."

For the first time, a genuine smile stretches across his face. "There you are. Pleasure to meet the real Mr. White." The smile drops away and he continues, "You know that's not how this works. I ask, you answer. And please keep your hands where I can see them, I'd hate to have to shoot you."

I know Detective George meant what he'd said and if I made a stupid move, he won't hesitate to shoot me. While this isn't a real concern as far as me being injured, it would be difficult to explain why I wasn't dead. I have no weapons near to hand and there is far too much distance for me to cover between us to make it before he could draw and fire. Besides, I have no desire to hurt this man who is simply doing his job.

I smile and hold my hands up around shoulder high,

palms facing him saying, "Detective you are in no danger here—"

The large, double wide window in my living room exploding cut through my words, throwing glass and wood splinters over both of us. The detective and I respond instinctually, me, turning to face whatever came through the window. Detective George shoots to his feet, a Glock semi-auto magically appearing in his hand.

A large, hulking figure bounds through the empty window frame and lands with a thud, shaking the walls and making my dishes rattle. The shaggy fur that reminds me of a buffalo cape and the glowing red eyes leave no doubts in my mind what or who had come to call. The missing werewolf, Harry Crowe has just been found.

I hear George exclaim, "What the fu…" before we are all moving at once.

The detective moves toward his left to get a clean line of fire away from me. I move to my right, crossing in front of George, charging for the kitchen and my Browning twelve gauge. Crowe drives straight ahead, claws flailing, trying to connect with either of us. An inhuman snarl emanates from his distended snout.

Crowe draws first blood by swatting me in the back. The hit sends me flying straight into the bar separating the living room and kitchen. George is next into the fray and drills four forty caliber slugs into the werewolf with absolutely no effect. Stunned, it takes a couple of seconds for me to recover, but I bounce up and reach across the bar to where the twelve gauge is leaning. I bring it around with a yell and open fire.

I let loose with both barrels and miss, the silver buckshot shaving hair from Crowe's enormous back and bury themselves in the sofa. It is enough to divert his attention away from the detective and he charges me with amazing speed. I scramble backward trying to get over the bar and into the kitchen. I know the bar won't slow the beast down, but my spare ammo is in a drawer beside the sink and I desperately need it.

I am not fast enough.

Grabbing my skull in both of its huge paws, the werewolf hurls me over its back and I crash into the far wall. The dry wall disintegrates, the studs give way, and I find myself laying partially inside my closet. I rise up in time to see the beast sling my sofa out of its path and advance on where I now lay.

George yells, "Hey, over here, you bastard," followed by the sound of gunshots.

The slugs hit Crowe dead on, but he doesn't even flinch from the impact. He snarls a warning at George before resuming his advance on me.

It is all the time I need. The wall I crashed through was the back side of my weapons cache and shotgun rounds lay scattered about on the floor. I grab two with one hand and thumb the latch that breaks the shotgun open with the other. The spent shells eject and I quickly load two new ones before snapping the barrels up. Not bothering to aim, I point in the direction of the beast and let fly with both barrels.

The werewolf is huge and so close it would have been impossible to miss entirely. The buckshot strikes him low in the legs, knocking his feet out from under him. Crowe crashes to the floor as a terrible howl bursts from his mouth. As fast as I can, I reload the shotgun. I know this reprieve to be only temporary and I have to finish the beast off before it recovers.

I see George advancing on the thing that rolls in agony on my living room floor. Trying to reload, I yell at the detective, "Stay away from it."

Before he can respond or I can reload the Browning, Crowe leaps to his feet with a final howl and vaults back out the window. I scramble around, pick up loose shotgun shells and stuff them into my jeans pockets. George stands open mouthed, his Glock now forgotten at his side after what he's just seen. Finding no more shells, I crawl out of the chaos of my destroyed closet and move to the window to try and see which way the beast went.

I get just a glimpse of it as it limps around the corner onto Sycamore Street. George joins me at the window and

I glance at him. The look of disbelief shows as he stands there trying to catch his breath. I know what has to be done. The beast is wounded and we have to find it and finish the job before it has time to heal.

I pull back into the room and say as gently as I can, "Come on, we have to find it. It's hurt now and should be easy to track."

He turns toward me. "What the hell was that," but before I can respond, he continues, "Oh, that doesn't look good."

I follow the direction of his gaze and looked down at the front of my shirt. Just below my rib cage and almost center of my body, a large sliver of one of the two-by-four studs extends through the fabric of my T-shirt. Blood soaks the shirt and front of my jeans down to knee level.

I have to agree with his assessment. "No. No it doesn't."

Detective George pulls out his cell phone and starts punching in numbers. "Are you calling for an ambulance?" I ask.

"Yes. Don't do anything until I've got EMS on the line, they should be able to give me some advice," he replies with a concerned look on his face.

The idea to have a little fun with him crosses my mind, but I think better of it. I'm not sure if he even has a sense of humor. "Hang up the phone." He looks at me like I'm crazy but I repeat, "Hang up the phone. I need your help and we don't have a lot of time. We can't afford to let that thing get away."

He misunderstands, thinking I've given up and decided to die. "Stay with me. I've seen people make it with worse injuries. I'll stay with you until EMS arrives."

Frustrated, I step across to him and yank the phone out of his hand. Clicking the disconnect button, I toss it back to him. This time, the look on his face more resembles indignant than anything else. I need to start easing him into the truth of the situation. I can already feel the healing process beginning, so I say, "Look, it's really not that bad. If you give me a hand, I can get this out."

"We are not touching that," he replies, looking at me like I'm crazy. "When the paramedics get here, they'll get you to a hospital. It's going to be fine."

Without another word, I walk over to the wall and forcefully ram the sharp end of the splinter into it before he can stop me. A good portion of blood soaked wood pops out of my back, just to the left of my spine. I reach back, grasp the splinter, and withdraw it from my body. It hurts like hell, but it had to come out. The look on George's face is priceless. He never says a word, but looks like he might puke.

"If you're going to puke, do it out the window," I tell him as I point with the bloodied splinter in my hand.

"What…what the hell did you just do that for?"

"I told you it wasn't that bad." I examine the hunk of wood with a shrug then drop it on the floor. The hole is already closing and I start to tell the detective that we need to go when someone knocks on my door.

We both turn to look at the door and hear a raspy voice say, "Tony, you open this door this minute." My landlady, Betty, has arrived on the scene.

"Shit." I say and cross to the door. I wish I'd thought about the bloody, torn T-shirt before I pulled the door open. Too late, I open it and say, "Yes, Mrs. Betty?"

She takes one look at my blood soaked clothes and without another word faints dead away, falling face first into my apartment. "Damn," is all I manage to mutter. I turn and look at George who still stands where he was when I pulled the splinter out of my back.

The situation is beginning to spiral down and I need to do some damage control before it gets worse. The police had probably been called and we need to be out of the apartment before they show up. Harry Crowe is my first priority now. The silver will keep him weakened for a few hours, but he will eventually heal. I want to finish him before that happens and now I have my elderly landlady passed out in the doorway.

I take charge, "Detective, get over here," I yell in a stern voice. That gets through to him and he quickly moves and kneels beside me. "I need you to look after her. I'm going to change clothes. I will explain everything if you give me the chance, but I need your help right now." He seems to be able to grasp that and nods to me. "Good, I'll be back in a minute." With that, I stand and sprint to my bedroom.

Changing takes only a few seconds and I think about my depleted wardrobe again. I am going through clothes at a lightning pace and will need to go shopping soon. Finished dressing, I go to what is left of my weapons cache and select another kit bag, drop my large knife with a silver coated blade and all the shotgun shells into it. Next, I grab a full flask of holy oil and a clean leak-proof bag for the werewolf's head. Geared up, I go back to Detective George. He has Betty turned over onto her back and is holding a damp cloth to her brow.

As I approach, he looks up and says, "She's still out, but nothing's broken. We should get her off of the floor."

I agree, "Help me pick her up and get her back to her apartment. We don't have time to stay with her."

He nods and slides his hands under her arms. I grab her legs and together we carry the frail old woman back down the stairs. I don't see any of my other neighbors, who are most likely too scared to come out to see what happened. We prop Betty up on her sofa with a pillow under her head and George covers her up with one of the handmade throws she has lying across the back of every chair in the apartment.

Satisfied we have done as much for the tough old bird as we can, I look at George and say, "Let's go." Without waiting, I turn and go out the door, the detective right behind me. Part of me is honestly surprised he follows and doesn't try to tackle me to the floor with cuffs. I decide that this detective is definitely a keeper if he doesn't get killed by Crowe first.

Exiting the front door, we start down the steps toward the street. A dark blue, slick top Crown Victoria sits directly behind my car.

I assume it belongs to Detective George. "We'll take

yours. You drive." He doesn't hesitate and goes straight for the driver's side as I stand at the passenger door. He'd just unlocked the door when we hear the wail of a siren obviously bound for us and rapidly getting louder.

Looking over the top of his car, I ask, "Can you fix that?"

NINE

Detective George doesn't acknowledge my question. Instead, he jerks the door open, reaches in and grabs the mic for his radio. After identifying himself, he asks, "Do you have a call for service at The Magnolia House on Cherry?" A female voice replies in the affirmative and that marked Police units were en route. George acknowledges her and says, "I'm on the scene, you can cancel the call." The woman questions him if he was aware that it was a shots fired call and the detective answers with, "Yes, but it wasn't. One of the residents tried out his new home theater system and it got out of control. I happened to be driving by and stopped to check it out. Everything's fine."

By this time, the sirens were right around the corner and they went silent as two police cruisers turned onto Cherry Street. I guess the dispatcher bought the excuse. Instead of the cruisers screeching to a halt, the lead car stops beside Detective George as the second swerves around and continues down the street.

The driver of the first car rolls the passenger window down and addresses George, "Everything okay, detective?"

"Sure is, Officer. I'm just having a talk with this young man about noise and that if anyone has to come back tonight, how sorry he's going to be." He looks at me sternly for emphasis as I try to look chastised. The officer in the car laughs and tells George to call if he needs any help, then pulls away. We watch until he turns the corner at the end of my block, then George says, "Let's go."

By the time I'm seated in the passenger seat, Detective George has the car started and already in gear. He asks which way and I tell him to make a U-turn and then a left at the corner. We drive in silence until he straightens out on Sycamore and drives north. He looks over at me and orders, "Start talking." A man of few words.

"Well, let's see. Where do I start?" I mutter thoughtfully.

"Smartass. You can start with what the hell that thing

was," he interrupts.

"A werewolf," I answer. He turns and opens his mouth. I know what he intends to say, so I stop him. "I know what you're going to say, so don't. It was a werewolf and all the protesting in the world won't change that fact. They exist. And so do a lot of other things you probably don't believe in. You'd better get your brain wrapped around that fact or we're going to be in trouble."

For a second, I think he planned to have a fit, but he calms down and says, "Okay, suppose I believe you." Then he takes a deep breath and asks, "Do you have anything resembling a plan?"

Well that was fast. "Yes," I answer. "Find it and kill it. I like to keep things simple." That, 'I'm going to have a fit' look returns to his face, so I let him off the hook by saying, "Keep going this way and look for an old blue Chevy pickup. It belongs to our werewolf. Find it and we find him."

A look of curiosity crosses his face as he asks, "They drive?"

"Sure. They drive and several other mundane things that humans do. This one actually lives in the apartments where you and I first met."

A little of the 'having a fit' look returns as he asks, "The one with the broken window?"

"Yep." I smile at him. "His name is Harry Crowe and I've been tracking him for over a week. I planned to kill him three nights ago, but that obviously didn't happen. I guess he decided he'd make sure I never got a second chance."

We drive in silence for a few minutes. Cruising slowly up the street, we scan out our windows looking for any sign of the beast. Detective George finally breaks the silence. "Who got thrown through the window?"

I knew there'll be a lot of explaining to do after my next statement, but say it anyway. "Me."

He handles it better than I thought he would, stating, "You're getting around pretty good for a dead guy."

"Thanks," I reply and continue to search for the

werewolf through the car's window.

"So, he threw you *through* his apartment window and then took off?"

I already know this is going to be a long night and that I'd be answering lots of questions, so I decide to get it over with, "No, he didn't throw me through the window. That was a demon." The loud screech of brakes precedes my sliding forward in the seat and smacking my forehead on the windshield.

I sit back rubbing the sore spot and look at him. George turns in his seat until he's facing me. He points his finger at me and says, "I've had about all I can stand of this shit. I want to know what's going on and I want to know now. No more bullshit."

"Fine," I respond as I rub the growing bump. "But it's going to take a while."

"Don't care. I'm not moving from this spot until I'm satisfied you're not fucking with me."

"Can you at least pull over out of the street? We're going to attract attention sitting here. I promise I'll tell you all of it." He doesn't look happy about it, but he pulls over against the curb.

After putting the shifter in park, he once again turns toward me and says, "Okay, let's hear it."

"You're going to have to understand that what I'm telling you must remain a secret and you cannot disclose it. This fight has raged for centuries and the knowledge could destroy the very fabric of our world."

"Really?" he asks expectantly.

"No…" I answer smiling, "But I would appreciate it if you kept it to yourself all the same."

He turns back toward his window, muttering a curse under his breath.

"Just trying to lighten the mood. You need to relax, detective."

George nods and says in a much calmer voice, "Call me David."

"Alright, David. As I've already said, the monsters you've always been taught are myth, do in fact exist." I go on briefly to explain the current situation with what exists and that my job is to stop them from killing and feeding on humans. I pause to let that sink in before I continue.

I start to relax slightly as I become more comfortable telling David about my current case. "The beast you encountered tonight is a werewolf and has been hunting a woman who recently hired me to protect her. In the last two weeks, I've faced more unnatural creatures in close proximity than I ever have in the past and I've been doing this a very long time."

He interrupts me, "It couldn't have been that long. You're what, twenty-two, twenty-three?"

I smirk. "I'm older than I look, trust me. What's important right now is you understand the nature of the enemy we're facing. These things are death, pure and simple. They have no remorse, no regrets, they only want to kill and feed and we don't have much time. Crowe is injured, but he'll start to heal soon. We have to find him and finish him before that can happen."

I pause to see what his reaction will be. I can tell he wants to ask more, but we are running out of time to find Crowe. "David, you can ask all the questions that you want later, but right now, we don't have time." To his credit, he shifts the car back into drive and eases away from the curb.

Easing up the street, continuing our search, he says, "Tell me what your job really is. What are you even called?"

"I'm called a Cleanser and it's my job to cleanse our world of the things that go bump in the night. I'm not alone. There are several of us scattered around the globe and we all serve the Vatican."

"So you're a Priest?" he questions without looking over.

"No, I'm a private in the Swiss Guard. My rank means nothing, it's simply a requirement to be a member of the Guard." I reply. "I do have a contact who is a priest, Father Salvatore. He and ten others are assigned to the secret section of the Vatican that deals strictly with unnaturals. Those are the men I report back to after I've cleansed one of the evil brutes."

"Why?" he asks.

"Why do I do it?" I ask to verify his question. He nods, so I answer, "Like most of us, it's personal. Something was taken from me years ago and this is my revenge." People in his line of work understand the concept of revenge. It's the most basic form of punishment, so he let that one go.

"And the Church is okay with revenge?" he asks. "I thought they were all about forgiveness."

I snort, then answer with my own question, "Do you have any idea how many people die each year in the name of religion? The Church is more pragmatic than most people think. Besides, the things I kill aren't human any longer. The Church considers them to be an abomination that must be cleansed." I turn to look at him and continue, "I'm surprised you don't agree. These things kill a lot of people."

"I didn't say I disagreed. I simply asked if revenge was acceptable to the Church. It's really no different for cops. We want justice, but we can't always get the justice we truly want. Too bad we can't have any people cleansers," he adds bitterly. Then he turns to look at me. "That thing in your apartment needs to be put down."

"Good, we're in agreement then," I reply and continue my search through the window. "He couldn't have gotten far with a load of silver buck shot in his legs."

"So, the silver thing is true?"

"Yeah, silver to kill a werewolf. Wooden stake through the heart for vampires and holy relics for demons. Keep in mind that most everything written down in myths and stories is just plain bullshit and mad ramblings of demented writers."

"Where did they come from, these monsters? I mean, what I saw was not from somebody's imagination."

I'd asked the same question many times. The first to try and answer it was my original Vatican supervisor, Father Perroni back in 1885. He didn't know the genealogy of the monsters, only that they were in the histories in one form or another. He told me the Church believed they were the spawn of Satan, thus evil and must be cleansed. His lack of curiosity and simple outlook suited my purposes fine back then. I sought revenge against witches and the Church provided the opportunity to exact it. Along the way, I learned that the other fiends were just as dangerous and I added them to my personal score. The Church didn't care why I chose the profession as long as I did their bidding.

I relate this information to David and he seems satisfied for the time being. We drive in silence for a while, searching for Crowe. It has been nearly an hour and we are running out of time. He will heal soon and we will lose our advantage.

After a few minutes of silence, David turns and asks the question I knew was coming. "What about you? What are you? I talked to the coroner the other night and he said you had an arm ripped off and your neck was broken. And tonight... Nobody pulls a two-by-four out of their guts and doesn't even ask for a Band-Aid."

"You can rest assured that I'm human, I'm just different." I sigh heavily trying to repress the anger that always arises when I talk about my particular situation. "I'm cursed."

"What kind of curse?"

"It's such a little thing, really. I'm immortal." The word is barely out of my mouth before I feel him turn to stare at me and I have to remind him he is driving. He turns back to the road and I continue with my story. "I was born one hundred and sixty-four years ago in Italy. In 1848, circumstances caused me to be in Rome where I took a job working in a bakery. The proprietor, a man named Alberto Gazzola, had a daughter. Her name was Lilith."

I smile as I remember that day, running into her father on the sidewalk outside the bakery causing him to drop several loaves of freshly baked bread. He was angry, but by the end of our conversation, he'd given me a job. He told me to go inside and find his daughter to get a broom to clean up the mess, so I did.

"David," I say, still smiling like a giddy school boy. "Have you ever met someone that takes your breath away the first time you see them?" I don't wait for an answer. "That's what it was like the first time I saw Lilith. Hair so black you got lost in it and perfect olive skin." If I close my eyes, I can remember the peasant blouse she wore that showed a fair amount of cleavage and the loose, flowing skirt did nothing to hide the rest of a body that would make an artist weep with its perfection. "She was beautiful, but it was her eyes that captured me. So green, they looked like polished jade." I glance at him and he looks uncomfortable with my detailed description of Lilith's charms.

"She sounds... nice."

I laugh at seeing him uncomfortable again. "She was sixteen, well into the age where she should've been married. At twenty-one, I knew about women and the look she gave me when I asked for the broom told me she knew about men. When I told her that her father just hired me, she gave me the kind of smile that makes a man melt and sashayed into the back of the shop. She returned a few moments later with my apron and the broom." I close my eyes again as the usual feelings made my heart flutter in my chest as I think back to that day. She'd stepped so close to me when she handed them over that I stepped back to take them. But in that few seconds of closeness, I knew I wanted her more than I'd ever wanted a woman. "Luckily for me, I guess, she felt the same way."

"I have a feeling that this story does not end well."

I laugh lightly. "You can see where this is going already, huh?"

He shrugs. "Call it a detective's hunch. You going to tell me what happened next or make me guess?"

I grin, but decide there are some aspects of my life with Lilith that David probably doesn't want to know. Right after starting work, the baker gave me a room at the back of the shop and inadvertently gave his daughter access to me. Our romance built quickly and in a short time, we were together almost continuously. Of course her father didn't know how we spent most of our time or just how well I had gotten to know Lilith. But every moment we could find to steal away, we were either in her bed or mine. She was passionate and energetic and when I was with her, I could forget Repen, *The Puttana*, Captain Caprisi, and Vincenti.

"I spent close to a year working at the bakery," I finally answer. "In all that time, I never slept alone. Her father seemed oblivious even when she would be all over me in front of him, he never said a word and no one ever mentioned her mother."

"Must have been a blind old fool," David mutters. I'm about to ask if he has daughters when he curses out an idiot driver and tells me to get on with it. He knows I was getting to the good part. I nod and think back to how quickly my almost-perfect new life went and jumped off a very steep cliff…

I had my twenty-second birthday and as a present, Lilith suggested we have a picnic. I spent a good deal of my meager earnings to buy a feast for the two of us. She told me not to bother buying wine. She had a special bottle she'd been saving and she would bring it. We packed our food, wine, and blankets and left early that morning. We hiked up into the hills overlooking the Tiber and Rome and spread our blankets under a stand of Maple trees.

Of course we satisfied each other before we satisfied our appetites and it was while making love that I made my biggest mistake. In the throes of passion, she expressed her love for me and in return, I told her I loved her as well. She told me she wanted us to be together forever. I thought it was just pillow talk, so I agreed. That's when she offered me some of the special wine she brought. I drank straight from the bottle and felt the effect immediately. I swooned and passed out. My last image was of her sitting atop me, sweat glistening on her naked breasts. In that moment, life was perfect.

When I awoke later, she had already dressed and had the food spread out, so I dressed and joined her. During the meal, she spoke continuously about what our lives together would be like. I nodded and smiled at the appropriate times, but inside I wasn't sure how I felt. At that particular moment, though, she was happy and I enjoyed her company so I figured I'd see where it went. What was the worst that could happen?

A week later, I found out. We were in my bed in the little room at the back of the shop, both of us naked with me on top of her. That's when her father walked in. It's as if he saw us together for the first time and he became furious. He had a large bread knife in his hand and before I could do more than raise up, he plunged it into my back. Lilith's screams were the last thing I remembered as I died for the first time.

I came to several hours later in a sewer. I crawled and swam through God knows what until I came to where the sewer exited into the Tiber River. I remembered being stabbed, but for some reason, I felt no pain and I couldn't find any wound. I made my way back to the bakery and found Lilith sitting on my bed crying.

When she saw me, she stopped crying and shouted, "It worked, it really worked."

When I asked her what she meant, she told me. Oh, and what she told me, unbelievable. She told me I would live forever just like her. She admitted to being a witch and that she made a potion meant to be given to her chosen mate. It had been the special wine and I had drunk it. We would never age and no disease could harm us. We would remain just as we were and be together forever…

"And that, David," I say, letting my mind wander back to the present as I finish my story, "is how I became immortal. Any questions?"

TEN

David only asks one question, "What happened to Lilith?"

It takes a second before I answer. "I killed her."

By this time, we had driven several blocks up Sycamore and hadn't seen any sign. I suggest to David that we need to turn around and start back toward my apartment. I don't believe it possible for him to have gotten this far in front of us.

Without a word, David makes a U-turn and speeds back the way we came. Scanning the side streets, I nearly miss the vehicle driving toward us with its lights out. I glance left just in time to see Crowe's beat up truck slide past.

"Hey, was that it?" David shouts a split second before I start yelling for him to turn around. He spins the car around again and speeds after the truck speeding away.

I adjust the Browning where it rests across my legs and thumb the twin hammers back in preparation for firing. We quickly catch up to the decrepit truck. David looks at me. "Now what?"

"Pull up on the driver's side," I reply, rolling down the window.

David swerves left and accelerates until he comes even with the blue Chevy. Crowe's hideous face turns toward me and he snarls as I poke the barrels of the shotgun out the window and fire. The driver's window of the truck explodes and a pattern of quarter-inch holes appear in the door. The vehicle swerves right, jumps the curb, and rams into the side of the Dry Cleaners building. David slams on the brakes and as soon as the car stops, I jump out, breaking the shotgun open and ejecting the spent shells. As I dig two fresh ones out of a jeans pocket, I see the passenger door on the truck force open.

I call to David, "Watch the passenger side."

He moves to a position to cover the door as I finish loading the Browning. Snapping the barrels up, I rush to the door on the truck and stick the barrels through the window, my eyes looking over them. Surprisingly, there is nothing there. David is standing at the right rear of the truck. "Did you see him get out?" I ask.

"No. He's not in there?"

I take a closer look inside. Blood covers the dash and seat so I move around behind the vehicle to David's position. "No but he's hurt. He won't get far."

I start down the sidewalk in the direction he would have had to go, David close on my heels. A short distance later, we come to an alley. This has to be where Crowe went, so we cautiously enter. David takes the right side and I the left as we walk toward the rear of the buildings. We see nothing as we enter an area for parking and unloading behind the row of buildings, but Crowe is nowhere in sight. I can't understand how he'd managed to get away from us again and with a second load of buckshot in him.

I look at where David stands covering his side of the alley and state, "I think we could use some help."

David nods, "Yeah, but it would be hard to explain what we're doing here."

"I already have somebody in mind." I pull my cell phone out and call Alonso. Again, the call goes straight to voice mail. I find it odd, Alonso wouldn't still be asleep and he hasn't returned my earlier call. There has to be something wrong, but I will have to wait to deal with that. Right now, I have a wounded and pissed off werewolf to find and kill. I look back at David, "No answer. Do you have a twelve gauge in your car?"

"Yeah, in the trunk."

"I think we're going to need it."

"Cavalry not coming?" he asks, turning back to his car.

"No," I answer, more to myself than him. It worries me that I haven't been able to get in touch with Alonso. It's never taken more than an hour or so for him to get back to me. Usually, it's within minutes. This isn't normal and I'll have to find him after Crowe's handled. David returns with a Remington 870 pump in place of his Glock and I hand him my last three silver buckshot rounds. He loads them and resumes covering his side of the alley.

"He's got to be close. He's got a face full of silver now," David says.

I signal and point to an area of bushes and tall weeds across the gravel lot. David gives me a confirming nod and together we move toward it, weapons up and ready. The detective circles around to the right while I go left, making sure we keep the muzzles of our weapons clear of each other. We make it to less than twenty yards before I hear it. A low rumbling growl, like an idling engine, comes from the heart of the weed-choked area. I wave with my support hand to get David's attention and when he looks, I points at the overgrowth.

It all happens at once. We reach a point about ten yards from the area when the beast bursts from the weeds, lunging for David. We both fire simultaneously, me with both barrels and David pumping the slide fast until we are both empty. The sudden violence and noise that envelopes the gravel lot and the silence in the aftermath feels heavy and cloying. I stand, panting, my heart jack hammering in my chest and as the smoke clears. The werewolf lies unmoving about three feet from David, who stands with the empty shotgun still pointed at the creature.

I move to where Crowe lays and prod him with my toe. There's no movement from the fur-covered body. I tell David to back up while I go back to the car to retrieve my kit bag then jog back to the body of the werewolf and kneel at its side. I roll it over as I rummage in the bag for the flask of holy oil. David watches while I perform the ritual mandated by the Vatican. Once I complete it, I draw the silver knife and David takes a step back, unsure about what I intend. Without explaining, I set to work removing Crowe's head.

Blood pours onto the ground around the incision and with a sucking sound, the ugly thing rolls free. Placing it in the leak-proof bag, I look at David and say, "Let's get out of here."

"What about the rest of him? We can't leave that here."

"We'll drag him back to the truck and burn it."

It takes all of our remaining strength to get the heavy

beast back into the truck. I drop the kit bag containing Crowe's remains into David's trunk while he sticks a road flare in the opened gas cap. I crank the engine on the car and David strikes the igniter on the flare. We both crawl into the car and he puts it in gear and floors the accelerator. We are a short distance away when the fuel tank goes up with a muted thump, not the explosion and fireball Hollywood has made famous. We both turn to look and watch as the truck becomes fully engulfed in fire.

David looks at me. "What now?"

"I need to find someplace to burn the head."

"Why not toss it into the truck and let it burn?"

"Never together. These things can regenerate after a lot of abuse. I never risk it. This way I'm sure it can't ever come back."

"I know a spot," he says and gets into his car. While David drives, I pull my cell phone out and try Alonso's number again. It goes straight to voice mail. He knew I'd be contacting him and would never ignore my calls. David looks over at me and sees the trouble on my face. "Problem?"

"Yeah. I can't get in contact with my friend."

He smirks and asks, "You actually have a friend? One that knows about you?"

"Now who's the smartass," I mutter. "He works at the Medical Examiner's Office."

David nods knowingly and says, "Big, black guy. Something Jones, right? I figured he knew more about that body disappearing."

"Alonso. Yes, that's him, he's just protecting me and now I can't get in touch with him. I'm worried."

"Why? Is he involved with this?" he asks.

"He was helping me last night, but we weren't together. We were supposed to contact each other today and he's not answering." I try his number again with the same results. Tossing the phone onto the dash, I turn to David and ask, "Is there any way you could find out if he's been involved in an accident?"

"Yeah, sure. Can you give me his plate number or social

security number?"

"No, all I have is his name, but I know his address and what kind of car he drives," I reply hopefully.

It surprises me when he starts to use his cell phone instead of the radio. When I ask, he says, "I don't want everybody on the radio knowing about what we're doing. By calling the dispatcher, I can get the information quietly. We already broke about a dozen laws tonight," he adds with a huff. He goes back to the phone and speaks softly with whoever answered.

After a few minutes, I hear him ask, "Where?" and then, "Thank you." He puts away the phone and turns to me. "Your friend's vehicle is in the impound yard. Apparently it was involved in some kind of accident."

"What about Alonso?"

He shrugs "I don't know. The vehicle was abandoned when it was found. Maybe he's just sleeping one off."

"Alonso doesn't drink," I reply defensively. "Take me to the impound lot. I want to see his car."

The impound lot is on Ponce De Leon Avenue in the north east of the city and it takes several minutes for us to make the drive. When we arrive, David gets out and speaks to a uniformed cop who let us in. David drives slowly between rows of vehicles of all descriptions, some in good shape, others not. Eventually, we come to an area that holds wrecked vehicles and David tells me Alonso's car should be here.

When I see the car, it takes a second or two to realize it's Alonso's. I ask David to stop and open the door as soon as he does. Walking over to the car, I wish it wasn't his. I can see four slashes across the roof, the edges of the metal turned up like the edge of an opened tin can. The top of the driver's door has been pulled out until the window frame was parallel with the ground. The windshield is smashed and I can see blood spatter on the seat and dash.

David walks over and stands beside me for several seconds before asking, "Is this it?"

"Yes," I say as I continue to inspect the damage.

"Any idea what happened to it? Doesn't look like wreck

damage."

"It wasn't a wreck. He's been taken." I kick the door in frustration as I answer.

"Taken by who?"

"Not who. By *what*. He was taken by a demon and I think I know which one. Can you find out where they found it?" When he bobs his chin, I continue, "I want to go there, now." Without another word, we both walk back to the Crown Vic.

Driving out of the lot, David makes another call to get the location where the police found Alonso's vehicle. After a minute or so, he clicks off and drops the phone in the console. "It's not far, they found it across the street from the Euclid Avenue Yacht Club."

"Yacht Club?" I ask, puzzled. "I didn't know there was a lake anywhere around here."

He laughs and says, "It's not really a yacht club, it's more of a dive bar. You know the kind of place that sells T-shirts with the bar's logo on them."

"Sounds like my kind of place."

"What do you expect to find?"

"If Alonso's dead, there's a body somewhere. I assume if he'd been in the car, you would have been told." He nods so I go on, "If he's alive, he's out there and I need to find him. Demons leave a trail I can follow. Besides, I owe this particular bastard."

"The window?"

"Yeah, the window." We drive in silence the rest of the way.

*****

At eight p.m., the Euclid Avenue Yacht Club is a busy place and David has to park a block away. We cross to the south side of Euclid and walk back toward the location Alonso's gold Honda had been found. The spot is fairly obvious with glass and small pieces of the car lying on the ground. I find blood and that's what interests me most. I walk around the area noting the location of the blood spots and it doesn't take long to confirm they describe the three points of a triangle with each side about ten feet long, a door for demons to enter our world from Hell.

The Thaumaturgic Triangle is often used by humans to summon a demon, the triangle is the door and the circle is the boundary. This is how the human maintains control over the demon. The triangle without the boundary circle indicates this demon has been knowingly released and is not under the control of a human. Bad news for Alonso. In the center of the triangle, where Alonso's car had sat, I find the offering used to summon the demon. A small bag had been burned and I bend to examine it, the smell confirms it as feces, probably human.

I explain all of this to David and he seems to accept it well. It has been a big night for him and he's done great for someone who just learned that monsters are not just metaphoric. There is no more sarcasm in his tone as he asks, "Where do we go from here?"

I point across the street at the Yacht Club, "Let's get a drink." He shrugs and falls in beside me as I walk toward the bar.

It takes a minute to locate a table though the crowd. When we are finally seated, David asks, "Are you looking for something or were you just thirsty?"

"Places like this have a usual clientele. I bet several of the people here tonight were here last night. If we ask around, we might find someone that saw Alonso," I have to speak louder than I normally like to be heard over the music. It doesn't take long for a waitress to appear and both David and I order beers.

When she returns with our drinks and as she sets them on the table, I ask, "Excuse me. We're looking for a friend of ours. We were supposed to meet him here last night, but didn't make it. I wonder if you might have seen him."

She is a cute girl. Slim, petite, long auburn hair, wearing jean shorts and a Yacht Club T-shirt. I notice her name tag reads Bella and she smiles sweetly as she answers, "I don't know, maybe. What's he look like?"

"He'd be hard to forget. Black guy, six feet, four inches and about four hundred pounds."

She looks thoughtful for a moment, and then says,

"Yeah, I remember him. He was here about ten last night."
Before I can ask another question, she turns and disappears
into the crowd.

David can see that her demeanor frustrates me so he
leans close and says, "Don't worry, she'll be back. Drink
your beer."

He turns out to be right and Bella reappears a few
minutes later with two fresh beers. She sets mine down
first and it gives me a chance to ask another question "Did
you happen to notice if my friend was with anyone last
night?"

Again, she pauses in thought before answering, "Not
that I can remember, but he sure seemed interested in a
woman that was here. Every time I noticed him, he was
staring at her. Can't say I blame him, she was beautiful."

The alarm bell goes off again. "Did she have red hair?"

Bella smiles, "Yeah, do you know her?" Once more
before I can respond, she moves to David's side of the
table and as she places his beer, she leans over and
whispers in his ear. He laughs and Bella turns and vanishes
into the crowd.

With my frustration building I inquire, "What did she
say?"

He looks sheepish and says, "She said it might be worth
my while if I met her in the men's room." He shrugs again
before saying, "I might have been tempted if it wasn't for
her breath. It's been one hell of a day."

"What about her breath?" I have a bad feeling I know
what his answer will be.

He pinches up his face and says, "It smelled like shit."

I come to my feet instantly and dash in the direction
where she disappeared. "Come on," I say to David, not
waiting to see if he follows as I move toward the
illuminated Men's Room sign. As I push the door open, I
sense David right on my heels so I rush inside and look
around. A strong smell of human excrement pervades the
air, more than you'd usually expect.

From behind me, David says, "Whew, something must
have died inside whoever did that."

That's when I notice the triangle scratched into the concrete floor, in front of the toilet stall. "You have no idea."

ELEVEN

We are still standing in the men's room when David asks, "You mean it's her?"

"It's not a *her*, it's an *IT*. But yes, Bella is the demon." I go to the triangle and pull the flask of holy oil from my rear pocket. I don't have a knife, so I ask David if he has one. He reaches into his pocket and grabs a small folding knife then hands it to me. I open the blade and pour some of the oil onto the blade as I speak a short prayer.

I set the flask down and as I prepare to destroy the demon door, he asks, "What's the liquid?"

I smile. "You're not Catholic are you?" He shakes his head 'no,' so I explain, "It's Oleum Infirmorum or oil of the sick used to bless them. It's also used in exorcisms and I use it to bless the unclean things that I kill." I proceed to destroy the triangle by scratching a cross over it in the concrete. I hand the knife back to David and he follows me back into the bar. I tell him we may as well leave and turn toward the door.

As I step out onto the sidewalk, I glance across the street and there she stands in the middle of the triangle where Alonso's car had been. I swear and reach into my shirt for the Saint Benedicts medal I always wear as I stride across the street toward the demon. Knowing the demon's real name is a vital part of getting rid of one and I now know this bastard's. The female human form, her attempt to tempt David, and the human excrement as an offering identified the creature. The female form stands with its hands clasped in front, a smile on its lips as I approach.

I close the gap and, clasping the medal in my hand, say, "Belphegor, I know you."

But before I can begin the Saint Benedicts prayer, the demon raises its hand and wags its finger saying, "If you speak one word of that infernal prayer, your friend dies. Horribly." As she had hoped, that gets my attention and I pause. Her smile widens as she says, "That's better, now, let's talk."

I stop in the edge of the street with David beside me. Trying to control my anger I say, "Speak, Belphegor."

"Oh, stop being so formal. I prefer Bella, now play nice and maybe you can save your fat little friend and your trained monkey." she says, pointing at David. He opens his mouth to tell her what he thinks of the monkey comment, but I hold my hand up to stop him. He remains quiet, but doesn't like it.

"What do you want?" I ask.

"Now, I want you to understand I don't have anything against you, personally. I was completely satisfied keeping my cute little ass in hell, but I've been summoned, so I have a master and a job to do. It's my master, you see, that seems to have a bone to pick with you," she says, the smile never leaving her face.

"I don't care about you or your master. You need to release Alonso or I will destroy you."

She actually laughs and seems to be enjoying herself. All at once, she turns serious, "If you threaten me again, I will pull Alonso's guts out through his mouth and eat them. Right now, he's unharmed." She shrugs and smirks a little. "Well, mostly. Anyway, if you want him to stay that way, you'll listen to me."

Swallowing my anger, I nod. I couldn't let my own anger get Alonso killed, so I take a deep breath and listen.

"Better. I told you the human that summoned me doesn't like you very much. You're trying to help a woman named Erin and my master doesn't like her much, either. There are some filthy little things trying to have their vulgar way with her and you've been getting in the way. You will stop and you will let her suffer and die or I get to take Alonso back to hell with me. I don't need to tell you how much fun I can have with him for eternity." Her smile returns as she finishes. "Once this Erin is dead, Alonso will be released no worse for the wear." She shrugs again. "Well, more or less."

What a predicament. On one hand, I have the only friend I've had in years. On the other, I have a woman that I hope to have a relationship with after all this is over. I need to stall for time to try and come up with a plan, but the demon isn't having any of it. She asks, "So, what's it going to be?"

"All right, I'll stop protecting Erin." I pause for a second before continuing, "I have your word Alonso will be released unharmed?"

Bella laughs again and claps her hands, "Oh, you are such fun. I know you're lying, but either way, I get what I want. If you fuck up, I get Alonso. If you don't, I'm going to take the asshole that summoned me…" She glances at David and then back at me. "You know it's my nature to deceive, so giving you my word on anything is pointless, but once I'm back in Hell, I have no intention of ever coming back to this place again. You won't have to worry about running into me again. But I really hate my master and would seriously enjoy spending some quality time with him."

She has my attention. It might be possible to still come out of this with all of us alive. It depends on what she says next. "I'll give you a hint. Alonso is alive and he'll stay that way as long as you stop protecting Erin, but who are we kidding? You've already killed the wolf and two of the blood suckers and I know you'll go after the rest. You Cleansers always do. There are three more vamps and if you manage to kill them before tomorrow night, you will buy the woman some time." She tilts her face as if calculating something. "I'll mislead my master and give you time to find and save your friend."

"That doesn't sound like much of a hint," I snap, losing my patience.

She grins and her eyes darken with demonic glee. "Perceptive aren't we? Fine, here's your hint. Alonso is in the absolute last place you'd think to look." She looks exceedingly pleased with herself as she asks, "What do you think?"

"Why are you doing this?" I don't want to commit to anything with the treacherous creature. I know it will double cross me if it suits its purposes.

She pouts and says, "I told you, I hate my master and

want to eat his guts."

I have one more question I need an answer for before I complete any deal. "Why should I trust you?"

"Trust me?" She cackles for several seconds before wiping a fake tear of mirth from her eye. "You shouldn't trust me, ever. I'm simply giving you an alternative that might benefit both of us. If my master were to give me a better proposition, I'd turn on you in less time than it takes your heart to beat. I'll just give you until daylight, day after tomorrow, about thirty-six hours. I won't say anything to my master until then and you can do whatever you want to do. How's that?"

"All right—" before I can say anything else, there is a sizzling sound, then a pop and she is gone. David curses and once again the Glock seems to jump into his hand of its own accord. I tell him to relax and go to one of the blood spots and wipe it away with my foot, closing this demon door.

David recovers quickly and after putting the gun away asks, "Do you believe her?"

I think a few seconds before I answer. "The one thing you can count on with a demon, they will always do what's in their best interest. Part of what she said is truth, the rest, who knows? We don't have a lot of choice at this point."

He accepts that much better than even I do. "What now?"

I look at him and smile. "How do you feel about helping me kill a few vampires?"

*****

A short time later, as we drive back toward my apartment in David's car, he asks what our next move will be. It catches me by surprise how quickly he deferred to me. At the beginning of the evening, he was the confident investigator, sure of where he intended to go and now he wants to know what we need to do. I decide not to point this out. He might not appreciate it, but I will take advantage of it. He knows weapons and how to fight, so with a little adjustment toward adversaries, he became an asset.

I tell him we'll go back to my place for weapons and then I'll need a place to stay. I don't want to risk staying at my place until this case is over. Besides, I need to do some major redecorating before my place will be habitable again.

David surprises me further when he says, "Why don't you stay at my place? I'm not married and I have plenty of room, plus it will make it easier for us to plan for this fight."

"If you don't mind, that would make more sense right now."

Happy that I have an ally, I mentally run over a list of equipment we will need to tackle the vampires in the sump. I only have the one crossbow, but I can arm David with weapons that will slow the creatures down long enough for me to make a clean shot with the olive wood arrows. My only concern will be preparing him mentally for what he will face during this cleansing. My mental gymnastics eat up the time and before I know it, David pulls up in front of The Magnolia House.

I exit the car and David follows. Inside the foyer, I notice Betty's door is closed tight and I can't hear any noise, so we go up the stairs to my place. I didn't bother to lock the door when we left and I don't hesitate grabbing the door knob and entering. The destruction inside still shocks me even though I'd been present when it occurred. The double windows are completely blown in and the wall separating my closet from the living room will have to be rebuilt. This is actually the first time in decades a fight had been brought into the sanctity of my own home and the thought rattles me more than I like. The monsters are supposed to stay beyond my walls, not charge through my windows to kill me.

I try to shake off the feelings and turn my thoughts toward Erin instead. My feelings for her are so overwhelming that I nearly forgot why I am here. If David didn't ask if I need help, I might have sat down and given into the fantasy. He snaps me out of it and in short time, I have my weapons cache cleared out and another bag for clothes ready to go.

Thankful that I'd made it out without running into Betty or my neighbors, I settle into David's car for the ride to his place. Traffic is light and it only takes around ten minutes to reach his apartment. He lives in a recently remodeled older building on Auburn Avenue across from John Calhoun Park. He has a ground floor unit with two bedrooms that has to eat a lot of his pay check.

His decor, like mine, I call single male Spartan. He has a ratty old couch and a new recliner that had to cost more than all the rest of the furniture in the place. He shows me to the spare bedroom with a bed and night table and nothing else. It is all I need and I feel at home immediately.

David wants to get started right away, so after ordering a pizza, we sit down for me to explain my plan. I already know the location of the lair, back at the industrial park at the end of Baxter Road. I also give him the details of how we have to enter. He doesn't look as keen after I tell him about the crawling in the sewer part, but I have to give him credit for not backing out. I show him the weapons we'll be using and detail how I want to attack the vampires.

I plan for both of us to enter the sump and I'll use a secret weapon to attract the vampires. As soon as they all show, David will open fire with the shotgun. The buckshot won't be fatal, but even a vampire would be slowed down for a few seconds by a load of double aught. That few seconds will be all I need to plant the wooden arrows in their black hearts. David seems a bit grossed out when I explain the secret weapon, but it is the only way to really get the vamps into our trap.

Being immortal has its advantages and I plan to use my blood to attract the vampires. We still have a few hours until sun up, plenty of time for me to recover from draining some of my blood. I'll open a vein and fill a couple of bottles and once we enter the sump, I'll smash them on the wall. The vampires won't be able to resist the smell.

David digs a couple of glass jars from under the kitchen sink and, using his pocket knife again, I cut my left wrist. I fill both jars, and then bandage the wrist so it will heal faster. Feeling weakened, I tell David I need to get some sleep. He tells me he'll be just down the hall and sets his alarm for six a.m. I think that will work, so I go to my bedroom. As soon as I lay down, I remember there's still a werewolf head in the trunk of his car. I chuckle to myself and think I'll have to remind him of that in the morning. I'm sure he'd be pissed if I left it in there. The mental image of him opening the trunk sometime next week to find the decapitated head of a werewolf decomposing inside causes me to chuckle again.

*****

The dream invades my subconscious more vividly than ever before, as if I were experiencing it all over again.

I stood in the small backroom of the bakery that served as my bed chamber. Lilith cried and yelled, "It worked, it worked!" I quieted her down and asked where her father was. She told me he'd gone to a tavern, evidently upset after finding his daughter and me making love and subsequently murdering me. I could understand that, I felt a little distraught as well.

I asked her to explain what happened and in between sobs she told me. "Papa came in and found you on top of me. In the past, I've always put a spell on him when I wanted to be with you. He could see us, but he couldn't see what we were doing. To him, it looked like we were working. This time I forgot." When I questioned her about spells, she admitted, "I'm a witch. I have been since I was a child, so was my mother." While I processed the fact that my lover was a witch, she continued, "I love you and I know you love me. At our picnic, I told you I wanted us to be together forever and you said you did, too. I had my special wine, which I'd mixed a potion into that made you immortal, just like me. You drank it and now we can be together forever."

I sat on the bed, feeling faint. I couldn't tell if it was from being stabbed or finding out that I'd been fed a potion that made me immortal. I looked at her and asked, "I can't die?"

"No, you will live for eternity. You'll never be sick and you'll never get any older than you are today. I took it the same day and now we're the same," she said.

"How do you know?"

"My father stabbed you. You died and he carried you to the sewer and dumped you in. The fact that you're back is proof it worked."

I had no idea if I had really died, but I did remember being stabbed and I no longer had a wound, so there had to be some truth to it. As I ran all of this through my mind, Lilith reminded me gently that I'd spent a couple of hours soaking in the piss and shit of several thousand Romans and needed a bath. I nodded, unable to think clear enough to speak. She led me to the bathing chamber and I sat on a bench trying to think while she heated water and poured my bath.

Once the tub was ready, I undressed and climbed in without thought. I sat there like a child while she bathed me. I don't remember much beyond that. I knew I wanted to get out of there before her father returned. If he'd killed me once already, I didn't relish the idea of giving him another chance. I still wasn't sure about the whole immortal thing and I was afraid he might get it right the next time.

After getting dressed in fresh clothes, I told her I needed to take a walk to think about all she told me. She wanted to come, but I convinced her I needed to be alone. She finally relented and I quickly ran from the bakery and wandered the city trying to decide what to do. The only thing that kept coming to mind was to run and that's exactly what I did. I never went back to the bakery and I hoped to never see Lilith again.

The next couple of years were still a blur. I spent most of my time drunk or passed out in a gutter somewhere. I roamed all over the Italian countryside, from Tuscany in the north to Sicily in the south. I spent a considerable amount of time in Naples and that's where I found out that Lilith had been correct, I couldn't die. I became involved with some criminal types and during an attempted robbery, I got stabbed. This time in the heart and died almost immediately. Thankfully, my friends didn't dump me in the sewer. They left me in the alley where I'd fallen. I awoke a couple of hours later with the wound healed and feeling no ill effects.

I left Naples and traveled back north. After several weeks, I found myself back in Rome. I survived by stealing and eating out of the trash. I wandered back to Vatican hill, hoping to beg some food from the priests and that's where I ran into Lilith. It surprised me that she recognized me, dressed in filthy rags, my hair long, unshaved and unwashed. She looked just as she did on the day I left.

She ran to me, calling my name, the love for me reflected on her face. The feeling was no longer mutual in any regard. Rage filled me instantly and I blamed her for all the terrible things that had befallen me. My vision narrowed and thoughts of murder flooded my brain. As she spread her arms anticipating an embrace, I drew the dagger I kept tucked in my belt. She stepped close and I lunged forward.

The blade went in so easily, hardly any effort to stab the woman I thought I might have loved, stabbed her to death in the street like she was nothing.

The look of love disappeared on her face to be replaced with one of surprise and then anguish as she collapsed at my feet. I stood looking down at her body and laughed. I think that was the closest I came to insanity during the entire time. I dragged her into an alley and out of sight as I decided what to do with her. All of my worldly possessions were carried in a large sack I slung over my shoulder. It's all I had, so I dumped my things onto the cobbles and set to work.

With the dagger. I disarticulated her arms and legs, stuffing them in to the sack. I removed her head and then dug into her chest cavity, removing her heart. I placed these into the sack also. Her torso I disposed of the same way her father had gotten rid of mine when he'd murdered me, I dropped it into the sewer. The sack I carried to an isolated hollow where I spent the next two days burning them until nothing remained.

I had no idea how to kill a witch at the time, but by sheer blind luck I fell on the one true way. Remove the head and heart, then cremate them. With the deed finished, I fled north and for another year, I wandered, a drunk and a beggar, until I stopped in Bavaria. Another woman found me and took pity on me. With her help, I came back from the edge and came to terms with my situation. Of course, my relationship with her resulted in my next experience with dying.

TWELVE

The light coming in wakes me up. My eyes flutter open and I look toward the door.

David is there. In his gruff detective voice he tells me, "Six a.m., coffee's on," then disappears back down the hall.

I sit up feeling dizzy. Apparently I haven't completely recovered from the loss of blood. I also don't feel rested and wonder if the dream is to blame. The details did not fade with waking as with most dreams and are still clear in my mind.

I force myself to my feet and stumble to the bathroom. I undress and step into the shower, turning the water on cold hoping the frigid temperature will refresh me. It works somewhat and after the initial shock, I turn up the hot water and finish showering. I don't bother to shave, only brush my teeth. My ablutions complete, I make my way back to my bedroom and dress.

By the time I join David in the kitchen, I feel better, but still not a hundred percent. David hands me a cup of coffee and as I take a sip, he says, "You look like shit. Are you sure you're up to this?"

I nod. "I'm fine, bad dreams."

"I'd have thought you'd be used to them by now. As old as you are and doing what you do, you're bound to have seen some really horrible things. Bad dreams come with the territory."

"Some are worse than others. Last night's was particularly bad. I dreamed about Lilith," I mutter more into my coffee mug than to him.

I can see he is considering what to say, we don't know each other that well and he probably fears he will offend me if he pries too much. He isn't that far of the mark either, I don't usually like talking about myself to others and I've already said I don't like to answer questions. In this case though, I wished he would ask. Maybe I need to talk about it with someone. It's been over seventy-five years since I attended confession. As David continues to try and figure out what to say, I let my mind wander back to those days when I actually cared enough to go to confession.

*****

In 1885, Elspeth and I traveled from what is today Germany to Rome where I volunteered to become a Cleanser. Over the next several days, I was inducted into the ranks of the Swiss Guard. At the time, Cleansers were the only non-Swiss allowed to enlist and then I made it into the ranks of the Cleansers. Elspeth introduced me to her mentor, Father Perroni. He was young, twenty-six, and hadn't been a priest for that long. Although I'd been born many years before him, we took an instant liking to each other. He became my mentor as well and I learned much about the unnaturals from him. Two years later, when Elspeth was killed, Father Perroni helped me through my grief.

Our friendship lasted until his death in 1939 at the age of eighty. During our fifty-four years together I told him everything about myself. He heard my confession on many occasions and at the time, he was the only living person to know my secret. Telling him about my curse was a difficult conversation because I had to admit that I was an unnatural, the thing I had sworn to destroy. After hearing my confession, he agreed we needed to keep the information secret. He was a good friend and never violated my trust, even though his position dictated that he do so.

We both had a good laugh when I confessed about my criminal past and he only said one thing, "It's a good thing you've dedicated yourself to God's work, you weren't a very good robber."

I had to agree. It had been after a night much like last night that I told him about Lilith and what I'd done to her. He had a very pragmatic attitude concerning the whole affair. He told me that my killing her had been completely fine as she was a witch and thus not under God's protection. I pointed out that I had not been a Cleanser then and I had killed her for entirely personal reasons. He dismissed this as insignificant, but it has always troubled me.

Lilith's death was the only one that haunted me. She loved me and I killed her for it. I know that's not exactly how I should look at it, but it's how I do. Father Perroni tried to assuage my guilt and yet, I still carry it today.

*****

I slowly drift back to the present where I stand leaning against the counter in David's kitchen. He must have sensed that I need to talk, but his choice of topics surprises me when he says, "Tell me about Alonso."

I laugh, a perceptive man, David. Instead of asking about Lilith, he tries to get my mind off her by talking about Alonso. "Well, considering my audience, the first thing I'd have to tell you about Alonso is he's not crazy about the police."

David smiles. "He's not the only one. In a lot of cases, we are our own worst enemy. What people seem to forget is that we're just people ourselves. No better, no worse."

"True, people simply don't like being told what to do or what not to do. With Alonso, I think it goes a little deeper. He hasn't told me a lot about his family, but he did tell me that his ancestors were slaves here in Georgia and of course his grandparents and parents grew up in the south. I don't think trusting the police was part of his upbringing."

He shakes his head and says, "Yeah, not one of our greatest moments in history, but I don't believe in institutional prejudice. I don't care what color you are, if you're wrong, you're wrong. Unfortunately, sometimes I think I'm in the minority."

His remark makes me laugh. "It would be better if more people felt that way. As for Alonso, he's a good friend. I think he nearly had a stroke the first night we met. Before coming here, I lived in Nashville. There's plenty of work for a Cleanser up there with all the runaways trying to be country stars and a pretty substantial homeless population. I'd been hunting a real nasty vampire. He killed four or five victims a night, sometimes right out in the open. Just grabbed them right on the street and go at it."

"I thought they looked…weird," he says with a frown. "Wouldn't someone notice that?"

I shake my head. "He hadn't been changed long enough to go through the physical transformation, so he still looked human. The Metro cops were going nuts trying to catch this guy. I started hunting him and he figured out quick I knew what I was doing because I'd gotten close on a couple different nights. He took off, but I'd been ready for that and I followed him here. First night, I confronted him thinking I'd put him down and get back to Nashville."

"Something tells me that didn't happen."

"I shot him with the crossbow, but I missed his heart," I admit. "He charged me before I could reload and as we collided he punched me in the chest. That's it, one punch to the chest, crushed my sternum and drove my ribs into my heart. I died before I hit the ground and I ended up in the morgue. Alonso had been writing my information on the intake sheet when I sat up. I wish I had a video of the look on his face." I look at David and ask, "You know those priceless commercials?" David nods so I go on, grinning, "His look was priceless.

"I got him calmed down. He said the thing that saved his life was his Momma's cooking. When I asked what he meant, he told me that everything she'd fed him when he was growing up had been fried in lard and it was all that hog fat that kept his veins and arteries lubricated. His answer made me laugh as I sat there and finished healing right before his eyes.

"We had a long conversation that night," I said. "Kind of like the one we had and he decided he wanted to help me. He watches the morgue for me and lets me know if anything weird comes in and I keep clothes there in an empty locker, so when I come in as a client I have something decent to leave in." I get up and pour another cup of coffee. After sitting back down, I resume the story, "Two nights ago, while I hunted the vampire nest, Alonso followed Erin. The last time I talked to him, they were on Euclid Avenue. She was with a man in a new Mercedes, that's the last I heard from him. The demon got to him at the Yacht Club and you know the rest." I sit back and sip my coffee.

"How do we get him back?" David asks.

"I have no idea. All we have is the hint that Bella gave us."

David scoffs, "That hint isn't worth much if you ask me, 'You'll find him in the last place you look.' Well, no shit."

I think a moment then said, "No, that's not what she said. She said, 'He's in the last place you'd *think* to look.' I know it's important, if I could figure it out."

"Any ideas?"

"Not a clue." After a pause, I go on, "When she referred to her master, she said 'him' which means that her master is male. I think that's important, I'm just not sure how yet."

"You told me you had the feeling you were being set up on this case from the beginning. What made you first think that?" David is thinking like a detective and maybe that's what we need.

"The fact that every time I went after one of the creatures, they seemed to know I was coming. It's like they already knew who and what I was. My every move was blocked by them somehow."

"Okay," he says, warming to the discussion. "What's the one thing that's been consistent?"

I answer without hesitation, "That's easy, the victim, Erin. Bella already told us that her master was trying to kill Erin. I don't know how that helps us."

He contemplates what I'd said. "There's something there, I can't see it yet, but it's there."

"What?"

"Stay with me. You said Alonso followed Erin on Euclid Avenue and that was the last time you talked to him, right?" I nod and he continues, "Alonso told you a man in a new Mercedes picked up Erin. We know from Bella that Alonso followed them into the Yacht Club and that she took him when he went back to his car. Someone at or around the bar had to draw the demon door and burn the offering to bring Bella to his car and, according to Bella, her master is a man." I nod again, trying to follow his train of thought. He looks straight at me and asks, "Is it possible that the demon master and Erin's mystery date is the same guy?"

Ding, ding, ding, we have a winner! It is as if the proverbial light bulb went on over me. So obvious, why didn't I see it? This whole Erin thing had begun to be too much. I remember why I had been mad at her now. She wasn't supposed to leave her house and she went on a date, possibly with the guy that was trying to kill her. Then he asks me the really hard question.

"Is it possible that Erin is involved?"

I set my coffee cup on the table and think long and hard before answering, "Possible? I'd have to say it's possible, but not probable."

"Why?" he asks.

"She simply doesn't seem the type." It sounds pathetic, but I don't want to say any more about it. I want to believe it more than anything else that she isn't involved. To be honest, I really don't know anything about her, other than she is a beautiful woman and every time I see her, I want to get her into bed. "Why would she be involved though?" I continue. "I mean, she's the one in danger from the vampires. What's she trying to accomplish?"

"I don't know, but something doesn't make sense." He stares at his shoes, thinking, then, "We need to find this mystery man she was with. It seems strange that she wouldn't have mentioned him. How well did you check her out before you agreed to help her?"

I start to become angry. He points out a serious flaw in my character and I'm not happy about it. Erin had batted her pretty green eyes and I'd rolled over like a puppy wanting its belly scratched. This has happened before and always causes problems. I'm angry at myself because he's right, but it manifests as anger toward him.

"I just kill the fucking things, you're the detective. Figure it out." As I walk toward the bedroom, David's expression never changes. He watches me until I close the door, those eyes of his already knowing the answer to his last question.

I sit on the edge of the bed and take several deep breaths. I regret blowing up at him as soon as I did it and I need to get myself together. I need him to help destroy the vampire nest and can't afford to lose him because I'm acting like a petulant child.

After a few self-admonishing words, I walk back to the kitchen to apologize to David. He's standing exactly like he was with the same calm expression as if I hadn't stormed out.

When I sit back down at the table, he sets a fresh cup of coffee in front of me and asks, "Feel better now?"

I look up at him as I try to formulate my response. I finally decide on, "Yeah, sorry." I've never said I was eloquent, but surely I can come up with a better explanation than that. I open my mouth to try and David holds his hand up to stop me.

"Don't, it's not required. I understand you're blaming yourself for Alonso and I understand you're blaming yourself for screwing up with Erin, but that's behind us. You need to focus on now. The past is the past, so get over it. You're the expert, so I'll do whatever needs to be done, but I need your direction. Can you do that?"

"Yes, and you're right, I have to focus and that seems to be my problem lately. I haven't been able to focus. Hopefully that changes right now. Let's get to it."

He nods and asks, "What do you want me to do?"

"I need some blank paper and a pen." David leaves to find the items while I collect my thoughts and get down to the business of planning the attack on the vampire nest.

He returns and sets a spiral notebook and pen on the table in front of me. I open it to a blank page and draw a map of the industrial site. David stands beside me, bending slightly to watch as I render the warehouses. When I finish with the map, I tear the page out and hand it to him. While he studies it, I draw a map of the tunnel system.

After studying both maps, he sits down beside me. "So, we're going down into this?"

"That's what I did last time and what I initially planned for us. There is a problem, though. When I went down, I did it before first light so I could be there when the vampires returned from their nightly hunt. This time, they will already be there and we have to make it all the way to the sump without alerting them. I don't think we can do that."

I point to the map of the tunnels and sigh as I realize we will have to come up with a different plan.

"The last part of the approach is about a hundred yard crawl through a corroded three-foot diameter drain pipe." I pause to let that sink in a moment and then, "Both of us, with equipment, I don't think we can do it and not alert them to our presence. Their hearing is incredible and if they caught us in the tunnel..." I leave the sentence hanging, letting David fill in the blank.

"I agree it seems fool hardy to try sneaking into that sump. I don't relish the thought of being stuck and trying to fight in that drain," he adds with a mock shiver.

I smile at the theatrics and say, "Not a pleasant thought, that's why we aren't going to do it that way. I think it will be best to make them come to us."

"What's your idea?"

I lay out the plan of how we'll draw the vampires to us, where we can kill them in relative safety. I explain what I need him to do and how he'll have to be positioned. I also describe that since I have the experience, I'll be the bait. I add, "You have to be sure about your understanding. I will be under pressure when I come back up that tunnel and you have to be ready."

He answers confidently, "Don't worry about me. I'll be ready."

"Good." I continue and explain the equipment we'll need to be able to make the plan work. I split the list of needed items in half and we spend the next hour or so making calls to find some of the harder to get pieces. After finding vendors for everything, it is finally time to get started. We agree we can make better time if we split up, so our first stop will be to take me back to my car.

We carry the stuff we already have out to David's Crown Vic and as he sticks the key in the trunk to open it, I stop him. Thinking about the image I had last night before falling asleep, I say, "Ah, I should probably remind you that Harry Crowe's head is still in there."

His face screws up and I prepare myself to catch hell for leaving a decapitated werewolf head in his trunk, but it never comes. He calms himself, apparently getting a handle on the fact that this new extension to his reality will take some getting used to.

"I want that thing out of my car, today."

I nod and he raises the lid, setting his items inside. I follow suit and he closes the lid, trying hard to ignore the slight smell of decomp coming from the bag stuffed into the side of the trunk.

He gives me an unhappy look as we load into the car and he drives toward my apartment. He has a few more questions concerning my plan and I explain them in detail so he knows exactly what his part will be. When we both feel comfortable that we know what is expected of us, I bring up the last item I need to tell him. I'd kept this until last, mainly because I feared he would see it as show stopper.

"There's one last thing you need to know." He glances at me and his look says it all. He already expected this to be bad, so I rush on, "Because of my condition, my curse, I don't have anything to fear from a vampire bite. Whatever it is that makes me immortal protects me from such things. You don't have that protection. If you get bitten and it doesn't kill you, you will become a vampire." This news doesn't make him happy, but he doesn't start screaming and he doesn't tell me to go to Hell. I figure that's worth something so I go on. "If that were to happen, what do you want to do?"

"You mean do I want you to kill me or leave me to be a vampire?" he asks.

"Not exactly. You were partially correct in do you want me to kill you, but I can't let you remain a vampire. If you are bitten, you will change and nothing you do can stop that. You will kill to feed no matter what your previous outlook is. You won't have a choice, that's the nature of the change. What I'm asking is do you want me to do it or do you want to do it yourself?"

"Would I be able to do it myself?" David asks seriously, considering my words.

"If you did it soon enough, yes. But I'd have to finish it." He knows I mean the decapitation. "If you wait too long, the vampire instinct to survive will begin to influence your thinking and you'll no longer have the ability. If you get bitten, you'll need to do something almost immediately or it will default to me." I give him an apologetic shrug. I hate to be the bearer of more bad news, but I feel he needs to know exactly what he'd gotten into. Now would be the test of his resolve. I won't blame him if he tells me to get the hell out of his car.

What he says makes me feel better about him and I appreciate his help all the more, "Got it. If I'm bitten, I'll let you know and you can kill me."

THIRTEEN

When David turns onto my street, I notice two work trucks sitting in front of The Magnolia House. Betty didn't let grass grow under her and repairs to my apartment were under way. There is no need for me to go in and I don't look forward to the confrontation with my landlady. I have David pull up next to my Jag and, after agreeing on a time and place to meet back up, I hop out. David pulls away and I enter my car and follow him to the end of the block. Once back on Sycamore, he goes one way and I go the other.

Our quest to find all the equipment we'd need to pull off a successful cleansing of the three vampires will take both of us across Atlanta. We have serious time pressure now. If we don't collect the equipment quickly, we won't have time to get set up and carry out my plan before we lose the sun and the sun is an all important part of the plan. My first item takes me to a medical supply company. Portable ultra violet lights are available from several sources, but most of these are long wave UV. For my purposes, I need the more dangerous short wave UV that is slightly harder to come by.

The damn things are expensive at a bit over three hundred dollars each and I need six. I also choose the variety that runs off disposable lantern batteries as I don't have the time to charge the rechargeable kind. I pick up the batteries next and with my shopping list complete, race to the rendezvous with David at the industrial site on Baxter Road.

I don't expect him to be there yet, so I'm not disappointed when I get there first. I use the time wisely and tear into the packages holding the UV lanterns and install the batteries. In short order, I have all six working and then I set to work on the rest of my equipment. I set out the two jars of my blood and then lay out my weapons. The large curved blade knife, my crossbow and, of course, the olive wood arrows.

The crossbow doesn't require much to make sure it works. I check it over carefully and turn on the sight unit and adjust the intensity. With the bow ready, I turn to the quiver of arrows. I have eight left of the original twenty-four. I lay them out and inspect the shafts for straightness, then the fletching and the points. I carry a small file and touch up the sharpness of each arrow. As I lovingly handle the arrows, I remember back to when they were given to me.

*****

I had been a Cleanser for nearly ten years and had seen many terrible things in that time. The only sure way of private communications in the day was to do it face to face. This required the Cleansers to travel to the Vatican each time we successfully cleansed a beast. My mentor, Father Perroni, and I had agreed we would meet on a quarterly basis and I would report on all the cleansings accomplished during the preceding three months. This saved me from having to make as many trips to Rome, but it made it difficult for me to receive intelligence about sightings or attacks.

I decided whenever I had been away for a month or six weeks, if there had been anything going on, I would make a trip to Rome and the Vatican to see if anything particularly nasty had popped up. During one of these trips, Father Perroni and I went walking so we could have a private conversation. We crossed the Tiber and soon found ourselves strolling the streets and alleys of Rome proper. We stopped at a cafe on the Via del Tritone and we so enjoyed the weather and our conversation that it became dark before we decided to stroll back to Saint Peters.

During the walk back, I experienced the feeling of being followed and tried to find the source of the feeling. Father Perroni had neglected to tell me about the disappearance of several Priests during the last month. He told me later that no bodies had been found so there had been no evidence of unnatural involvement. But as we walked through the streets, I realized we were being hunted.

I told Father Perroni what I suspected and he tried hard to put on a brave face. I knew he was scared. His knowledge of the unnaturals and the ways to destroy them was all academic. He had never even seen any of the creatures he sent me out to kill.

In those days, I carried all of the weapons I needed on me at all times. I carried an officer's model 1889 Bodeo pistol loaded with 10.4 millimeter silver bullets and an Italian Navy cutlass with pure silver work on the blade, along with a German made crossbow. I carried so many weapons that I clanked when I walked, but I was ready no matter what beast I encountered. On that night it would be a vampire, a female that had a hatred for Priests.

I steered us into an alley, away from the prying eyes of passersby. She came at us from above, dropping down from a roof top. Father Perroni was petrified with terror at the appearance of the hideous thing. He stood in front of me so that I had to fire the crossbow over his shoulder. My shot went high, striking her in the throat. While the shot was not fatal, it did give me time to draw the cutlass. Grabbing the terrified Priest by his cassock, I pulled him behind me, at the same time swinging the blade. The narrow confines of the alley slowed the power and speed of my arm and I only managed a deep slash to the vampire's neck.

Black blood spurted across the alley covering both myself and Perroni. She staggered and went to one knee. I drove the heel of my right boot into her chest before she had a chance to recover, forcing her to the cobbles of the alley. With my foot on her chest, I hacked at her neck until finally the head rolled free. It most definitely wasn't my cleanest kill, but she was dead.

Father Perroni came up to examine the creature and added the contents of his stomach to the mess already polluting the scene. The ugliness of the vampire and the speed of her attack amazed him and he thanked me profusely for saving his life. I told him that had I known he was going to vomit on me, I would have waited until after she had killed him.

He didn't think it was funny.

I wrapped the head in my cloak and had the good Father carry it while I carried the rest of the body. We made our way back to the Vatican through back alleys and side streets and the bisected corpse was cremated in the center of Saint Peter's square. The Cardinals were not happy with us. They finally backed off when Father Perroni pointed out this was the creature that had killed the other Priests. They were still not appreciative of the stinking corpse that now littered the square. I figured I would leave while the getting was good, so I said my goodbyes to my mentor and road back out into the country.

A month later, when I returned for my scheduled meeting with Father Perroni, he presented me with the gift of twenty-four of the finest crossbow arrows I'd ever seen. He told me that each one had been blessed and that they would help me to more effectively kill vampires. I knew it was a thank you for saving his life. We never talked about it again.

*****

I hear a car coming and turn to see David's Crown Vic pulling through the dilapidated gate. As my car's the only thing in the empty decaying parking lot, he steers straight for me. When he gets out of the car, I can tell by the sour look on his face he isn't happy. I incorrectly assume it has something to do with his not being able to procure some piece of needed equipment.

He corrects my assumption by saying, "Get that stinking piece of shit out of my car."

I immediately realize the source of the problem. Midsummer in Georgia, the blazing sun rests high in a typically cloudless sky and the temperature hovered around ninety-five degrees, Fahrenheit. The temperature in the trunk of his car probably exceeds one hundred and twenty, combine this with a decapitated head and you have the makings of a real disaster. When David raises the lid, the incredible stench hits me in the face. Apologizing was pointless, so I reach in and pull out the bag containing all that was left of Harry Crowe. Holding it at arm's length, I carry it over to the same spot where I cremated the remains of the first two vampires.

I don't bother taking it out of the bag. Instead, I set the entire thing on the ground and collect wood. David eventually ambles over to help, the sour expression still on his face.

While we pile the wood onto the pyre, David says, "I'm surprised no one called the police. You should have seen the looks I got every time I stopped at an intersection." I can't help myself and start laughing. His expression intensifies and he loudly announces, "I'm glad you're enjoying yourself." His attitude only serves to make me laugh harder and a few seconds later, he joins me.

I manage to get the fire started and we continue to laugh as we stand watching the last remnant of Harry Crowe go up in smoke. I finally stop laughing and feel better, more focused. The therapeutic value of a good laugh should never be underestimated. It's a common phenomenon, nothing cures a case of nerves before battle better than a good laugh.

Calm now, David asks, "Are you ready?"

"Yeah, let's get your gear and move to the building."

He agrees and falls in beside me. At our cars, we load up with the equipment and make the short walk to the rundown office building. Setting everything on the ground, we divide it into piles. The first pile, items that we need to carry down into the tunnels we pick up and carry inside. We have no reason to wait any longer and go straight to the steps.

It takes us a couple of trips to get everything into the tunnel and forty-five minutes later, the tunnel trap is set. David and I move back up into the old office building and prep the equipment we'll need there. With everything inside ready, we go out and collect more wood for the pyres we'll need to cremate the three vampires we hope to destroy. An hour and a half after we start, we are ready.

If we are going to complete this cleansing before sunset, we need to get started. The whole plan hinges on getting the three vampires to come to us. If we fail at this crucial part of the plan, our only recourse will be to go into the sump and neither of us thinks that's a good idea.

"Let's go over the plan one more time," I say.

*****

The plan, while not simple, isn't overly complicated, either. I've found that the more complicated a plan is, the more likely it is to fail. I try to keep all of mine as simple as possible. God knows they go bad enough without me increasing the odds of failure. This plan requires some timing and a bit of luck, but I think it has a better than average chance of success. It relies on the nature of vampires. When they feel threatened, they attack and I intend to make them feel threatened. Also, they can't resist human blood. I will sweeten the trap with two quarts of my own vintage.

David starts with, "We both go down into the tunnel, me with the shotgun and you with the blood. I hide in the last storage room before the drain that feeds into the sump."

I take over, "Once you're hidden, I'll start by pulling the grate out of the floor, making sure to be as noisy as possible. One jar of blood gets smashed in the drain pipe. The noise combined with the smell of fresh A positive will get them moving our way. The second jar I'll use to pour a trail up the tunnel to the stairs. That will help to mask your smell, but you have to be as still and quiet as possible. If they spot you, we're screwed," I add.

David takes up relating the plan again with, "Got it, I'll be as quiet as a church mouse." Glad that he didn't said as quiet as the dead, I nod and he continues. "Once they go past me, I turn on the UV lantern and place it inside the drain pipe. That will keep them from being able to get back to the sump." Again I nod, prompting him to go on. "Then I follow them to the stairs where I turn on the rest of the UV lanterns forcing them to remain on the main level."

"Correct, if they try to escape, hopefully those lanterns will keep them out of the tunnel, but if they make it past them, the one in the drain should slow them down until we can catch back up. While you're doing that, I'll confront them upstairs in the old office. With luck, I can catch them by surprise and get an arrow into at least one of them as they come up the stairs. This is where it gets a little dicey. You have to be Johnny on the spot and get up there with the shotgun to help me. I can't hold three off indefinitely."

He grips the shotgun in his hands and nods once. "I'll be there. You just make sure you're out of the line of fire because I'm going to start shooting as soon as I get back topside. I'll pump double aught into them to slow them down and you put the arrows through their hearts. When they're down, we use the grapnel hook and rope to drag them out into the sun and then you do your thing with the heads."

I finish with, "And if everything goes right, we leave here having cleansed three vampires and us all in one piece."

"It's a good plan. Not a lot of moving parts and the odds aren't that bad, two against three. I've had worse." He shrugs to cover up the slight quaking of his body. I can't blame him. This is only his second monster fight and it is going to be a big one.

I don't bother pointing out that fighting three vampires would be like fighting three times that number of humans. Probably better I don't correct him at this point, so I pat him on the back. "Let's get going."

He picks up his 870 and racks the slide, loading a shell into the chamber and starts toward the building. I pick up my crossbow and arrows and fall into step beside him. He enters first with me right on his heels and crosses through the empty rooms to the top of the stairwell. He pauses and looks back at me. One last nod passes between us and he turns on his flashlight. I think about that first step again as he starts down. I reach the bottom a second behind him and together we move down the tunnel to the drain.

Neither of us speak. Any communication from here on out will be hand signals. About twenty feet from the end of the tunnel, we come to last storage room. This will be David's hiding spot. He sweeps his light around the room, ensuring it was empty, and then enters. I go on to the tunnel end and the floor grate. I notice a quick flash of purple-hued light illuminate the store room as David makes one last check of the UV lantern. As I watch, his arm holding the flash light extends out into the tunnel and wags up and down. His signal to me that he is ready.

It's up to me now. I take a long, deep breath to calm myself, letting it out slowly and with a short prayer, bend and slip my fingers through the cross section of the grate. The plan calls for me to make as much noise as I can while removing the grate, and the rusty metal square cooperates nicely. A loud, metallic screech fills the silence as the grate slides out of its frame. Once it comes free, I stand and from about waist high, release my hold. The grate drops and slams into the concrete floor. A tremendous clang echoes up and down the damp corridor. That had to have woken them up and I'll find out soon enough. I pick up one of the jars of blood, watching the red liquid slide back and forth thickly within the glass. If they are awake, the blood will be more than they could ignore.

Raising the jar high, I slam it down into the drain. Rewarded with the satisfying sound of glass shattering and the coppery scent of blood, I know the trap had been set. Now we have to wait and see if our prey takes the bait.

The noise I made fades away and silence fills the tunnel once again. I strain my ears for any sign that the vampires are on the move and they don't disappoint. A hiss like air escaping floats up from the drain, quickly followed by a soft scrabbling sound. I lean down to hear better and listen as the scrabbling intensifies, coming closer.

Here comes the party. Grabbing the other jar of blood, I unscrew the lid and splash the thick liquid onto the wall opposite of David's door. I make my way back up the tunnel as fast as I can, making sure to leave a good trail of my blood.

My timing is nearly perfect as I run out of blood just as I reach the alcove with the stairs. Pausing to listen, I almost wait too long. When I finally hear them over the sound of my own breathing, they are only thirty or so yards away. I drop the empty jar and run up the stairs, my legs pumping with all I have. I shoot out of the stairwell and run for the next room. Once through the door, I turn and take up a firing position with the crossbow.

Raising the weapon to my shoulder, I whisper, "Come on, you bastards." And then I wait.

FOURTEEN

I'm sure it's only seconds, but it seems like hours before I see the first sign of the creatures at the top of the stairwell. Evidently, they sensed a trap and are being cautious. I hold fire, wanting at least two of them to completely clear the top of the stairs before launching my first arrow. I hope David has the first lantern deployed, if he can come up behind them and fire at them with the shotgun, it might drive them into the open.

Several seconds pass before I see any more movement. Then a scrawny, pale arm attached to a clawed hand reaches up into the room above the stairs. It is quickly followed by the head and body of the first vampire as it slides out of the stairwell. It emerges completely into the open and looks around the room. I'm sure it feels safe because it turns and, looking back down the stairs, makes a short, sharp screeching sound. Soon, another shadow comes into view as the second vampire creeps out of the sewer.

From my place in the darkness of the adjacent room, I carefully move the red dot of the halo sight over the heart of the second vampire. As the index finger of my right hand touches the trigger, a loud, explosive boom sounds so loud that I jump. In an instant, the vampires that had just come up the stairs turn and disappear back down. Two more booms follow in quick succession. I realize it is David's shotgun and he had engaged the vampires from behind. I make a rapid shift and bring the sight onto the first vampire. His position will not let me make a heart shot from where I crouch, I will have to move.

As I rise up from my crouch, the vampire zeroes in on me. It advances too fast for my eyes to follow. I fire reflexively, hoping for a heart shot, but I miss. My arrow goes high and lodges in the creature's left cheek. The force of the impact rocks the vampire's skull back and forces it off its path. Most likely the only thing that saved me another trip to the morgue. I dodge to my right and the creature shoots past me into the other room. I cock the bow again and fit another arrow. The vampire recovers quickly and turns to face me once more.

We both move at the same time. I raise the bow to my shoulder and the creature charges. This time when I pull the trigger, I hit my mark. The vampire's momentum carries it into me and I crash to the floor under its weight. The distant reports of the twelve gauge tell me that David is still in the fight, but I know he can't stand long against two of them. I try to push the paralyzed vampire off of me and fail. The weight isn't the issue, I'm completely exhausted. My breathing comes in rapid, shallow gasps and my heart hammers inside my chest.

The fight has only been going on for a few seconds and I already feel spent.

I concentrate to force my breathing to slow. After a few deep breaths, I heave at the dead weight again and push the vampire off. I climb unsteadily to my feet and grab my crossbow. My breathing has slowed and my heart rate has come down, but it still takes three tries to get the bow cocked again. As soon as I reload, I run for the stairs. I have to use the hand rail and I slip once, but make it to the bottom. David's life is on the line. I don't have time to get myself gathered completely and I have to push through it. Stop to grab one of the UV lanterns, I run down the tunnel, looking for David.

Black, rotten blood stains the floor of the tunnel and is proof that David's shotgun had done some damage. There have been no shots since I started down the steps and I dread what that might mean. I continue down, taking care in case something is hiding in one of the side rooms. I come closer to the end of the corridor and at the very edge of my light's reach, I can see a foot lying on the floor. I know it belonged to David because of the shoe.

I pause, not wanting to go further, not wanting to see what I know waited for me.

As I draw closer, it surprises me to see that the foot is still attached to a leg and the leg becomes a whole body. David is sitting on the floor, legs splayed, leaning against the side of the tunnel. His eyes are closed and I prepare myself for the worst. I stop a short distance from him and thumb the switch, turning on the lantern. A deep purple light fills the corridor and I raise the bow, preparing to make the shot that would end David's transformation. His eyes flutter open and his face turns towards me. I place my finger on the trigger and apply pressure.

He smiles. "It's about time you got here."

"I'm sorry," I say, but I wasn't talking about being late. My finger readies to apply the last ounce of pressure needed to let the arrow fly.

A split second before I fire, David asks, "Are you going to help me up?"

I breathe for the first time in several seconds and ease my finger away from the trigger. Before lowering the bow I ask, "Were you bitten?"

"No. Just had the wind knocked out of me. Help me up."

I'm relieved that I won't have to kill him. "You scared the shit out of me." I bend over and grab his outstretched hand, pulling while he struggles to his feet. Leaning against the wall, he fights to get his breathing under control, I know how he feels having just experienced it myself. Now that he's up, I get right back to work. "Where did they go?"

He inclines his face toward the far end of the tunnel, "Back down the hole."

Surprised, I ask, "They made it past the UV?"

"It fried them pretty good, but yeah they made it." He points to where the shotgun lay on the floor and without having to ask, I hand him the gun and he feeds shells into the tubular magazine. He racks the slide and asks, "What about number three?"

"Paralyzed up top," I answer, still trying to figure out how the vampires made it past the UV lantern. I step closer to him and try to take his arm to help him back up the tunnel.

He shrugs me off. "What are you doing?"

"I'm getting you out of here. We'll finish the one upstairs and try to figure out what to do next."

"Like hell," he replies, stronger and with more

conviction than I thought he'd be capable of. "Those things are hurt. The light burned them badly and I put two or three loads of buckshot into each of them. We have to go after them now, before they have time to recover."

I look at him with a newfound respect. "Okay, let's go."

At the grate, I kneel and look down. The UV lantern lay smashed in the bottom of the drain pipe. That explains how the two vampires had been able to get past it. That close to the light source would have melted the skin off them. Whichever one smashed the light had to be seriously hurt, which means David's right. He kneels beside me, ready to climb inside. It occurs to me there's equipment upstairs I need, so I ask him to wait. He nods and I run back down the tunnel to the steps.

Back upstairs, I grab my kit bag, check to make sure the vamp is still lying uncomfortably on the floor, then hoof it back to David. He's sitting on the floor with the shotgun pointed at the hole, obviously still in pain.

I look at him questioningly and he says, "I'm fine, just resting."

"Sure. I'll go first." He doesn't argue, so I slide into the hole and then reach back up to drag my gear through. As I push the UV light in front of me, David looks down through the hole and I whisper, "I'm going to start crawling. I've got the light and my bow. I need you to bring the bag." And with that, I start forward, knowing he'll catch up.

The crawl seems longer than I remember. I know it's mostly due to my exhaustion, but I labor on, pushing the light in front of me as I keep the bow tucked under my right arm. I figure with the light in front, neither of the vampires will try and attack us from that direction. I hope they aren't behind us. If they are, David will have to deal with it. I can hear him behind me breathing hard, but still moving. Once more, I feel thankful that I still have the body and endurance of a twenty-two year old. David, in his mid-forties, is suffering.

After what feels like an eternity, we reach the end of the drain. Like the last time, I swivel around on my ass and drop to the sump floor. I turn and pull the bag out of the pipe as David pushes it to me. Following my example, he scoots his legs out and drops down. This is his first glimpse of what Hell must look like.

"Jesus…" isn't the worst thing he could have said, but we don't have time for him to try and process the horror of the scene to come up with anything more colorful.

"Get it together, David, it gets worse and we need to move."

He nods then grabs the kit bag, slings the strap over his shoulder, and raises the shotgun. With him ready, I turn and heft the UV light. Purple-hued light softens the overall appearance of our location, but brings one aspect into stark focus. UV light causes body fluids to fluoresce and the walls and areas around the drain pipes glow with splashed and spattered fluid stains. I try to take my own advice and ignore the disgusting mess as I search for the vampires.

Keeping with my usual practice, I keep it simple. I move to the first drain to my left and plan to work my way around the sump one drain at a time. I tell David to follow and cover behind us with the shotgun. We move together to the first drain. I quickly shine the light inside, *then* look to see if anything is there. It's empty, so I move to the next drain. This time, as I shine the light inside, I hear a screech and something moves. Easing one eye past the edge, I look in. Lying on the bottom of the pipe flailing around, I can see the vampire that smashed the light at the grate. It is horribly burned and the light I shined on it did more damage. As I watch, its skin bubbles and boils, turns black and begins to slough away.

I keep the light aimed at it and reach inside, grabbing it by one leg. Pulling it as hard as I can, I draw the injured vampire out of the pipe to fall to the bottom of the sump. I don't bother with the bow, there is no need. I pull the knife at my belt and hack off its head, avoiding its claws and chomping jaws as it fights with its last strength. Setting the big light box on the ground, I pull a leak-proof bag out of the kit slung across David's shoulder.

He turns and glances at my handiwork. "That thing

stinks."

"Yeah, I know. They don't smell much better before they're burned." I lift the head and place it in the bag.

He turns back to continue covering our rear and that's when the third vampire makes its appearance. Idiot. I set the UV light facing the damn wall, giving the vamp his chance to attack. It shoots out of one of the drains behind me at a speed too fast for a human to perceive. It strikes David, knocking the shotgun out of his hands and sending it spinning across the sump. David falls back against the wall, slamming into the concrete, leaving him conscious, but dazed.

The vampire continues on its course, slamming into me and driving me back against another wall. I drop the bag with the head and my bow. The vampire and I grapple, each trying to gain an advantage over the other. Ordinarily, it would have made short work of me, but this one, like its friend, had been injured by the UV light and David's buck shot. Weakened as it is, I still need more luck than I possess to win in a hand-to-hand struggle. I weaken and seeing it has the advantage, the vampire slides both its hands around my throat. Squeezing and pushing at the same time, it raises me off the floor, pinning me to the wall.

I fight back, striking it repeatedly in the face with my fists. I might as well have been using a feather pillow. My punches lose their strength and my vision blurs, and then fades completely. With my arms hanging limply at my sides and my sight almost gone, the vampire smiles at me, exposing its needle-sharp teeth, and then I black out.

*****

I awake on the floor of the sump with a sore throat and something sticky covering my face and hands. Slowly, I sit up to see David standing over the vampire, shotgun still smoking in his hands. He still has the thing aimed at the vamp, which is hissing and moaning on the floor. Though how it's doing either of those I'm not sure. Half of its cranium's missing due to the nine thirty caliber rounds of buck shot he must have fired at it.

"Good, you're alive. I'll let you do the messy part," he smirks as I slowly sit up. "And watch behind you."

I turn to see more gore splattered all over the wall. "Fantastic. You couldn't have just chopped the thing's head off," I mutter, getting to my feet and picking up my bow.

"Nope, thought I'd save the best part for you."

I grimace as I check to see if the bow is loaded then move toward the vampire.

It's difficult to look at the pitiful thing. Most its head had disintegrated, leaving only half its face and one eye. It still writhes around, attempting to regain its feet while the single eye blinks, looking for an escape from the sump.

I raise the bow to my shoulder and recite the prayer I'd learned years ago, "May the Holy Cross be a light unto me and may the Dragon never be my guide." I pull the trigger and send an olive wood arrow through its foul heart. There is no drama, no death throes, it just seizes up and stops moving. I pull the knife at my belt and, kneeling by its side, sever the neck.

David steps up beside the body and me. When I look up at him, he asks, "I thought you always did that thing with the oil."

"I do, but I really want to get the hell out of here. I'll do it up in the parking lot."

"No arguments from me. What can I do to help?"

"Take the light and check the rest of the drains, just in case. I'll collect the heads and then we're out of here."

He nods and drops the kit bag at my side. I rummage around for another bag and slip the remains of the second head inside. Going back to the first creature, I drop its head into the kit bag along with the other one. David finishes his search of the drains and comes back to where I stand. When I look at him, he signals negative in answer to my unasked question. Our task finished, we load all the gear into the drain and I help David to climb in. Once inside, he crawls back toward the entrance, pushing our gear along the bottom of the pipe. Taking a last look around, I climb in and follow.

The trip back to pipe entrance takes several minutes because we are both exhausted and beat to a pulp. Eventually, we make it and help each other climb through the grate. In the tunnel, we drag our sore and bruised bodies back to the steps. At the top, in the stairwell room, I go to the first vampire where it still lay, paralyzed and complete destroying it.

After pulling my arrow from the body, David and I carry it to the steps and pitch it down. I don't worry about anyone finding it because decomposition will take care of everything but the skeleton before long.

I carry the three heads out to the parking lot and drop them onto the pyre where the last of the werewolf smolders. David helps me to pile more wood up and I relight the fire. He and I sit down on the overgrown asphalt and watch in silence as the fruits of our gruesome labor burn.

Finally, he asks, "Is this how it always goes?"

"Pretty much. If it can go wrong, it usually does. I've always got a plan, but when you're dealing with monsters, nothing is ever easy."

"I can't believe you've been doing this for as long as you have. This is my first and I'm ready to take up knitting or something. Anything but this," he says, running a slightly shaky hand through his hair.

"That's why I don't have anyone helping me. No offense, but people just don't have the constitution for it. I like you, David, and I understand how you feel, so don't worry if you want out."

After a few seconds thought, he looks at me smiling and says, "Nah, I'm good. Besides, the way you've been getting into trouble lately, you'll wind up getting yourself killed again without me around."

I smile and slap him on the back, which causes him to wince, but I don't care. I'm just glad to have someone to help me, especially someone capable and that I trust.

FIFTEEN

It sometimes amazes me how fast a plan can go down the toilet. As we stand there watching the heads burn, I go over how close our plan had come to screwing us over. I'm still not sure how we were able to pull this off. If I had pulled the bow's trigger one second earlier, or if David had waited one second to pull his trigger, it all would've been different. Now we had the whole spilled milk thing going on, so instead of bitching, I ask David what happened.

"I heard them when they came up out of the grate," he replies while his eyes focus down on the burning heads. "I couldn't see anything, but I could hear them and I knew when they went past my door. After they went by, I counted to ten and then slipped down to the grate and turned on the lantern."

I nod. So far, so good, though I'm surprised he didn't wait just a bit longer.

"I made my way back up the tunnel toward the steps and had no trouble all the way to the alcove. I could see a little and as I reached to turn on the first lantern, one of the vampires turned and looked right at me. I didn't know what else to do, so I shot it. Put a load of buckshot in its chest and it ran right past me like it was nothing. I pumped the slide and that's when I got hit the first time. I guess it was the second vampire, I never saw it," he growls angrily. "Took a slam in the kidneys and went down, but I came back up fast and put two more rounds in their direction."

"You're lucky they didn't just finish you off right there," I state with a grin. "You are one lucky S.O.B. tonight."

He drops his chin and smiles, "What can I say?" He continues with his story, "I started down the tunnel after them while I reloaded and caught up to them at the drain. I pointed and fired as fast as I could, hoping it would slow them down enough so you could get to me and finish it. Next thing I know, I'm on my ass again, this time from a punch to the gut. That one hurt. I crawled over to the wall and that's where you found me."

The fire begins to burn down, so walk a short distance away to gather more wood. I come back and drop a few sticks on top of the baking heads, the sound of fat sizzling mixed with the sound of wood popping as the fire consumed them fills the air. I sit back down beside David and we spend the next several minutes staring into our grizzly camp fire.

After a time, I look at David and say, "Don't sweat it, there wasn't anything you could have done different. Like I said earlier, if it can go wrong, it usually does."

Nodding, he adds, "It wasn't what I expected, they're so fast and man, can they hit. I've never been punched like that." He looks at me. "You were right, never underestimate these things."

"It still happens to me. As long as I've been doing this, I sometimes forget how hard they are to kill. With me, I take a few chances because I'm not worried about getting killed. You, though. You only get one chance, so be careful."

Again, he nods and we resume our vigil over the fire. It takes a couple of hours for the fire to do its work and once more, I use the broken post to smash the skulls into powder. Late in the afternoon, we finish and return to our cars.

David looks toward me and I know what he intends to ask. It had become his favorite question. "What now?"

"Back to your place and try to figure out how to find Alonso. We have until day light tomorrow morning, so no rest for the wicked tonight."

"No problem, I'll sleep when I'm dead."

It surprises me how sad his last statement made me feel.

*****

It takes several minutes for us to collect our equipment, but we are finally able to sit down in our cars. David pulls out first and I follow him as we convoy back to his apartment. After being on the road for a few minutes, my cell phone rings. I answer and hear David's voice. He tells me he plans to stop off at one of his favorite take out places and pick up dinner for us. I agree it will save us some time and after telling me where his hideaway key is located, he clicks off.

The great thing about summer is the long days and we still have a few hours of daylight left when I get to the apartment. Finding the key, I enter and go straight to the shower. As I undress, I looked at my pitiful clothes and sigh. Another set for the trash. I drop the nasty smelling jeans and T-shirt on the floor and kick them aside trying to remind myself that at some point, I'll need more clothes. David's shower is much better than mine and the higher water pressure feels like the water is blasting the crud off instead of washing it away. Lobster red on exit, I begin to towel off when I hear the detective come in. I acknowledge that I hear him to avoid accidents. Most people might worry about someone entering and catching you naked. With me and folks in martial lines of work, who usually go around carrying a variety of weapons, a surprise can result in a more fatal form of embarrassment.

Towel wrapped around my waist, I leave the bathroom and as I pass near the kitchen en route back to the spare bedroom, I am greeted with a wonderful smell. By the time I get to the bedroom to dress, my mouth had begun to water. I hadn't realized how hungry I was and I have no idea what the food is, but it smells fantastic. I dig into my travel bag and pull out another pair of jeans and a T-shirt. Dressing quickly, I slip on a pair of ankle socks and my last pair of soft, grip shoes. These are a pair of old and well-worn New Balance runners.

I can hear David in the shower as I come into the living room. The smell of the food continues to drive me crazy, but I wait until my host can join me.

He finally comes out dressed similarly to me and says, "Come on, let's eat."

That's what I'd been waiting for and jump up, feeling more energetic than I had earlier. I step into the kitchen as he sets plates out and pulls flatware out of a drawer. I stand with my tongue hanging out, drooling like Pavlov's dogs. David looks at me, laughing, and tells me to get a couple beers out of the fridge. Opening the door, I grab two bottles of Red Brick Ale.

I hold them up toward him and he nods, saying, "Opener is on the door."

I pull the magnetic opener from the door and as I pry the tops off, ask, "A beer snob, huh?"

He smirks. "Army. Spent a lot of time in Europe, the beer's great. When I came home, American beer tasted like piss, so I have to find the dark stuff and I like the micro brews. That one's made here in Atlanta."

I set his on the table, taking a long pull on mine. Giving him an appreciative look, I say, "Not bad, tasty. Speaking of tasty, what is that heavenly aroma?"

"Southern barbecue. I've got shredded pork, some brisket, and all the fixings. Mustard potato salad, vinegar slaw, and corn cakes. Dig in."

That is all the encouragement I need. I don't know what barbecue is, but the heavily peppered and smoke flavored meat smells amazing. I tell him I'd never had it before and he says, "I can't believe your buddy Alonso hasn't hooked you up with it."

As I scoop large helpings from all the containers onto my plate, I answer, "We're friends, but we don't spend much time hanging out. In case you haven't noticed, I don't have much of a life outside of being a Cleanser."

"Well, you need to take some time and savor the special joy that is barbecue." Shoveling a fork full into his mouth, he adds, "You gotta love a good hog."

*****

After dinner, we grab another Red Brick Ale each and sit in the living room. My belly full, I have to fight the urge to take a nap and the comfortable chair doesn't help. David's the detective, so I defer to him for a strategy for finding the man with the ponytail that, as of right now, is our prime suspect for sending the demon to take Alonso. David sips his beer, looking at the floor, deep in thought.

After several minutes, he says, "As I see it, we don't have enough information to even begin to find our mystery man. There's one person who should know who he is."

Looking directly at me, he says, "We need to ask Erin."

I consider his opinion and can't find any fault with his conclusion, "I agree, it's the only answer."

"Besides, if she's as beautiful as you've said, I need to meet her," he adds with a huge smile on his face.

"You're not her type, not old enough." He starts laughing and I continue, "I'm ready whenever you are."

Turning his beer up and draining it, he stands. "Let's go." I finish my beer and follow.

Outside, I transfer my weapons and equipment to his car again. We climb into the Crown Vic and he pulls onto the street, heading southwest toward our confrontation with my client, Erin.

With light traffic, we make it to Erin's house in less than twenty minutes. Pulling to the curb in front of the stucco house, David parks and we exit the car. I wait until he comes around and we walk to the porch side by side.

I can't help feeling troubled and like a traitor as I step up and prepare to knock on the door. It's hard for me to believe that Erin is involved with what has been going on or in Alonso's disappearance. I knew David suspected her, but he's a cop and cops don't trust anyone, at least that's what I keep telling myself. At the door, I hesitate with my hand raised. David steps around me and knocks forcefully, like a cop, on the door.

When I look at him, he says, "We don't have time to pussy foot around."

I know he's right, but that doesn't mean I have to like it, so I keep my mouth shut. We wait for a couple of minutes and hear nothing from inside. David knocks again, louder this time, actually making the glass rattle. Several more minutes pass with nothing from inside. David steps close to the door, shading his eyes with his hand, attempting to see inside.

Seeing nothing, he looks at me, "I thought you told her to stay in at night?"

"I did."

Of course it wasn't dark yet, but it would be soon. She should've been home by now. Every time I've been here, she was also. Though I'm starting to wonder how much she actually listened to me.

David starts toward the edge of the porch and says, "Stay here. I'm going to walk around back. Maybe she's in the yard and didn't hear us knock." He smiles and slips around the corner.

I continue to stand there, thinking about her. It's as if there are two sides warring inside me. On one hand, as David pointed out, there is some evidence that she could be involved. On the other hand, I can't stop thinking about how I feel when I'm around her. I make myself knock on the door, hoping that with David gone, she will open it so I can see her again.

Again, several minutes go by with no answer at the door. Eventually, David comes back around to the front and the look on his face tells me something is wrong.

After he steps up on the porch, he asks, "Have you ever been inside this house?"

"Yes, of course I have," I answer defensively. I don't like his tone and as I prepare to tell him about it, but a nagging thought enters my mind. No, I haven't actually been inside. She asked me to come in each time I came here, but I always declined. I'd meant to go in to help her install the UV lights and show her where to place the wards, but for some reason, I'd backed out at the last instance. I gave her the stuff on the porch and told her how to install it.

He can tell something is troubling me. "What is it?"

"I'm sorry, that's not true. I've never been inside the house. I don't know why I said that," I apologize and then, "Why, what's wrong?"

"There isn't anything inside except for the front room. No furniture, nothing."

"What? You have to be mistaken. She lives here. I've been here and talked to her here, right here on this porch."

He motions for me to follow him and says, "Come on, see for yourself."

I follow him as if in a daze, wondering what the hell is going on. We walk around to the side and he indicates I should look in a low window. I step up, peer through the glass, and curse. The room is empty and doesn't appear to have been lived in for some time. Without waiting for him, I move around to another window. Looking inside gives me the same results, nothing. I continue to move around the house looking in every window I come to, feeling more and more panic the further I go.

By the time I make it back to the front of the house, there isn't any conclusion to be had except the fact I'd been made a fool. Angrier at myself than anything else, I sit on the edge of the porch, my feet in the grass. I can't grasp the situation. The harder I try, the more I try to find a reason. David steps up in front of me and when I look up at his face, it is obvious he is angry. I can't blame him, I feel like such an idiot.

I don't know what to say, but know I need to say something. I open my mouth and at that moment, a dark blue Mercedes slows in front of Erin's house. Seeing it, I raise my arm pointing as the big luxury car accelerates and speeds away up the street. David turns, seeing the car and we both realize that our prey is in sight.

Without a word, we sprint for the unmarked police car. David has it started and as I close my door, he pulls away, accelerating fast, trying to catch up. Already two blocks in front of us, the Mercedes turns left and vanishes. David presses hard on the accelerator, trying to close the distance. He turns left at the same intersection and I barely catch a glimpse of the Merc as it turns right almost three blocks ahead. As soon as the Crown Vic straightens out, David jams the accelerator to the floor and rockets toward the next turn. Driving with one hand, he digs around in the console and comes out with a small pair of binoculars.

He pitches them to me and as I catch them, he says, "Next time we get on a straight away, see if you can get a plate number."

I take a few seconds to check the focus on the binos. A thought occurs to me and I ask, "Can you call in for assistance?"

"And tell them what? We want to talk to the owner

because he might have made a pact with the devil to use a demon to kill his girlfriend?"

"Well, when you put it that way…"

"Just get a plate number, okay?"

"Okay."

I go back to trying to get a look at the Mercedes. David makes the next turn and again, I have a second long glimpse before the mystery car makes its next turn.

David swears. "I can't make up any ground. We have to find a way to get closer, this isn't working."

At the next intersection, instead of turning right, he continues straight. "I hate to be Captain Obvious, but you missed the turn."

"If he keeps up the pattern he's been following, his next turn will be to the left. If I go down three blocks and turn right, I should be on the same street he'll turn right on." Not a great plan, but it is a plan. Again, I don't want to point out the fault in the plan, but figure I'd better, just in case. As I open my mouth, David cuts me off, "Don't say anything. I know it's a fifty-fifty shot, but we aren't getting anywhere this way. So just keep your mouth shut and let me concentrate."

I close my mouth and face back to the front. We are both tired and frustrated. It won't help either of us to let our tempers flare. I know David is still angry about what we found at Erin's house. I'm sure he thinks I'm an incompetent ass because that's what I feel like. How I managed to get myself into this mess and hadn't bothered to check the background or verify anything about Erin was beyond any reasonable explanation. This isn't like me and I think that's what bothers me most. Yes, I've made stupid decisions in the past where it came to women, but not where it came to dealing with the monsters. I know my personal life is a disaster, but being one of the top Cleansers in Vatican service had made it bearable. This made me look like a joke.

All of this flew through my mind in the few seconds it takes David to drive to what he felt should be the intercept turn. With the tires screeching their protest, he throws the

Ford around the turn, the rear end breaking loose momentarily. He fights the wheel for a second and the car comes back straight and shoots down the street. In as much time as it takes to think it, we cover half the distance to where he expected the Mercedes to appear. Just as I thought we'd lost the big Merc, it slid sideways into the intersection. The driver fights to get it under control and it looks like he was losing. He fishtails back and forth several times, but finally straightens out speeding away in the same direction we were going.

I glance to my left at David, I see him cut his eyes toward me and smile. He knows I'm impressed and I tell him so.

"Don't be. We were lucky. That's all."

I don't push it and turn back to the front, hoping to get a look at the Mercedes' plate. David has us three car lengths behind the blue car and I can see the driver is male, but no details. The plate is easily legible from this distance, so I didn't need the binoculars. As I prepare to call the Georgia plate out to him, he grabs the microphone and calls the dispatcher. I listen while he calls the plate in and a check is made of the registered owner.

In seconds, we have the information. The car belongs to Brunelle Pannier, twenty-five years old and has an address close to the corner of John Portman Boulevard and Williams Street, near the garment district in North West downtown. As soon as the dispatcher finishes relating the information, David takes his foot off the accelerator. The Ford slows and the Mercedes continues to speed to the next corner where it turns left and vanishes. Now that our car has slowed to a more reasonable speed, we maintain on straight.

He knows I was about to ask, so he explains, "If we keep this up, someone is going to get killed and I'm not about to risk some kid to get this guy. Besides, we know where he's going."

Impressed, I say, "So that's how cops do it. Not as glamorous as the movies make it look."

He snorts and shoots back, "This way is safe. I like safe.

I'll take safe over glamorous any day of the week."

SIXTEEN

David intentionally drives slower than the speed limit allows in order to calm down from the adrenaline high of the pursuit. I feel antsy and fight to control my anticipation. His professionalism serves to inspire me and eventually the adrenaline wears off. He makes it look so easy, never getting excited, never letting his emotions get the best of him. Always in control, but never having to announce it to the world. I like working with him and think we would make a good team if given the chance.

Street lights are coming to life and the vehicles we meet on the way to Pannier's address have their lights on. Night has arrived and we now have less than ten hours to find Alonso. We have to find Pannier and get the answers we need. My single hope is that he isn't a dead end. The fact he ran when he saw us seems to indicate he doesn't want to talk to us. I've always considered myself a pleasant conversationalist and I want the chance to show him— whether he likes it or not.

As we pull onto the block that contains Pannier's address, David points, "That's it, up there on the right."

It is an old building that has been updated and now contains offices for several different companies and businesses. Parking appears to be along the street as there isn't a parking lot or structure visible. I can see an empty parking spot in front of the main door and point it out to David.

"Not so fast, let's do a drive by first," he says as he slowly cruises up the street past our target.

"I didn't see the Mercedes," I say, turning almost completely around in my seat to get a longer look.

"It's not there. Did you notice the building directory on the front of the building?"

Annoyed again that he is a step ahead of me, I answer, "No, I'm assuming you did." When he nods, I ask, "Anything you'd like to share?"

"Pannier Bakeries home office is on the first floor. I

didn't get the room number, sorry." I know he is being sarcastic with the sorry, so I don't acknowledge it. The fact this is a bakery isn't lost on me. I don't know what it means, but I don't believe in coincidences. When I finally get the chance to talk to Mister Brunelle Pannier, I will ask him about that.

David drives completely around the block holding the building to get a look at it from all sides. Our reconnaissance proves that the only parking seems to be the street in front of the building. The blue Mercedes still hasn't shown up and I ask him what our next move should be.

"Be patient," is all he says. He cruises past the front once more, finding a parking space about a half block away, on the opposite side of the street. Pulling a U-turn, he pulls in and shuts the car off. Before I can ask, he explains, "The car isn't here, so our man isn't here. Going in and talking to them now will only alert them and him. So, we wait." He settles back and gets comfortable.

"So, this is a stake out?"

He laughs before answering, "Yeah, I guess it is."

"This whole cop thing is a lot different than what I thought it would be. Where's the excitement?"

"I told you, this is safe. The golden rule is, if it's exciting, it's not safe. I'll do whatever needs doing, but I don't go looking for trouble. If I intend to go home at the end of every shift, I play it safe."

I know this doesn't make him a coward because I've seen him fight and know he won't run. What he's talking about is being careful and keeping the advantage. I decide to be patient and see what happens.

An hour later, I've just about reached the end of my patience. I need to find Alonso and we are running out of time. It is almost ten. How do we even know Pannier will come back to his office this late? I turn to say this when David holds up his hand and tells me to wait. Two seconds later, the big blue Mercedes drives past and executes a U-turn just as we had and parks in front of the building. I watch as a tall, slim man, very well dressed in a dark blue suit that closely matches the car, opens the door and gets out. I can see his ponytail clearly. This guy fits Alonso's description exactly. He has to be the man that picked Erin up at her house.

I look over at where David sits leaned back as comfortable as the car seats allow. I expected that we would follow our prey into the building to confront him, but it doesn't appear David plans on moving.

He looks back at me with that same calm face he always has and says, "He doesn't live here and he wouldn't hold your friend here. All he has to do is tell us to get screwed and then we've got two options. Either we beat the crap out of him here where someone will call the police and we have to try and explain what we're doing. Or, wait outside and follow him to his home where we have a little privacy." He turns back to looking out the windshield before asking, "Which option do you think's best?"

I hate it when he's right, but he does make sense. Tracking humans, it seems, takes more patience than hunting monsters. With me, as soon as I see one, I go after it. To wait might cost another person their life and I can't handle that. With people, although they are as capable of killing each other as the monsters are, as long as they aren't actively engaged in a crime, I guess we have some time. It is still difficult to sit here when the person that might have information about Alonso is within reach.

*****

David's calm demeanor never changes during the hour and some few minutes that we sit watching for Pannier to show himself. I'd already made up my mind that if he didn't show by midnight, I would go in and confront him. Thankfully, that doesn't happen because at around eleven-thirty, he comes back out and gets in his car. Without a word, David starts the engine of his Ford and prepares to follow.

Pannier pulls away from the curb and rolls slowly down Williams Street past our car to the corner and turns right. As soon as the Mercedes is out of sight, David spins the car around in a tight U-turn and accelerates to the corner and turns after it. We can see the blue car about half a block in front of us. David stays back several car lengths and matches the Mercedes' speed. Pannier seems in no hurry and to keep us from being spotted, David parks against the curb several times while the other car sits at traffic lights.

After several minutes, it becomes clear we're traveling toward the northeast part of the city. We continue to follow as Pannier pulls onto Ponce De Leon and drives east. We follow him all the way to the affluent neighborhood of Druid Hills and after several turns, stop at a house on Normandy Drive. As the Mercedes pulls in and rolls down the excessively long driveway, we cruise past and continue to the next intersection. David pulls over and makes a phone call to the dispatchers. After clicking off, he tells me the house is listed as property of the Pannier Bakery Company.

"Okay, what's next, expert?" I grin as he glances at me and curses at my sarcastic comment.

After a moment of thought, he says, "We'll pull back up toward the house with our lights off and we'll sit and watch for a few minutes."

"What're we waiting for this time?"

"I didn't say to wait, I said to watch."

"Oh, sorry. What're we watching for this time," I correct, trying not to sound too annoyed. I really wish we were hunting monsters.

"Anything suspicious or that might lead us to Alonso. This isn't rocket science. It would be nice to know if there's anybody else at home, too. Get the binoculars out and let's see what's going on before we go barging in there."

I surrender. I won't be able to get him to go until he's good and ready. He'd deferred to me when we were hunting the vampires, the thing I'm supposed to be an expert at. I need to defer to him on this and so far he hasn't let us down. We have his car, his place of business, and his home and we haven't even met him yet. I nod and try to relax. I pull the binoculars out as he turns about and, with the lights off, pulls back up Normandy to a place where we can watch Pannier's house.

It is after midnight and the clock is running out. Because he can tell it won't be long until my head explodes, David agrees that we'll watch until one a.m. and then we'll pay our mystery man a visit. My side of the car faces the house, so it is up to me to watch. I adjust the binoculars and scan the front of what can only be described as a mansion. In all honesty, I've been in castles that were smaller. During the time I watch the house, I see Pannier pass in front of a window on the ground floor one time. That's the only thing I see.

David's facial expression never changes as I rage about our continued sitting, instead of actually doing something to find Alonso. He points out that I said I'd follow his lead on how we approached our man. I tell him that I am following his lead, but I don't intend to do it quietly. That makes him smile and we both have a little laugh about my childish behavior. A few minutes before one a.m., David finally gives in to my constant bitching and agrees to make our visit.

He starts the engine and as he puts the shifter into drive, I decide to take one more look at the house. Good thing I did. Just as David pulls forward, I notice the on the garage door start to rise. I reach back and tap him on the arm, at the same time saying stop. He takes the opportunity to tell me he wishes I'd make up my mind. I ignore his jibe and tell him our target is leaving. He doesn't reply, which prompts me to turn around and look at him. He sits there with a very pleased expression on his face. I knew it was coming and prompt him to go on and get it over with.

He can't resist, "Told you."

"Yeah, yeah, you got lucky."

"Lucky or not, we have two locations tied to him and now we're going to have another. Maybe some more suspects and, if we're really lucky, he's going to check on Alonso."

As I watch, Pannier backs out of the garage and turns the Mercedes around. We sit still while he pulls back down the driveway and out onto Normandy, driving back toward

Atlanta. David gives him to the count of ten and pulls out to follow. It becomes obvious that he intends to go to Ponce De Leon. David takes the opportunity to go on a different street to keep from getting us caught following on the slower residential streets.

Correct once again, which causes me no small amount of ass pain, I watch the blue Mercedes slide past on Ponce de Leon. David looks at me and smiles as he pulls onto the bigger road driving west. I tell him about how he's making my backside hurt, this elicits a small laugh, but he quickly goes back to work concentrating on following Pannier without getting caught.

When our objective turns onto smaller streets and angles southwest, a thought occurs to me and I ask, "Is it possible he's going back to Erin's house?"

David considers that for a moment, and then answers, "He just might."

*****

In the southwest part of the city, we follow the only person who might give us a clue about Alonso's location. It does appear that Pannier plans to return to Erin's house. David decides to take a chance and break off tailing the big luxury car. He turns onto a cross street and speeds up.

I ask what he's planning and he replies, "I want to get there first. I don't want him to see us driving on the same street. At this time of the morning, with so little traffic, it might spook him."

I agree with the strategy and sit back while he accelerates hard, attempting to get in front of our quarry.

David has the driving under control, so with nothing for me to do but sit back and enjoy the ride, I doze off. More tired than I thought, I drift down into a deep sleep where the dreams always wait for me. This time was no different and I find myself transported back to 1850s Europe. I recognize the time as right after Lilith's death.

*****

Still existing as a beggar, I hadn't come to grips with the fact of my immortality and with the added guilt over the recent murder of my once lover, I wished for death.

Rome had always been a city blended from people of different nationalities, but with the reunification talk beginning, foreigners were finding it not as pleasant a place as it once was. The Sardinians were pushing the Italy for Italians agenda and, even though I'd always considered myself Venetian because of my grandfather, everyone else considered me Austrian.

I realized I wasn't welcome in Rome, not just me, but thousands of street people were being persecuted. Even in places where we'd been tolerated before, like the Vatican. I decided to get out of Rome while I still had the chance and the only place I could think to go was Trieste. With no other form of transportation available to me, I walked out of Rome carrying all my worldly possessions in a sack slung over my shoulder.

Several weeks after starting my journey, I finally reached Trieste, hitching rides and walking until my feet were numb. It had been twelve years since I'd been there last and in that time the city had grown and spread out. I nearly didn't recognize the place until I saw the harbor again. Only then did I feel like I was home. I spent the night the same way I had when I'd been here the first time, huddled under fishing nets. The next morning, I set out on the longest and hardest part of my trip, the one-day walk to Repen and my family home. By nightfall, I would see my parents, my brothers, and sister again. I tried not to think about the questions they'd ask and counted on the fact they would welcome me back with loving arms.

It wasn't to be, though. I guess the cliché about never being able to go home is true. When I reached Repen, it was simple to find the paths that led to where I grew up. I trudged up and down the hills and hollows on the goat trails to my family farm. I knew when I reached where our house had stood, but nothing remained. The animal pens, the well my father had dug by hand, the little mud and stone hut, all of it gone. What little energy I had left, I expended running from hill top to hill top thinking I might have lost my way, knowing all along I hadn't. Eventually, my energy gone, I gave up and sat down on what was left of the stone foundation that had been the home I grew up in and cried.

As low as I had sunk, I sank lower, but I also learned an important lesson. Hoping to die, I sat on that stone for five days and in all that time I did not eat or drink. Surely, I thought, starvation and thirst would kill me, but it didn't. Then and only then did I realize I could not die. Tired, hungry and thirsty, but still very much alive, I put my feet to the path again. I visited all the farms around the area trying to find information about my family and to beg for food. After another week, I found no one that knew anything about them or what happened to them.

I clearly no longer had a home and I had no more desire to be a farmer than I did at fifteen, so I left Repen and Trieste for the north. Considered Austrian because of the location of my birth, I headed for Austria. The German Confederation, which included Austria, had been embroiled in a war with Denmark for over a year and most of the country was in turmoil. I stayed in the mountains, away from Salzburg and Vienna and eventually made my way to Innsbruck in the Tyrolean Alps. It was here, while trying to find myself and what this new life of immortality meant, that I met Baroness Nina Schaller.

Nina, the wife of Baron Bruno Schaller, lived in the Inntal Valley near the village of Flaurling and had come to Innsbruck to visit family and friends while her husband was away on business. Obviously wealthy, I approached her to beg for a few coins so that I could eat that day and, for some reason, the Baroness took a liking to me. Instead of a few coins, she took me to a cafe and fed me and then back to her hotel where I had my first bath in several months. To this day, I can't tell you why because she never told me and I never asked, but two days after meeting her, I had new clothes, finer than anything I'd ever worn and I was clean with a full belly.

At twenty-seven years old, she believed me to be younger than her and I think she derived some joy from parading me around in front of her friends who clearly thought we were lovers. In fact, I didn't climb straight into her bed. It took a couple of months, but in the end that's where I landed.

In those days it was common for men to be away from home for extended periods of time and as a Nobleman, Baron Schaller spent a great deal of time in Vienna. I'd been his wife's lover for almost a year before I had the displeasure of meeting the fat, old bastard that had the luck to marry one of the kindest and most loving women I'd ever met.

The Baron of course didn't appreciate me keeping his sheets warm for him while he was away. It didn't matter what story she told him, he knew the score and to show Nina exactly what he thought of me, he had me hanged from a large oak tree at the entrance to the estate.

He intended to leave me hanging there until I decomposed as a warning for anyone that might have had designs on taking my place as the Baroness' boy toy. The fact that I wasn't dead and would hang there until the end of time instead of rotting away would have caused a lot of gnashing of teeth on the Baron's part if it hadn't been for the fact Nina really cared for me. She paid one of the stable hands to bury me, thinking it a kindness. Lucky for me, on the night he cut me down, I awoke lying in the back of a cart while he dug my grave. Taking advantage of the darkness, I slipped away and left Flaurling forever.

I learned quite a lot during my time with Nina. She brought me back from the edge of insanity and introduced me to a world I'd only seen from a distance. I had to thank her husband as well. He taught me the meaning of discretion and that Lilith's curse was a fact. The three days I spent dangling from a limb by my neck were the longest I've ever experienced.

SEVENTEEN

The car coming to a stop wakes me and as I rise up, David says, "Good morning, sunshine."

I turn to look at him and he gives me a cheesy smile. "Sorry about that. I didn't mean to conk out on you."

"No problem, but we need to go. Pannier should be here any second."

We both exit the car and I see we were on the opposite side of the street from Erin's house and about half a block west. We stay in the shadows and walk toward the stucco home of my client. David and I have gone around twenty-five yards when we notice headlights coming toward us. Slipping deeper into the shadows, we watch as the blue Mercedes we'd been following all night rolls down the street and stops in front of Erin's house. Seconds later, Brunelle Pannier steps out and makes his way to the front door. Proving this wasn't his first time here, he produces a key and opens the front door. He doesn't knock, just goes straight in and closes the door behind him.

"Well, him having a key says something," David points out. I nod, not liking where this appears to be going. I ask David what we should do now and he says, "We'll move up to the house. There aren't any security lights I can see and it's dark all around except the front. We should be able to get right up to the house and hopefully see in a window. I want to know what he's up to."

Again I nod and together we move toward the house. David has us cross the street before we get there so we can slip around the edge of the landscaping in the neighbor's yard to stay concealed. So far, we haven't run into any dogs or early morning risers. Always using the shadows for cover, we continue to move until we are on the side of the house toward the rear and the darkest part of the yard. David starts to move toward the house and I stop him with a hand on his shoulder. He turns to look at me with a quizzical look.

I whisper, "I'm the sneak remember, you stay here and

let me do this part."

I can tell he doesn't like it, but he knows I have more experience at slipping in and out of places. He hunkers down by a large Azalea bush and watches as I weave my way in a crouch toward the house. A large maple tree stands about thirty feet from the wall and provides the last cover before reaching the house. I stand behind it for several minutes, watching the windows closest to me for any sign of movement. The windows remain dark with no sign anybody is watching from behind them, so I make the last rush to the outer wall.

Keeping my back to the stucco, I ease around the side to the back and peer in the windows. The first two I check had completely empty rooms behind them. It's the third that causes my heart to skip a beat. I slip up to the edge of the frame and ease over until my right eye can see inside. It is only lit by candles scattered about the floor, but that is all the light I need to see. Pannier is the only occupant in the bare room. He kneels in the center of the floor using blood to draw a Thaumaturgic triangle. As I watch, Pannier places a bucket in the center of the triangle and I have a feeling I know what the bucket contains.

Something touches my shoulder and I nearly piss my pants. I jerk around to see David standing beside me and I mouth, "What are you doing?"

He places his lips close to my ear and whispers, "You've been gone a while and I couldn't see you, so I got worried." I nod as I try to get my heart out of my throat and back down into my chest. He whispers again, "What's going on?"

I point at the window and mouth, "Pannier." He nods and drops down on his knees, crawling to the other side of the window. He stands and eases his eye around to see inside.

I turn in time to see Pannier drop a lighted match into the bucket. It flares for a second and as it burns down, a cloud of black smoke replaces the fire. A shimmer coalesces over the bucket and transforms into the shape of the demon I remember from Harry Crowe's apartment.

Eight feet tall, clawed hands and feet, tail, and horns, Belphegor stands inside the triangle. In a flash, the image of the demon transforms to be replaced by the image of Bella.

Now we had our proof Brunelle Pannier was Belphegor's master. I can't hear what he says to the demon, but Bella laughs and Pannier doesn't look pleased with her reaction. I know David and I need to get inside and get to Pannier before Bella slips her leash and kills him. I motion to David that it is time to move and he drops back down to his knees. I take one last look in the window and come even closer to pissing my pants than when David scared me. As I glanced in, Bella looks right at me and winks.

As he stands up beside me, I tell David, "We have to go, now!"

He doesn't question me and falls in beside me as I sprint to the back door. I don't slow down and hit the door hard with my shoulder. The latch gives and the door flies open, slamming against the wall. I don't have to look to know David is right behind me with his Glock in his hand. I continue through the room and down a short hall before coming to the room I had been watching from outside.

I come through the door and stop in my tracks. David steps up beside me, his gun up and aimed toward Pannier. Bella looks toward us and with a big smile on her face. "Hello boys, come on in. Join the party. I'm just getting started."

Bella had expected us, but from the panicked expression on Pannier's face, he didn't. He backs away, angling toward the window. David's Glock steadies on him and he says, "Mister Pannier, I don't want to shoot you, but if you don't stop moving, I'm going to." I don't know whether Pannier believes him or not, but he stops.

Bella continues to smile as she looks at each of us, settling her gaze on me, "Now, isn't this special? An intimate little gathering, me, you, and our trained monkeys." Neither David nor Pannier looks happy about her comment. "I wondered whether you'd make it or not. How did the first part of your mission go?"

"Accomplished," I answer. This makes her even happier and she claps her hands, bouncing up and down.

She turns looking at Pannier and says, "Well champ, it's almost time for me and you to have some fun." Pannier, who had been looking terrified, now looks confused. Bella turns back to me saying, "And you're ahead of schedule. You really are good at this."

"I can't take all the credit." I point to David, "I couldn't have done it without him."

Bella smiles at David. "You did well, for a trained monkey."

"Fuck you, lady… thing. Hell, just fuck you," David growls, never taking his eyes—or gun—off Pannier.

Bella laughs, "I wish you would." When David looks like he might vomit, she pouts and says, "Aw, don't be that way, slugger. You might be surprised, but I'm afraid that will have to wait." She looks back at me, asking, "Did you figure out my hint?"

"Still working on it," I reply tightly.

A disgusted look replaces her smile as she says, "Oh you humans are so stupid and I had such high hopes for you. Anyway…"

Pannier tries to regain some measure of control over what had gotten completely away from him by saying, "I want to know what the hell's going on!"

David's attention is already directed at Pannier and now Bella and I both turn to look at him. Bella starts first, "I'd almost forgotten about you. Although you haven't met, I'm sure you know…" She turns to me asking, "You go by Tony, right?" When I nod, she turns back to Pannier, "Anyway, you know Tony. He's here to ask you a few questions and his *friend*," she emphasizes the word, causing David to nod his thanks for not calling him a monkey again. She smiles and goes on, "Is here to do evil things to you if you don't answer Tony's questions. And, of course, I'm here to eat your guts."

For the first time, Pannier looks pleased with himself instead of scared, "None of you are going to *do* anything." Looking at David and me he says, "The two of you won't leave here alive." He turns to Bella and continues, "And you. I own you and you'll do what you're told."

Bella giggles. "Uhh, you're such a scary witch," she coos as if talking to a baby.

I interrupt before she can say anything else, "You! You're a witch?"

That look of panic returns to his face, but it is Bella who answers, "You didn't know that? I guess you really aren't as smart as I gave you credit for. Yes, he's a witch and he's got a secret too. Don't you, witch-boy?"

"I don't know what you're talking about," Pannier rebuts. "You'll tear them apart and do it now!" he shouts at Bella. She begins to laugh and the witch looks confused once more.

I try to explain things to the idiot. "Brunelle, you aren't in control of the demon any longer. You need to help me or it's going to kill you in a very, very terrible way." As if to prove to him that I'm telling the truth, Bella steps out of the triangle and walks right up to him. Now Pannier looks absolutely scared to death.

"Y-you can't d-do that," he stammers. "I'm in control of you."

I try once more, "Brunelle, you never had control. She's been loose from the beginning." She glances back at me and gives me a smile.

Turning back to her would-be master, she says, "You fucked up the incantation. The one you cast summoned me, but didn't let you have control, so good job genius," she claps her hands in front of her. Then she looks back at me and says, "Very good. I didn't think you'd picked up on that. My respect goes back up a notch."

I acknowledge her compliment and go back to talking to Pannier, "Why are you doing this?"

His attitude changes, I'm sure he figured he needs to do something to get someone on his side. "This isn't my idea. I'm just doing what I'm told. Look, I don't have anything against you, this wasn't my idea."

"Okay, I want to know why you're trying to kill Erin." I don't know why I start with that. I should have asked about

Alonso first, but that's not what came out.

Pannier looks even more confused and says, "I'm not trying to kill Erin. Why would I want to kill her, she's my…" but before he could finish, Bella reaches out with a hand that now looks like a claw and grabs his shoulder. He starts to scream, but it is cut short when she shoves her other hand down his throat. All that comes out is a strangled gurgle as she shoves her arm down until she is up to her elbow in his mouth.

David and I watch dumbfounded. There is nothing we can do to save him, but damn that is just gruesome. I try hard not to look away, not to gag. That would only give Bella something to use against me later.

Pannier's arms wave uncontrollably and his feet are sliding and skidding around on the wood floor, but she holds him fast. Then with a great heave, she yanks her arm back out of his mouth. There isn't any more noise coming from Pannier, he hangs from her hand a deflated wreck. In her other hand is a steaming, stinking mass that includes his heart, lungs, and a good deal of intestines. She raises his innards up at arm's length and opens her mouth. I watch her mouth open further and further until its inhuman size would accept the mass that had once been inside Brunelle Pannier.

She lowers the entire mass into the gaping maw of her mouth and releases it. She turns and looks at David and me as she commences to chew, making small groaning noises like she is eating the tastiest treat in the world. She finally swallows and licks her fingers while we continue to stand too stunned to do anything.

Finished with her meal, she drops what had once been Pannier and smiles at me, "What? I told him I was going to eat his guts."

I find my voice as I watch her lick her fingers clean. "What in God's name have you done?"

She doesn't look happy, "Don't say that name to me, you piss ant. I told you what would happen!" She calms herself and says, "I told you and him," pointing down at what had been Brunelle Pannier, "that I would do that.

Why are you surprised?"

"He's the only one that knew where Alonso is. Now you've killed him," I yell.

"Don't you raise your voice to me, Cleanser," she snarls and takes a threatening step toward me and David. Her shadow grows behind her and her fangs lengthen. I step backward, dragging David with me, waiting for her to kill us. After a moment, she calms down and flips her hair out of her face as her smile returns. "I've already told you where Alonso is. You need to use your brain for something other than pâté."

I look at David for a little help, but he's staring down at the floor, deep in thought. When I look back at her, Bella is gone and the demon Belphegor stands in her place. A low growling voice comes from the dagger-filled mouth, "Think and you'll find him." And with that, the demon reaches down, grasps Pannier's remains and vanishes.

"Bloody hell, what're we going to do now?"

"We need to figure this out," David says. When I look over at him, he appears to be onto something and I urge him to go on. "Bella said, 'Alonso would be in the last place you'd think to look.' Right?"

Frustrated, I answer, "Yes, we've been over this. I have no idea where that could be."

"No, you do, you may not realize it, but you do. She wouldn't have used it as a hint if you didn't."

"She's a demon and demons deceive. Everything that comes out of their mouths is a lie."

"She didn't lie about killing Pannier or how she planned to do it. Now think. It's got to be some place you know. The thing that's important is why you would not think to look there. Is it because it's difficult to get to or is it something else?"

I see where he is going and I try to think, "Technically, he could be anywhere so I can't think of anyplace I wouldn't look."

"She didn't say you *wouldn't* look there, so it's got to be something else. What would make you decide he wouldn't be in a place?"

"I don't know!" I say, feeling more frustrated. "This isn't getting us anywhere."

"We need to find Erin."

It is my turn to be confused now, "We do, but that can wait until after we find Alonso."

"No, I mean she will know where Alonso is. She and Pannier were connected somehow. She knows."

I still feel defensive when it comes to her. "Until I know different, she's the victim here. She wouldn't have anything to do with Alonso's disappearance."

I see it when he perks up. We look at each other and he asks, "So, there's no way Alonso would be here in this house?"

"No, why would he be here?" And then it hits me. I'm standing in the last place I'd think to look. David sees it in my face and smiles at me. "Start looking," I say.

We split up and check all the rooms. I start up the stairs when I hear David call me. I follow his voice back to the kitchen where he stands looking in a closet. When I get to him, he points in and I look to see a set of steps going down. The house has a basement, something I'd never considered. I start down without hesitation and as I hit the bottom step, I know we are in the right place.

There are several rooms off a central hallway and I rush from door to door, checking every room while calling Alonso's name. With one room left, I start to feel that maybe it isn't the right place. When I open that last door, it actually surprises me to see my friend sitting in a chair, hands and feet shackled to an eye bolt set in the wall and a gag in his mouth.

I stop, tears coming to my eyes and a catch in my throat, as I look at my friend where he sits, a prisoner. I can see relief in his eyes as he realizes he is safe. David comes up behind me and asks if I intend to stand there or release him. I laugh and walk over to Alonso.

I remove the gag first and as soon as he could speak, he says, "About damn time."

I laugh again as I try to get the chains off. David has come up beside us and Alonso looks at him. David says,

"Nice to finally meet you, Alonso. I'm glad you're okay." Looking at me, he continues, "I've got bolt cutters in the car. I'll get them." He turns and leaves the room, leaving me with Alonso.

Alonso looks back at me and asks, "Who's that dude?"

"Detective David George, Atlanta PD," I reply.

"You called the cops?"

"He's all right, he's been helping me hunt unnaturals and he's the one that figured out where you were. So don't be too hard on him." I slap him on the shoulder, saying, "Man, it's good to see you. You really had me worried."

"You? I've been so scared I've been about to mess my drawers. What the hell have you gotten involved in here?"

"I don't know, but we're going to figure it out."

"That's fine, but you got to get me out of here before that crazy mother comes back."

"Who?"

"The dude with the ponytail. He's one sick bastard."

"You don't have to worry about him anymore. He's dead."

"Good, I've never met anybody that deserved it more. You do it or the cop?" he asks as David returns with the bolt cutters.

"Neither. I'll explain when we get out of here. The important thing is you're all right."

David cuts the chain and he and I help Alonso up. He'd sat for so long that he'd gotten stiff and with his bulk, getting him moving again takes both of us.

It takes a few minutes to get him up the steps, but we finally make it and on out to the porch. David had pulled his car up in front of Pannier's car and we walk toward it. Alonso stops, looking at the unmarked police car. David and I stop and look at him.

I ask, "What is it?"

Alonso looked at me and said, "I'm not riding in the back of that thing. It's bad for my image." Even David laughs at that one and I tell Alonso he can ride up front. He nods and we get into the car.

Once we're ready to go, David asks, "Where to now?"

"Let's go by my place first, I need to get some more clothes and then we can take Alonso home," I reply.

David nods and Alonso says, "I don't care where we go as long as we stop at a drive through first before all my lovely fat disappears." We all laugh this time.

EIGHTEEN

There isn't much said for several minutes after leaving Erin's. Our first stop turns out to be a fast food joint and Alonso loads up on all the things he'd missed while chained in the basement. David watches in wonder as Alonso wolfs down burgers and fries in massive quantities.

Glancing into the rearview mirror at where I sit in the back seat, he says with a straight face, "Kind of reminds me of Bella's last meal."

"Oh, don't remind me of that," I mutter, trying to push the mental image away.

Alonso turns to look at both of us and with a mouth full of cheese burger saying, "What?"

"Never mind, I'll fill you in later," I reply. "For now, I want to know how you ended up in that basement."

Between mouthfuls of food, Alonso tells us how he'd been abducted. "Well, you know about how I started following that redheaded bitch." He doesn't look at me when he says it, but David glances in the mirror at me. The comment pisses me off, but I let it go. I figure Alonso gets a pass after spending a couple of days chained to a chair. "I followed her and the guy with the ponytail…"

"Pannier," I interrupt. Alonso turns, asking who, so I explain, "His name is Brunelle Pannier."

Alonso continues, "Anyway, I followed her and Pannier to that bar. I parked across the street and watched them go inside, then I followed 'em. Place was pretty crowded and it took a few minutes and they weren't alone. They were sitting at a table with two other women. One was maybe in her late teens, red hair like your girl," he glances back at me when he says it. "She had a nice body, dressed kind of slutty, but the other woman, now she was a looker. Older, maybe forty, auburn hair and dressed real expensive. It seemed she was the one in charge."

The more Alonso tells us, the more my gut is starting to tell me something is seriously wrong with what Erin had originally told me. It is beginning to sound like witches, not

Wiccans. If that is the case, things are going to get complicated real fast.

"I took a table where I could watch them. They sat there for a long time and then the older woman looked over right at me. I mean, we made eye contact, so I knew she knew I'd been watching them. She turned and said something to that Pannier guy and he looked over at me. He got up and I thought he was going to come over, but he went outside instead then came back a few minutes later. They went back to talking and I kept watching." He pauses to shove the last handful of fries into his mouth. After he swallows he goes on, "Eventually, they looked like they were leaving so I went out to my car. When I opened my car door, I noticed this young chick walking over. I thought it was funny because I didn't see her as I crossed the street and then, there she was."

I sigh. That would've been the demon. Too bad Alonso didn't know how to tell a demon from a real lady, though that knowledge probably wouldn't have saved him either way.

"She knew my name, which was weird. I tried to remember if I'd seen her before, but couldn't. She started hitting on me. I thought she was kind of hot except her breath stunk. Really smelled like shit."

David glances in the rearview and I nod to him. I hadn't noticed until I feel the car decelerate that Alonso's story filled the car ride all the way to The Magnolia House. David parks and I start to get out.

Alonso says, "I'll come with you."

"Might as well," David says and shuts the engine off. The three of us go up the steps and I open the front door. As we walk into the foyer and I shut the door, Betty appears in her doorway. Feeling a little guilty, I utter a hello and start up the stairs.

Betty stops me. "Tony, I'm so glad you're back. I was afraid something bad had happened to you."

"No ma'am, I'm okay," I reply and start up the steps followed by Alonso and David. I look back once and notice that Betty came up with us. Swearing to myself, I try to think of something to say that will get rid of her. At my door, I pause, realizing I don't have my keys. Betty elbows her way past David and Alonso until she stands beside me at the door. She pulls her keys from a pocket and then proceeds to open my door.

I thank her and as I reach for the knob, she says, "Now, Tony, I don't want to have to say this anymore. I want this door cleaned off, the other residents are complaining about it."

I start to say okay until I realize I have no idea what she was talking about. "Mrs. Betty, that's the second time you've said something, but there's nothing on my door."

Before she can respond, Alonso says, "Man that shit wasn't there before." I look at the door and then back at them. I still don't understand what they're talking about. I just want to get inside and rest.

That's when David speaks up, "I asked you about this the first time I came here and you told me the door was like this when you moved in."

"Like hell it was, I keep this place presentable," Betty grumbled. "Lucky for you, Tony. I'd never allow something like this from my other renters."

Once again, I look at the door and then at them, unable to understand what they mean. Confused, I shake my head and start to go in to my apartment, that's all I want to do. Alonso turns to David and says, "I don't know what he told you, but I know for a fact that shit wasn't there two weeks ago when I was here."

Betty pipes up, "No, it's been there almost two weeks. Ever since that floozy showed up."

David looks interested and asks, "The redhead?"

"Yeah, the one with the big knockers," Betty answers. I stand there open-mouthed, confused as hell. The whole conversation is about me, but I'm not part of it and can't figure out how to get things back on track. I need to get inside my apartment and then everything will be all right.

Alonso looks at me and asks, "Tony, did you put that shit on your door or not?"

I yell angrily, "I didn't put anything on my door!" I

point to the door and continue to yell, "There is nothing on this door. I don't know what you people are talking about."

They all stand there looking at me then David finally asks, "Tony, you can't see anything on this door?"

"No, there's nothing there to see," I say, trying to calm down. Why won't they let me go inside? It's all I want to do right now.

Alonso shuffles up beside me and places a hand on my shoulder. In a calm and soft voice, he says, "Tony, there are symbols written in what looks like blood all over your door."

*****

I can't comprehend what he is talking about. I'm speechless for several seconds, then shrug his hand off and try once more to go inside my apartment. Alonso grabs me and pulls me back out onto the landing. He spins me around and pushes me against the wall. He places one of his big hands in the center of my chest and pushes slightly, so that I get the message I'm not going anywhere until he allows it.

"Tony, we aren't going anywhere until we get to the bottom of this."

David steps up beside him asking, "What is it, Tony? What are the symbols?"

I force myself to quit struggling and calm down. After several deep breaths I ask, "You both see symbols on my door?" They nod, so I ask, "What do they look like?"

David describes how the symbols are arranged in a circle at the top half of the door and that a trail of symbols runs down to the bottom. He also describes a different line of symbols across the top of the door. All of this begins to sound familiar. As my curiosity level rises, I calm further and Alonso removes his hand. I ask David to describe what the symbols at the top look like.

When he finishes the description, I know exactly what it is. "It's a spell." Betty had been standing there quietly and I ask her to please go inside my apartment and bring back a wet cloth. She agrees and disappears behind the door that

I'd longed to hide behind.

David asks, "What kind of spell?"

I laugh, realizing what had been going on for the first time, "The kind that keeps me from seeing the real spell on the door. It's called a 'Glamour' and it keeps me from suspecting that I've had a spell put on me by a very sneaky witch." I'm pissed at myself for being so blind this entire time.

Betty returns and hands me a dish cloth. I offer it to David and ask him to wash off the top symbols only because I want to see the main spell. He bobs his chin once and starts scrubbing the top of my door. In seconds, I notice a shimmering in front of the door and the symbols of the main spell appear. I step over and examine them closely. They are the same type I'd seen every time I went after a witch. Alonso had been correct, they were written in blood and I know whose.

"So, what is it?" Alonso asks.

"It's an infatuation spell." He gives me a confused look and I explain, "She couldn't make me fall in love with her, but she could make me think about her all the time and want nothing but to be around her. This spell kept me from seeing the real Erin or what she was up to."

I ask for the cloth back from David and when he hands it to me, I rub it across the symbols. As soon as they dissolve in the water, I start to feel different. The desire to get inside my apartment and the euphoric feeling go away. The more I rub, the more clearly I see what had been happening. All of the situations that I had attributed to bad luck crystallized as a concerted effort to cause me pain and suffering. All of it comes into focus and as the symbols dissolve, so do the effects of the spell. This is why I hate witches.

Alonso leans over close to my ear and asks, "You okay?"

"No, not really. I'm sorry, I should've listened to you." I look over at David, "And you. You told me she had something to do with all this. I wouldn't, couldn't, listen. I'm sorry." I turn to my landlady. "Mrs. Betty, I'm sorry I brought all this into your house. It's all my fault and if I can make it right, I will."

The old lady smiles at me, "Tony, I tried to tell you to be careful. I didn't realize that was a spell or I'd have wiped it off a long time ago. I thought it was something you'd put on there to protect you from the monsters."

Shocked I look at her and ask, "You know about the monsters?"

She gives a short cackle and says, "You aren't the first Cleanser I've known. You are the youngest, though—and the cutest."

Stunned, all I can think to say is, "Thanks, Mrs. Betty."

She pats me on the arm saying, "You're a good boy, Tony. You just need a good woman to keep your feet on the ground. You spend too much time chasing skirts." After that, she walks into my apartment. Alonso and David both look like they are about to bust from holding in the laughter.

"Not a word from you two," I say, wagging my finger in front of them as I feel my cheeks burn. I follow Betty into my apartment and my two cohorts follow me. Looking around, I can't believe my eyes. The place had been completely fixed. It's as if nothing happened, right down to my furniture being placed just as I had it.

Coming out of the bedroom, Betty motions me to follow her. She brings me over to the closet and opens the door. I walk over beside her and she moves my clothes to one side and points out the back wall. "I had them fix your gun hide out. I think they did a better job than you did. The door slides out a lot easier now."

After I pick my jaw up from the floor, I ask, "You knew about that, too?"

She smiles. "I know about everything," she replies and walks back into the living room. As I walk in behind her, she starts on Alonso and David, "Now, you two better start taking care of Tony. He's doing important work and he needs all the help he can get. If you let him get hurt, you'll have to answer to me." She points a gnarled finger at them for emphasis and walks out, shutting the door behind her.

We watch her leave and stand staring at the door long after she is gone. Finally, we all turn to look at each other and David and Alonso both start laughing. I try hard not to, but can't hold it long before I join in. There it is again, the therapeutic value of laughter.

After a good, long laugh I say, "All right, let's find that bitch and burn her."

*****

We don't grab our pitchforks and torches, and then go running into the night screaming for the blood of the witch, even though I have a feeling that would've been highly entertaining. I mean it in a more metaphorical sense than reality. What we do is grab some more clothes for me and get to David's apartment for some much needed rest. Then we will have a serious planning session on how to find and destroy the witch Erin.

On the way through the lobby, Betty pokes her head out of her door and says, "You boys be careful out there."

I assure her that we'll be safe and continue to David's car. On the way to the apartment, Alonso suggests we stop for something to eat. David laughs and asks where he can put it. Alonso explains that, as a big guy, it takes a lot of food to keep him going and as he'd been deprived for the last couple of days, he has some catching up to do. David and I both laugh at that one. I suggest barbeque again and receive agreeing comments from the other two.

What follows is a fifteen minute discussion between David and Alonso debating the attributes of various barbeque styles. Alonso subscribes to the wet rub and David thinks dry better. Alonso suggests chicken over beef and David has the opposite opinion, but they both agreed on pork.

I parrot David's earlier comment, "You got to love a good hog."

"Amen," they reply in unison. Eventually, a barbeque place is agreed on and David turns in that direction. On the way, I prompt Alonso to continue his story about his abduction.

"I stood there beside my car, talking to this girl you called Bella, until I saw the others come out of the bar. Redhead and ponytail got in the Mercedes and the other two women got in a black BMW. I told Bella I had to go and as I opened the door something hit me. I turned around expecting to see this little sprite of a girl, instead there's this eight foot tall monster that started tearing my car apart. I don't remember much after that until I woke up chained to that chair in the basement. I didn't know where I was until you guys pulled me out of there."

"What happened when you woke up?"

"First thing when I come to, I started yelling, but nobody came. I listened trying to see if I could hear anything, but there wasn't any sound. So I waited, I don't know how long, but finally ponytail showed up with his damn bucket."

"Bucket?" David asks.

"Yeah, made me relieve myself in it. Nasty. I told you he was sick. Then red showed up, she told me she knew I'd been following them. That's why they took me. I told her I'd been helping you and she said she knew that. That's when I knew for sure she's bad. Up 'til then, I wasn't sure, just had a feeling, you know."

"Yeah, I should've listened to you," I say.

He shakes his head. "Don't beat yourself up too much. I mean, she did have a nice ass and then there's the spell she put on you. So I ain't holding you responsible. I want to know what that thing was that took me, though, and who's this Bella?"

David answers him. "Bella is a demon. I don't know as much about this as Tony does, but I'm learning. Evidently, the demon, Belphegor takes the form of a young girl, Bella, when it's up here on Earth." He looks at me for conformation.

I nod. "And this particular demon is summoned with an offering of human excrement, your bucket." Alonso makes a sour face, but doesn't say anything. By this time, we've made it to the barbeque place and Alonso takes a break from his story while he and David order our dinner.

I stay in the car trying to make sense of all that happened in the past twenty-four hours.

The vampire nest, the demon, Pannier, and now Erin are involved in... in what? Why set me up from the beginning? Why would she go to all this trouble to get to me and why bring these other beings? Why didn't she just try to kill me? The obvious answer is that she knows about my immortality, though how she figured it out I have no idea. I don't exactly go around advertising it and she sure didn't get it from Alonso beforehand. There seems to still be part of this story I haven't figured out yet and that was probably the important part. If I could figure that out I might have my why.

David comes back out to the car followed by Alonso, the latter carrying several of the largest bags I've ever seen. He opens the door and hands them into me before climbing in himself.

After they are both seated, I ask, "Did you leave anything for other people?"

"Screw them, they didn't spend two days chained up in a basement having to crap in a bucket and not getting anything to eat," Alonso shoots back.

"Yeah, he's got a lot of catching up to do," David says, looking over his shoulder at me.

"Ah, I don't really need any help from you. It sounds kind of lame when you do it," Alonso tells David. I can't help it and start laughing. It feels good to have my friend back and even better now that I have two people I can count on. They seem to be getting along okay and if we can keep it together, we'll make a hell of a team.

Depending on what we are facing, a team right now doesn't sound half bad.

NINETEEN

After eating and further discussion about the witches and what we plan to do, I finally get to bed around five-thirty a.m. I sleep until around two p.m. when I awake feeling rested and refreshed. As I make my way to the shower, I see David sitting in the kitchen reading the paper and drinking coffee. He tells me good morning and I return the greeting, carrying on to the bath. After showering, I join David in the kitchen and as I sit he pushes a full cup of coffee in front of me.

I thank him and ask, "Alonso still in bed?"

He nods, saying, "I'm sure he didn't get much rest in that basement." He sets the paper aside, pours himself more coffee from the stainless steel carafe sitting on the table. "I've been thinking."

I smile and reply "That's never good."

He ignores me and goes on. "The thing that keeps coming to the front of my brain is, why? Why would she go to all this trouble? Why not just kill you?"

Turning serious I answer, "I know, it bothers me too. I thought of all that last night while you two were buying dinner. The first thing that occurs to me is she already knows I can't die. I don't know how, but she has to. And now she's torturing me."

David warms to the discussion, sitting forward. "That would indicate a personal vendetta. You're sure you didn't know her before meeting her on the street?"

"Never saw her before that day and yes, I'm sure I would've remembered. She's the most beautiful woman I've ever seen. That should've been a clue."

"Well, you've pissed her off somehow."

"Maybe or there's someone else."

Now really curious, David asks, "What do you mean 'someone else'?"

"Like I said, I spent a lot of time thinking about this last night. The way Alonso described Erin and Pannier's relationship sounded more like coconspirators than lovers.

When I asked, he said he never saw them touch or hold hands. Nothing that would indicate affection."

"Bella said her master intended to kill Erin."

After a sip of coffee I answer, "A lie. A deception. He almost told us right before Bella killed him. I think that's why she killed him. To protect the identity of her true master. I think they were working together, but for someone else."

"Who?"

"The older woman Alonso described seeing in the bar," I respond, feeling sure of my deduction after I'd said it out loud. He thinks about it as he sips coffee. I can see the wheels and gears turning in his mind.

David ponders my statement for a few moments and then says, "I think you might have something there. The thing that keeps bothering me is why would the demon defy its master to help you? You even said it in Erin's house, that Pannier never had control over it, why?"

"Bella said he had gotten the incantation wrong so he didn't have control. If he didn't have control, why did she do any of the things he commanded?"

"Because someone else was in control," he answers. "Any idea who she is?"

"None. I might if I could get a look at her, but from the description, I don't have a clue."

"I think our next move should be to find Erin and have a little talk with her."

Relieved that he had said 'our' next move, I ask, "So, you still want to help?"

"In for a penny, in for a pound," he answers, smiling. "Look, I've been a detective for eleven years and I've put hundreds of assholes in jail. In all that time, I've never done anything that feels like I'm making a difference. The people I put in jail this week are the same people that were victims last week. It just goes on and on, but I actually feel like I'm accomplishing something by helping you."

"Ahh, that's so sweet. Now you two kiss." We turn to see Alonso standing at the entry to the kitchen grinning.

David glances at me. "He's quiet for a big guy." I laugh

and watch as Alonso lumbers over and sits as David offers him coffee.

"Thanks, but I never drink that stuff, tastes like dirt. I'll take some tea if you have it." David gets up and rummages around in the cabinets. "We going after Red?" the big man asks.

"Yep, I assume by saying 'we' that you want in?"

"Hell yes, I owe her and I'd like to get some payback."

After setting a cup of tea in front of Alonso, David gets us back on track by asking, "Any idea how to find her?"

"All I have is her house and we now know it's not really her house. I'm open to suggestions."

Alonso sets his tea cup down and says, "You know Pannier's connected to her. What do you know about him?"

David smiles at him in appreciation saying, "That's good, Alonso." Turning back to me, "We know where he works and where he lives. I suggest we pay that visit to the bakery you wanted to make last night."

"But he's dead," I point out.

Alonso answers me with, "Yeah, but who knows that besides us?" When I look at David he nods.

"All right, as soon as we're ready, we go to the bakery," I decide.

Alonso finishes his tea and tips the cup at David. "I'd appreciate it if we could slide by my place first. No offense, but I'd like to shower in my own bathroom and change out of these clothes. They're getting a little gamey."

When I look at David, he shrugs his shoulders, I look back at Alonso saying, "No problem and I'm glad you recognize that you smell a bit."

"Don't even go there. The last time you came into the morgue, you smelled like the ass end of a three week dead buffalo. It took me two hours of scrubbing to get up all the blood and other stuff I don't want to think about off the damn floor. I smell pleasant by comparison."

"Well, if you ladies are finished comparing perfumes, I'd like to get going," David adds. We help David clean up the kitchen and a few minutes later, we're on our way to

Alonso's.

*****

Alonso doesn't have an apartment. He lives in a house that had been left to him by his grandparents southeast of Atlanta. Single story, ranch style, it's a nice homey place and he lives alone. David and I sit in his living room while he showers and changes. He takes forever and I expect David to get angry because he wants to get to Pannier's office, but he sits calmly leafing through a magazine. In due course, Alonso comes out dressed in jeans and a polo.

I comment that it was good of him to finally join us and he snorts, "There's a lot more of me to wash than your skinny ass." He looks over at David. "You got anything to say?"

David lays the magazine on the end table and replies, "Nope, I'm good."

"All right then, what are we waiting for?" Alonso asks. David and I stand and the three of us go to the car.

It isn't a long drive to our next stop. This time, David pulls right up to the front and parks. All three of us exit and start for the door. I see this as a potential problem so I stop, causing the other two to turn to look at me. "We can't all three go in there talking and asking questions. David, because you're law enforcement, why don't you do the talking?"

"And we'll stand around and look intimidating," Alonso says.

David pats him on the shoulder and says, "You do that, big guy." Looking back at me, he adds, "Good idea."

Inside, the first person we encounter is a receptionist sitting behind a counter to the left of the foyer. She asks if she can help us and David shows his badge and asks to speak with Brunelle Pannier. The young woman informs him that Mister Pannier isn't in the office, but his office manager is and does he wish to speak to him? David tells her that will be fine.

We wait quietly in the lobby. After a few minutes, a well-dressed man comes out and introduces himself as James Kenison. Kenison looks about thirty-five years old with conservative length blond hair and a tailored suit on his slim frame. He asks how he can help and David suggests they speak in private.

Kenison directs us to his office. Once everyone is seated, he asks, "All right, detective. How can I help you?"

"Mr. Kenison, I'm looking for a young lady and I have information that she knows your boss, Brunelle Pannier."

"As the receptionist told you, Mr. Pannier isn't here today," Kenison repeats, keeping that fake smile on his face.

"Do you know where he is or if he's expected to be in today?"

Kenison looks uncomfortable for a second, and then says, "I believe he's inspecting one of our bakery facilities today and no, I'm afraid he's not expected to be in today."

"I see, well maybe you've seen this woman around here with Mr. Pannier? She's about five feet, six inches. Red hair, green eyes, and is extremely attractive, curvy if you follow me. I believe her first name is Erin. Have you ever seen anyone like that with Mr. Pannier?"

Again the uncomfortable look from Kenison before he answers, "If you don't mind my asking, why are you looking for this woman?"

David smiles at him and very calmly says, "But I do mind you asking. It's part of an ongoing investigation, so if you could answer my question please, I'd appreciate it."

Kenison looks like he just swallowed something that didn't taste good and after several seconds he answers, "I believe the woman you described is Mr. Pannier's sister." That startles me. I'd been prepared for almost any answer but that one. His sister, well that removes any lingering doubts about whether she was involved or not.

"Thank you, Mr. Kenison, now that wasn't that hard was it? One final question, do you know if she lives at the same location as her brother?"

Kenison just wants us out of his office now and answers quickly, "Yes, I believe she does."

"Thanks again Mr. Kenison," David says and we all file out of the office. As David reaches the door, he turns back to Kenison and says, "Last thing, Georgia has a hindering law enforcement statute and it covers anything that's done to slow down an investigation. I'm telling you this because when I talk to the sister, if she's expecting me or I get the feeling she was warned in any way, I'm going to come back to see you. Understand?"

Kenison looks sick now, but he nods his understanding.

David points a finger at him and says, "So, no phone calls. Have a nice day."

Back in the car, David pulls into traffic and drives toward Pannier's house. Alonso starts chuckling and David asks him what was funny. "Dude, you had that guy pissing his pants. I think he was picturing himself in a cell with somebody like me."

We all laugh and I hope that Kenison takes the warning seriously. As a witch, Erin already has an advantage over us and advance warning we are coming will give her time to have a nasty surprise waiting for us.

I relate this to David, telling him what I'm worried about. Alonso turns serious and calls me a killjoy. David, always serious, acts like it is no big deal and simply shrugs his shoulders. Traffic picks up and it takes almost an hour to reach the Druid Hills area. Alonso comments on the size of the houses, saying, "These people are compensating for something." I understand what he means. Some of these places are enormous.

At last, we come to Normandy Drive and then to the Pannier estate. David pauses at the street end of the driveway and looks in the mirror at me. "Is there any way to capture her safely?" When I indicate that there isn't, he says, "I guess we have to kill her then." I agree and explain the procedure of removing the heart and head for cremation. They both acknowledge my instructions and David pulls down the drive toward the house as if this is the most normal thing in the world to do.

*****

David parks the Crown Vic and we walk to the front door. David takes the lead, planning to use his police credentials to get us inside, but as he prepares to knock I hear him say, "Uh oh."

"What?" I ask, moving forward to see.

"Door's open," he replies. He uses his toe to push the door fully open then glances back at me with a raised brow.

"That's not good," I reply. I notice he has his gun out again so I ask, "Do you think Kenison might have double crossed us?"

David looks thoughtful and says, "I'd have to say it's possible."

Alonso pushes past both of us saying, "Screw it," as he steps inside. David starts to follow, but I grab his arm. When he turns to me, I shake my head.

"Alonso, stop. If she's expecting us, she may have set a trap." He stops, but doesn't look happy. He has revenge on his mind and won't be deterred long.

I spend a few minutes checking the door, looking for spells or wards. I find nothing and step inside, again checking on this side of the door. I ease my way around the entire foyer area, finding nothing. I don't let this influence me, I have a bad feeling and I know the nature of a witch. Once they have someone in their sights, you have to kill them to stop them. It's just the way they are, single minded and evil.

I feel sure there will be a trap somewhere and, while it might kill me temporarily, it would be permanently fatal to my friends. Alonso asks what he should look for and I explain it could be anything, I'd know it when I see it. He doesn't like that answer, but it's the best I can give him. I ask them to wait and go back out to the car to grab my kit bag from the trunk. I want my knife and the flask of holy oil, the crossbow isn't much of a help when it comes to witches, sadly enough.

Back in the house, I tell them to follow me as I clear each room one at a time. David helps by suggesting a route that will make it easier and Alonso follows behind. We search one downstairs wing and the entire upstairs finding absolutely zip. We are on our way back down the central stairs when my nerves tingle and then vibrate a warning to my brain. I stop, holding my arms out as a signal for the other two. They freeze a couple of steps up behind me as I scan all around looking for whatever made my hair stand on end.

David asks, "What is it?"

"Don't move," I answer, trying to get a handle on what is happening. I circle around behind them trying to get back upstairs and find the same static electricity tingle feeling. Moving back down a couple of steps, I look at my friends and see the questioning looks. I tell them the truth, "We're screwed."

"Great," Alonso comments. David scans the area, alert, his gun up and ready to engage whatever came at us. I know it won't be that easy. There isn't anything coming for us, this is a trap and we'd sprung it. We can't go up or down, but the real question is what will happen next? There has to be a spell somewhere and it might give me a clue what we are up against, if I can find it.

We're safe for the moment, we simply can't move. I tell David and Alonso to relax as I search for the hidden spell. The inaction doesn't sit well with my partners, but they really don't have much choice. It doesn't take me long to find what I'm looking for. The stairs run from a central balcony down to the foyer, a wall runs along the right side and it is open on the left side, overlooking a large sitting room. A large-framed painting of a mountain stream hangs on the right hand wall. I lift an edge of the frame and there, beneath the painting, written on the wall in blood, is the spell.

I ask David to help me and together we lift it from its mounting hooks. We pass it to Alonso, who promptly drops it over the railing to the wood floor of the sitting room. Now revealed, the spell covers the entire area previously hidden by the painting. Written in an ancient script and impossible to decipher unless you were familiar with the language of witches, I can only understand bits and pieces of the spell.

As I study the writing, David asks, "Any ideas?"

"One thing comes to mind," I say. They both look at me, waiting for a revelation. "Whatever it does is probably bad." David snorts and shakes his head.

"I knew I should've stayed at home," Alonso says.

As much as I want to keep stringing them along, I let them off the hook, "I haven't figured it all out yet, but I can tell you it's supposed to hold us here. I haven't figured out yet what happens if we try or if it's supposed to do something else after a period of time, like a time delay. The important thing is we are safe for the time being."

"What could the time delay be for?"

I shrug at David's question. "It could be set to burn the house down or something equally terrible. I don't know yet," I say as I continue to study the symbols.

Alonso adds, "Oh, if I ever get my hands on that bitch she's going to wish she'd never…"

At that moment, he is interrupted by a feminine cough at the bottom of the steps. We all turn and my breath catches in my throat. Standing at the bottom of the staircase and looking as lovely as I'd ever seen her, is the current object of all our desires.

With hands on hips and a wide smile on her ruby lips, Erin looks up at us and says, "Hello boys."

TWENTY

Alonso takes a step down the stairs toward Erin and I grab his arm, pulling back hard to stop him. The smile never leaves her face, if anything, it grows bigger and has a touch of anticipation to see what will happen if Alonso steps past the barrier.

David raises the Glock preparing to fire and I yell, "No!" He hesitates and I go on, "She'd have thought of that. Nobody do anything, just stand still." My partners stop moving, but the look on their faces tell me they won't wait long.

Erin laughs gaily and says, "You're good, Tony. Very perceptive. He's right, boys, but you go on and give it a go if you want." That got through to them and they calm down. She has everyone's attention now, just what she wanted. "The spell creates a net around the three of you and has consequences if you attempt to break free or harm me."

"What kind of consequences?" I ask.

"You will die, no drama, no theatrics, you'll just drop dead. I wanted your undivided attention, I hope I have it," she replies. When I nod, she continues, "Now, while this won't have a lasting effect on you, Tony, your two friends will be truly and forever dead. Before we get started, I have a question. What happened to my brother?"

David answers her, "He's dead, like you're going to be soon."

She smiles again, "Keep it up. You'll just make it easier for me." Turning serious she asks, "How did he die?"

I answer this time, "The demon, Belphegor." She looks thoughtful for a moment and then it appears she reaches a conclusion in her mind. She smiles menacingly once more.

"Good enough, time for some fun then. Detective, you seem anxious to shoot someone, so I want you to shoot Tony in the chest." To say I'm shocked would be an understatement and I think David is even more shocked than I. Alonso gets angry and swears in very colorful terms.

Erin turns to him with a sweet smile. "I haven't forgotten you, but wait your turn." She focuses back on David saying, "I'm serious, I want you to point your gun at Tony and shoot him, now." Still speechless, David looks at me.

"Wait. Why?" I ask. "Why go to all this trouble to torture me?"

"Fun, the sheer delight of watching you squirm. The way you drooled over me and tried so hard to be a gentleman. Putting yourself in danger to protect the poor defenseless woman. It was like watching a fly trapped in a spider web, pathetic. Of course it's fun for the spider," she laughs.

"I don't think so," I shoot back. "I'm sure you did derive some sick pleasure from watching me, but you know it's because of the spell you placed on my door. If it hadn't been for that, you'd have been just another skirt." I smile as I say this, hoping to piss her off. If she's angry, maybe she'll say something she normally wouldn't.

Again she laughs, "I'd never be 'Just another skirt' to you. I know you, Tony—or should I call you Antonio? I know how easily you fall in love." Her gaze narrows as she stares at me. "I've watched you for some time."

"And I know witches. I've killed hundreds of your kind. If you had been watching me, you couldn't have resisted torturing me, it's your nature." I ignore David and Alonso, completely focused on her "Why involve your brother?"

"When I told him about you, he couldn't resist helping."

"Another lie. Your brother summoned a demon, that's not witch behavior. You'll use spells and incantations, but you won't use demons because you know how unreliable they are. You don't like the competition. No, there's something else going on here and you're being used."

That got to her and I watch her smile slip just a bit, "Witches don't get used by anybody."

I have to keep up the act, keep her talking. I laugh hard, "That's rich. You don't get used? You are a liar, but your brother told the truth in the end. Just before he died, he told me the truth."

Angry now, she screams, "What did he tell you?"

"He told me that the two of you were being used and attacking me and my friends wasn't your idea," I exaggerate a bit.

She swears under her breath and I know I got it right. Recovering quickly, she says, "He lied, trying to save his pathetic life."

"You sold him out from the beginning?"

"What do you mean, 'I sold him out'? He's my brother. I might think he was a coward, but I'd never sell him out."

"We know the summoning incantation he used to summon the demon was flawed and allowed the demon to slip its shackles. Whoever taught him that spell set him up to be killed."

"Lie, you're a liar!" she screams.

"So much for no drama. Calm down, sweetheart. You know I'm telling the truth, you knew it a few minutes ago when we told you he was dead. You knew that he'd been sacrificed. Your face gave you away." Her face turns stony as I go on. "Whoever is pulling the strings on this little caper sacrificed him and you know it. That's what he was, wasn't he?"

Her sad eyes suddenly darken and she grins with a little laugh, throwing her hands up in defeat. "All right, I sacrificed him, so what? I think I'm going to sacrifice the three of you as well. I'll summon the same demon and let it tear you three apart, what do you think of that?"

"Do it," I say. Alonso looks at me like I've lost my mind, but I'm not worried. I can see from the look on her face that she was stymied by my challenge. I don't believe she orchestrated any of this and I don't believe she knew how to summon Belphegor. I take a chance, but I also count on the fact the demon doesn't like those that summoned it.

She glares at me, getting angrier and angrier by the second. The fact she doesn't start a summoning spell tells me she was bluffing and I have to figure out a way to exploit it.

Alonso comes to my rescue, so to speak, when he asks,

"Hey, Red, who was the two bitches you and your brother were with the other night at that bar? That old one was fine. I'd sure like to spend some quality time with her. And that young one, you know, the one that looked like a slut. I bet she could…" That gets to her because she doesn't let him finish before she throws her hand up as she mutters a few words. The spell that hits him knocks him backward onto the stairs.

He tries to stand again, but she throws another that slams him back down, eliciting a grunt from him. I yell, trying to draw her attention back to me. "The graphic fantasy aside, who were they?" She lowers her arm, but the furious stare never leaves Alonso.

Eventually, she looks back at me, "No one you should concern yourself with. You should be concerned with what I intend to do with the three of you. You don't think I'm going to let you walk out of here do you? You've caused me a lot of aggravation and the fact you were able to find this house tells me you would be even more trouble if I allowed you to live."

Her refusal to answer my questions tells me we are on the right track, but I have no idea how to use this information at the moment. I decide to go for broke and see what happens.

"Erin, I know you aren't smart enough to have dreamed all this up on your own and your brother is too weak to have done any of this by himself. Neither of you can handle the demon, so I know there is somebody else running things and you should probably ask their permission before you do anything to us. She might be real pissed at you and we both know what she did to your brother. It was her that set him up with the demon and let it kill him. If you do this, you're probably going to be next. Why don't you call her and get her here so we can discuss it."

She looks at me for a few seconds and I can see anger boiling out of her. Then she becomes calm and that's when I get scared. She looks at David and said, "Detective, it's time. I want you to shoot Tony now or I'm going to see how much pain you can tolerate."

David asks me, "What do I do?"

Erin answers for me. "If you don't, I'll kill your big, black friend in a most painful way now instead of waiting."

I look at David and say. "It's okay, she's just torturing me. I'll come back. Don't let him do anything stupid while I'm gone." Alonso stands on the same step as me and I can tell he is barely in control. It won't take much to push him over the edge and he'll go berserk, getting himself killed.

David raises his pistol until it points at the middle of my chest. I glance at Erin, who wears a look of expectation on her face. I reach over and gently squeeze Alonso's arm, telling him, "It'll be okay. I'll be back in a minute." He doesn't move or speak and I can see the pain etched on his face. I pat him on the arm and turn back to David.

He asks, "Are you ready?" I nod and before I have time to think about it, he pulls the trigger.

I expected the noise to be louder, but I only hear a small pop and it feels like I've been punched hard in the chest. Almost immediately, my knees feel weak and I start slipping to the stairs. David grabs me by the shoulder and helps me down until I sit. Leaning back against the wall, I can see the guilt. I smile and try to tell him it will be okay, but before I can say anything, my vision blurs and then goes dark.

*****

I have no idea how long I was dead, but it couldn't have been long. My eyes flutter open and I start to breathe again. Automatically, my hand goes to my chest, feeling for a wound. It had already healed and I can feel my heart beating so I know I'm back. I look down at my chest and can see the hole from the bullet in my shirt and a large blood stain covering the entire front. I place my hand against the wall and use it to lever myself up until I stand, looking at Erin and she looks back at me with what I can only describe as glee.

David asks in a hushed voice, "Are you all right?" I reach back, grasping his arm and tell him I was okay. Alonso places his huge hand on my shoulder and squeezes in solidarity.

"It's so sweet to see such brotherly love. Let's test it, shall we?" We all look at her, knowing what is coming, but having no idea what twist her demented mind will put on it this time. "You," she snaps, pointing at Alonso, "I want you to wrap those great big hands around Tony's throat and choke him to death."

Alonso opens his mouth to tell her what she can do, but I stop him. When he looks back at me, I say, "Just do it, she's not going to stop until you do it and she'll kill you. Just do it." He looks at me pleadingly and I can see tears welling in his eyes. I place the palm of my hand on his cheek and smile at him. "It'll be okay."

We continue to look into each other's eyes while he places his hands around my neck. Alonso begins to squeeze and Erin giggles, "No cheating, I'll know." My vision starts to fade once again and a thought occurs to me. *I know.* I know how to break the spell. I smile as I die for the second time in less than thirty minutes.

*****

Like last time, the lights come back on and I wake up, alive. Before I stand, I reach out and grab David by the hand. He looks down at me and I pull until he bends over so I can whisper a question. He pulls back and replies, "Yes."

I hold my hand out and he places a worn Zippo lighter in it. I ask him to help me up and he takes my arm and lifts until I stand beside him. Alonso stands staring at Erin with hate in his eyes.

I think to myself, 'Hold on a few more seconds, big guy and you can do whatever you want.'

With his bulk serving to block what I do from view, I pull the flask of holy oil from my back pocket and open the top. Checking the Zippo to make sure it works, I hold it in my left hand. With my right, I quickly splash the oil across the spell-covered wall in the sign of a crucifix. Before she can do anything to stop me, I strike the lighter and hold the flame to the oil. It flares and a flaming cross appears on the wall.

Erin screams in frustration at seeing her trap broken. Alonso instinctively knows he is now free and vaults down the steps three at a time. Erin turns to try and flee, but she only makes it two steps before Alonso has her. He grabs a handful of her beautiful red hair and yanks her off her feet. She screams again, but this time in pain as Alonso swings her forcefully into the wall. A loud '*Oof!*' escapes from her lips as the air is forced from her lungs by the impact. He keeps up the rhythm of swinging her back away from the wall and then slamming into it over and over until she no longer makes any noise.

I walk down to where he continues to batter Erin and grab both his arms. He starts to shake me off and continue, but he stops and looks at me. Erin's shattered body hangs limply from his hands, her neck clearly broken. "That's good enough buddy," I mutter with a pat on his arm. "I'll take it from here." Alonso opens his hands, releasing the hold on her hair and she drops to the floor like a rag doll.

Reaching behind me, I draw the knife from my belt. Kneeling at her side, I plunge the blade down between her perfect breasts. I saw with the blade until I have a hole big enough that I can slice through the attaching tissue, veins and arteries until I remove the heart. Laying it on the floor beside the body, I start removing her head. It takes less time and effort than the heart and in a few moments, it rolls free from her body.

I stand and look at my partners and although they had hated her and wanted her dead, the mutilation of her corpse leaves them feeling sick. I ask David and Alonso to get some wood to build a pyre and they commence breaking chairs and tables. I carry the two parts of the witch outside. We build the pyre and I anoint her forehead with the oil, then I pour the remainder over the wood and set it alight. The three of us stand and watch as the fire burns trying to ignore the pop and sizzle of fat melting as Erin is consumed.

David asks, "What should we do with the body?" Alonso has a suggestion, but we ignore him while I consider what will be best.

"Alonso, keep the fire going, David and I are going to search the house."

David asks, "What are we looking for?"

"Anything that might lead to the other women, the ones we think are behind all of this," I explain. He asks if I think it's safe inside the house. I think about it for a minute and reply, "Yes, she thought she had us with the trap. Her arrogance would have convinced her it was all she needed."

He and I go in while Alonso tends the fire. We spend a couple of hours searching with zero results. We find nothing to give us a clue as to their identity or where we can find them. As a matter of fact, there isn't even a sign that Erin lived there. Only one bedroom appears to be used and there are clothes in only one closet and they all belong to Brunelle.

We eventually surrender and go back out to where Alonso's keeping watch over the fire. By the time we return, the heart had been completely consumed and the only thing left is a blackened and charred skull. David goes into the garage and returns with a shovel, which I use to smash the skull to powder.

We still haven't come to an agreement on what to do with the body. David isn't crazy about driving around Atlanta with a mutilated, decapitated body in his trunk. It might be hard to explain if we get stopped. I have to agree with him. Alonso suggests just leaving her and again David thinks it a bad idea as the police would definitely be involved and the hunt for a serial killer would bring out all the power of the Atlanta police. Besides, we had most definitely left DNA in the house.

The only suitable course of action seems to be burying her in the backyard and cleaning the house. Everyone agrees it's probably our best choice and we spend the rest of the evening cleaning blood from the floors and walls while Alonso digs a grave in the back and we bury what was left of Erin. Around one a.m., tired and dirty, we leave the Pannier estate and drive back to David's apartment. Too exhausted to eat, I take a shower and flop onto the bed where I fall asleep in seconds.

TWENTY-ONE

You might think this is the end of the story. The vampire nest had been destroyed, the werewolf Harry Crowe was dead, and the demon had gone back to hell. Erin and her brother were dead, but I still want to identify the two women Alonso had seen with our witches. I know there is more to this, but I have no idea where to start looking for them.

I still have no idea what their ultimate goal was. Maybe they just wanted to torture me for a while, but I don't think that is it. I hope that when they learn the plot failed and their co-conspirators were all dead, they'll do what these creatures always do, run and hide. That would give me time to recover and be ready for when they pop up again. That they will come back seems a foregone conclusion, but that is beyond my control. All I need to do now is file a report of the cleansing with Father Salvatore and I can put this behind me.

Alonso and I stay at David's apartment until evening. The sleep I had that morning, after disposing of Erin, was the first dreamless sleep I've had in weeks. It feels so good to be out from under Erin's spell and to be able to think clearly again. Just knowing that I'm not being influenced by someone else is a relief. I feel like my old self again and back in control. I want to get to my apartment, file the report with the Vatican, and then get drunk off my ass.

David suggests I swear off women for a few hundred years, he correctly identified my weakness for them as the source of most of my trouble. I seriously consider his advice, but know realistically my vow will last only until I see another beautiful, sexy woman. It is what it is, so instead I promise to be more careful.

Alonso laughs at me. "It's a good thing you're immortal."

*****

I drop Alonso off at his house and cruise to my apartment. As I pull up in front of The Magnolia House, I notice Mrs. Betty sitting in her rocking chair on the front porch, smoking. I know I need to have a long talk with her and now is as good a time as any.

She watches me like a cat watching a mouse as I walk up the steps to the porch, a slight smile curling the corners of her mouth. She sees my hesitation at the door and says, "Come on over and have a seat, Tony."

I take a seat on the rocker next to her and settle back for the discussion.

She continues to watch me in that predatory way of hers and then asks, "Did you find the redhead?" I nod in affirmation. "Good, I assume she's dead?" I nod again and she sits back in the rocker, puffing on her cigarette.

"Mrs. Betty, I have to ask, how did you know what I am?"

She doesn't respond immediately. Clouds of foul smelling smoke billows from her nostrils as she stares out across the street. I think she might not have heard me and prepare to ask again when she sighs. "Tony, I'm going to tell you a story. Not many people know this and I don't talk about it anymore. When this house was built in 1953, it was a brothel and there were ten girls working here. That's why the rooms are laid out the way they are. It was simple to change it into apartments with a little remodeling."

What she told me doesn't really surprise me. There have been brothels around forever. I've been in one or two and not always for what you might think. They're a great place to meet if you want to keep it private. Most of the customers don't want anyone to know they frequent such establishments, so whatever they might see or hear usually stays a secret and the girls of course don't say anything. They know the value of information and their reputations depend on being discreet. That's why throughout history prostitutes have been recruited to be spies.

What she says next does surprise me, though. "I worked here back then. As a matter of fact, it was my house."

Astonished by her revelation I stutter, "You were a, a…?"

"Whore is the word you're looking for, Tony. Yes, I was a whore and not just any whore. I was the Madame of The Magnolia House," she answers, not embarrassed or offended at all. It's my turn to sit back and stare out across the street. I knew her toughness, but this new information meant she was even tougher than I thought. A Madame has to be able to control the girls, who can sometimes be very rough, and all the clients. It can be a violent profession. "In the winter of 1956, a man came to the house, but he wasn't like the men I usually dealt with. He came in injured, that wasn't uncommon back then. To be a Madame back in those days, you had to be part doctor and part priest. Patch them up and listen to their confessions, then screw their brains out and send them away happy."

My eyes widen at her candid words. This is not the Mrs. Betty I've known since I moved into this house and it's actually quite refreshing.

"This fella didn't want to confess or have sex," she continues. "He just wanted help with the injury and I had never seen anything like it. Slashes like a razor all over his arms and back, but in neat little rows like from a claw. I'd seen people cut with a razor—hell, I'd even cut a few—but this was different."

I've seen injuries like that and I'd been killed by several over the years. "Did you ask him what did it?"

She laughs. "Of course I did, stupid woman that I was. He didn't want to answer, though. I was persistent and finally he told me a werewolf had been responsible. I thought he was making fun of me and got pretty riled up. Threatened to put him out on the street if he made fun of me again. He didn't say a word, just looked at me. It was that look that convinced me he was telling the truth."

"What did you do with him?"

"Over the next few months while he healed, we talked and he told me what he did and who he worked for." She looks over at me again when she says this. For the first time, I notice a crucifix hanging around her neck.

"You're Catholic?" I ask in surprise.

She bobs her chin. "A better one now than I used to

be. I don't go to mass as often as I should and my priest still turns red when I go to confession," she says with a wink that makes me blush. "I believe in God and I believe in evil. I know it's out there and I respect anybody that takes a stand against it. The man that came to me way back then, he stood against evil and I tried to help him. I gave him a place to stay here and I nursed his injuries whenever he got hurt. He stayed with me four years and we became very close."

"So the two of you were lovers?" I ask with a smile.

Her smile fades some and she takes on a look of melancholy as she answers, "No, but it wasn't for lack of trying on my part. I wanted to be his lover and I think he wanted it also, but it just wasn't to be."

"What happened?"

"He left for a job, something about a vampire stealing children from an orphanage in Birmingham and he never came back. To this day, I don't know what happened to him." She stares off into the distance and I know she isn't seeing the road anymore. "I'm sure he's dead," she says quietly. "If he'd lived, I know he would've come back here. Either way, I'm sure he's dead now anyway, he was much older than me."

She sits, silent for a few moments, then perks back up and the smile returns. "But that's how I knew what you were. I saw the same things in you that I saw in him and I've known every time you've gotten into a fight."

"How?" I ask, curious because I've always been careful not to leave evidence around—until recently.

"The bloody and torn clothes you keep dumping in the trash around back," she replies with a satisfied grin on her face. I guess I wasn't as careful as I thought I'd been and my face betrays me. "I check all of my occupant's trash. You learn a lot about a person by what they throw away and I like to know who's under my roof."

That sneaky old bitch. She'd been going through my garbage since I moved in and I never knew it. Prostitutes know that knowledge is power and use it instinctively to great effect. Blackmailing Johns for money is the norm.

Betty collected on all of her renters and stored the information away to be used if she needed an advantage in a situation. If she didn't need it, the information disappeared, but if she did, she'd pull it out and use it to get her way. Very effective and very impressive.

"Why didn't you tell me?"

She slides another cigarette from her pack and lights it. After a couple of pulls, she says, "I knew, that's enough. I'm too old to be of any real help to you and I know you like to keep what you are a secret. I tried to help in little ways, but mostly I stayed out of your way and let you do what you do."

I don't want to ask the next logical question. I'm sure that I won't like the answer, but I need to know, "Is my being a Cleanser the only thing you know about me?"

"Yes." Relief floods my mind and then she drops the other shoe, "And that you can't die."

My jaw drops. How the hell is everyone finding out about that? She said it so casually that for a moment, I almost can't believe that she actually said it. Betty doesn't say anything. She just sits back and waits, letting me process the information. For my part, I sit looking at a darkening sky, trying to decide how best to handle her knowledge of my situation.

Heat lightning flashes across the sky and the distant rumble of thunder foretells that a storm approaches. A common occurrence for summer in the south, an evening thunderstorm will cool the temperature and wash away the red clay dust that seems to accumulate on everything. I enjoy summer storms, watching the rain and the clean, fresh smell after, as long as they don't get too wild and develop into a tornado. The boiling black clouds promise that this will be a good one.

My eyes remain on the sky as I ask, "How long have you known?"

"Not long, since the fight in your apartment. I suspected something was different about you, but wasn't sure what. I told you I'd found the bloody and torn clothes. As bad as the clothes were, you had to be injured, but there were no bandages and you never seemed to be in pain. I know injuries don't normally heal that fast and the wound to your belly the other night should've put you down for a while, if not killed you." We look at each other and she finishes, "That's when I knew."

A loud clap of thunder rolls across the sky and serves to punctuate her words. As the sound dies away, I say, "I'll move if you'd like. I don't want to bring more trouble to your door."

She cackles for a few moments. "I don't want you to move. You're welcome here as long as you want to stay. Besides, you're the only tenant that always pays your rent on time."

I laugh with her as the wind begins to freshen, announcing the arrival of the storm. Far in the distance, I can just make out the first waves of rain coming along the breeze. It will be over top of us soon, so we step inside the house.

Betty pauses at her door and as she looks at me, I know she is staring into the eyes of the Cleanser she once loved. Her hand reaches up toward my face and I let her hold my chin. "Be careful," she whispers. I promise I will and she goes into her apartment. I think about what she said as I climb the stairs to my apartment, wondering about Mrs. Betty and her broken heart over a dead Cleanser.

The whistle of wind and the constant barrage of thunder greets me as I open the door to my apartment. As I step inside, the rain hammers the big windows in my living room and the sky has gone dark. I feel surprisingly good after the week I've had and the foul weather outside only serves to make me feel more at home in the cozy little flat.

I grab a bottle of Patron off the counter and drop onto my well-worn sofa for a little quiet reflection. It has been a strange two weeks, not only with the revelation that the entire mess had been some crazy witch conspiracy designed to torture me, but now I have a new ally in the fight against the monsters. Detective David George's assistance had been a welcome addition. He not only had been a great benefit during the fight with the vampires, but his investigative skills had kept me pointed in the right direction. It doesn't hurt that we seemed to like each other and now I count him among a very small list of people I consider friends.

The biggest surprise by far had to be Mrs. Betty's story. Two Cleansers, separated by a number of years, in the same house, what were the odds? And the fact that she'd been a prostitute, staggering! She had to have been a wild thing in her day. Of course, now that I know, it makes some sense. The predatory glint she sometimes gets in her eye and the way she slinks around Magnolia House at all hours. I simply thought she was a busy body and wanted to catch a tenant in an awkward moment.

Regardless, I have a newfound respect for the old girl and she definitely fit into the category of ally as well as David and Alonso. My little band of miscreants. There probably wasn't a Cleanser in history that had a more diverse group of associates. The skinny and taciturn detective, the large—okay, very large—black morgue attendant, and the eighty year old former Madame of a cat house. And of course, me, the baby faced immortal cursed by a witch, who now spends his time chasing around all the things that go bump in the night.

I laugh to myself as I take a long pull from the bottle of fiery amber liquid. The warmth of the tequila settles in my stomach and the rain continues to beat down outside. I sink further back into the sofa cushion and relax. Invariably, my mind turns to Erin, this time without the added help of the spell. No, this time I manage to think about her in a rational way. I try to puzzle out what it had been all about. All the twisted and convoluted paths she'd taken just to torture me, knowing that I was immortal.

It doesn't make sense.

She had to have known that I would eventually defeat the vampires and the werewolf. The demon could have given me more trouble, but even then, I would've prevailed in the end. This is what I did and even with all my faults, I'm pretty good at it. So there has to be more to the story, but for the life of me, I can't put my finger on it. There has to be a connection with the two other females at the Euclid Avenue Yacht Club. The biggest question that keeps jumping to the front of my thoughts has to be, *what is that connection?*

I assume they have to be witches as well, but had the older one been pulling the strings and Erin simply did as she had been told the same as her brother? Or had Erin been the ring leader all along and the meeting had nothing to do with the conspiracy? I remember something David said soon after he became involved. He said there's no such thing as a coincidence. Everything happens for a reason and if you think two seemingly unrelated occurrences were connected, they probably are. Trust your instincts, he said, and find the common denominator. It will always be there if you can see it.

That line of reasoning brings me right back to the fact that the other two witches had to be involved, but they disappeared. Maybe they'd accomplished all they could as far as making my life a living hell and the cost had simply gotten too high. They lost two of their own along with the lesser creatures that had allied with them. Hopefully, they had cut and run and I wouldn't be seeing them again for a long while.

With the cloud cover outside, the night seems black as a pit, occasionally lit by the strobe-like flash of lightning. I continue to mull over the questions about the case and Erin as I sip the aged Mexican liquor. I didn't turned on any lights when I entered and the only light comes from jagged slashes of discharging electricity quickly followed by the artillery rumble of thunder. Sitting in the dark, drinking tequila, alone seems a little pathetic so I decide to get up and turn on some lights, maybe watch a little TV, when a knock sounds at the door.

I immediately think of Erin, but quickly push her from my mind. After all, I'd cut off her head. The knock comes again and I reluctantly push myself up off the sofa and step to the door, flipping on the living room light as I go. Back to my old self again, I ask who it is before opening the door. The smoke-coarsened voice of my landlady comes through the wooden door, advising me she has a problem and needs my help. Smiling, I ask how I can help as I pull the door open.

The sight that greets me when I look out onto the landing is one that I'll never forget. Standing right in front of my door is a young girl in her late teens. Brilliant red hair that can't possibly be natural, cut short on the sides with bangs that swoop down across her forehead and obscure her right eye. Her left eye shines green as poison. I've seen those same eyes before. Her slim figure wears a white halter top spattered with what looks like blood and I can see a few droplets shinning on the green vinyl mini skirt below it. Her legs are encased in green and white stripped leggings down to her knees where red vinyl platform boots take over giving her the overall look of a twisted Christmas elf. An evil smile spreads across her face from ear to ear.

My attention turns to what she holds up in her left hand. It appears to be a rumpled leather throw wrapped in a flowery patterned sack. Then I notice the shock of curly silver hair grasped in her hand and the realization dawns on me that she holds the skin of my landlady, still wearing her house dress.

My eyes grow wide with shock and before I can move, the elf's right hand stabs forward, plunging a large knife to the hilt into my chest. As my knees grow weak and my vision starts to blur and darken, a thought pops into my mind. The witches are back.

TWENTY-TWO

My next conscious sensation is of a tugging feeling in the center of my chest. Almost immediately, my eyes snap open and I sit up with a gasp, pulling fresh air—well, disinfectant laced with piss and shit undertones—into my empty lungs.

Yep, back in the morgue, again. Just fantastic.

Alonso stands beside the gurney that supports the white vinyl body bag I'm lying in. He holds a large, bloody kitchen knife in his right hand as if preparing to plunge it back into my chest, a maniacal grin on his large, round face. If I didn't know him better, I would have thought this a problem.

Instead, I simply say, "Thanks."

"No problem, brother. May I have your frequent flier card so that I can stamp it? One more trip to the morgue this week and you win a toaster."

My ruined T-shirt has a three inch long gash dead center and is absolutely covered with my blood. The only thing I can say is, "Funny."

"Your landlady is in that bag over by the wall. What's left of her, anyway," a familiar voice comments from behind me.

I glance over to see Detective George leaning against the wall next to the top of my gurney. He points across the room and I turn in the direction he indicated. Another gurney is pushed up along the same wall where I'd lain the last time I came here. There are two body bags on top of it, the larger was shaped as you'd expect and a second, smaller bag rests on top.

"Her body, completely skinned by the way, is in the big bag. You can guess what's in the little bag. We found it on the landing outside your door, right next to you." After a brief pause, he asks, "Do you have any idea how it got there?"

"Yes, the same little bitch that stuck that in me," I snap, pointing at the knife in Alonso's fist.

Alonso shakes his head in disbelief. "Not *another* woman. Man, I done told you, you need to stay away from women for a while. Maybe become a monk, take a vow of celibacy or something."

"Stop, please, I wasn't trying to get laid. It's one of the witches you saw at the bar on Euclid, the young one. She knocked on my door and when I opened it, she was standing there with Mrs. Betty's skin in her hand like it was the best present in the world. Then she stabbed me. She shouldn't be hard to find dressed the way she is." I give the detective a physical description of the girl and what she'd been wearing.

"Sounds like a demented elf to me," Alonso mutters. David and I both look at him, he gazes back at us. "What? It's what it sounds like. Shit, tell me you didn't think the same thing."

I'm not ready to admit the same thought had crossed my mind right before she stuck the knife in me. David only shakes his head and goes to call in the description. I get down from the gurney and begin to peel off the sticky T-shirt. The wound had already closed up and only a hint of pink flesh shows where it had been.

Alonso points toward the shower. "Come on. Let's get you cleaned up again." I allow him to steer me toward the emergency shower like a child.

Once more standing in the spray washing blood from my body, I wonder how this could happen. The craziness obviously isn't over and I keep coming up against the same thought. What are they trying to accomplish? You didn't have to be a rocket scientist to have figured out by now that I'm immortal and all the mayhem isn't going to make a lasting impression. If they are trying to make me miserable by killing me on a regular basis, that wasn't working either. All it had accomplished was to piss me off and make me determined to find them and finish this.

They no longer have Erin's spell to keep me blinded and unless there are more monsters waiting for me, there are only the two witches left. They are determined, I have to give them that, but I'm aware and will be looking for spells and charms everywhere I go. The fact they had killed Mrs. Betty *really* pissed me off. As far as I knew she had no dealings with any of this, so her killing had been designed to cause me pain. That makes me consider whether Alonso and David are in danger. It's possible the witches will strike at those around me, the people I care about. I decide first thing I'll do after getting dressed will be to warn my friends about this possibility.

*****

By the time I finish getting dressed, David had returned and I share my thoughts about the danger with him and Alonso. David stands to one side deep in thought. Alonso on the other hand, has a little freak out.

"Man, I done spent days chained to a chair in a basement because of witches! I thought when we killed Red this would be over with." He paces back and forth across the cold tile floor and I let him vent. "I can handle the occasional vampire or werewolf, but this demon shit and the witch spells? I don't know. I should have stayed in church. My momma told me this kinda stuff would happen to me if I quit going to church. I should a listened."

He stops pacing and points his finger at the recently healed hole in my chest before saying, "The Reverend Theopolis Winslow of the Oak Grove Ole' Timey Southern Baptist Church told me when I was fifteen years old that the Devil was chasing me and if I didn't get washed in the blood of the lamb, the Devil would catch me and skin me!"

We all look over toward the bags containing what was left of my landlady, considering that the Reverend Winslow might've been right. "Are you finished?" David asks.

Alonso takes a deep breath and shrugs his massive shoulders, "Yeah. I'm good now. So, what's the plan?"

"I suggest whatever we do, we stick together. It'll be much harder for them to get close to us if we're all watching each other's backs," David answers.

I agree with David and Alonso asks, "I don't suppose we can do it at my house instead of either of your tiny apartments? I need the comfort of home."

David shakes his head and answers, "It's probable that

they already know where we all live and that would be the logical place to try and attack. They've already gotten to Tony at his place twice. I suggest an alternate location. Somewhere they aren't aware of yet."

"Yeah, like a church," Alonso interjects.

David ignores him and goes on, "We need a safe house where we can plan and rest, at least initially. They'll probably find it eventually if we can't end this soon, but we should have freedom of movement for a couple of days."

I smack myself on the forehead and say, "You're right and I don't know why I didn't think of it sooner. I always find an alternate place to live when I move to a new city. In case something happens to the primary one."

"You mean like the last two weeks?" Alonso asks, always ready to point out my shortcomings.

I ignore the implied insult. "I have a safe house and it already has a cache of weapons and other items. Damn, I'm really screwing up lately."

"Probably a result of the spell Erin placed on you," David offers. "Could the witches know about it?"

I think a moment before answering, "No, I don't think so. It's been a couple of months since I visited last. I try to stay away from there unless I need something so I'm not connected to it."

"Sounds like just what the doctor ordered. Where is it?"

"Far northeastern part of the city. On Nathan Bedford Forrest Avenue."

"Great! I get to stay on the street named after the guy who invented the Ku Klux Klan," Alonso grumbles.

*****

I pull up in front of 1503 Nathan Bedford Forrest Avenue and park the Jag in the short gravel driveway. The grass is knee high as I step out of the car and grab my travel kit out of the passenger seat. The small, single-story, gray clapboard house situated on a quarter acre lot looks slightly dilapidated and rundown, especially with the overgrown yard. I actually scare a rabbit out walking to the rear door. The rest of the neighborhood looks pretty much the same as my place. This is a poor section of Atlanta and no one seems to care much about the upkeep of their property or their neighbor's. Just the kind of place you can hide, not because you're invisible, but because no one cares.

I open the door leading into a small kitchen at the rear of the house with my key and step inside. The inside of the house doesn't reflect the same degree of neglect I'd cultivated with the outside. Although a little dusty, the inside appears neat and relatively clean. A quick wipe down of the surfaces and a broom and mop would have the place livable in no time. I carry my bag to the bigger of the two bedrooms in back and drop it on the bed. A pull-out bed in the sofa in the living room and the second bedroom in back will be for my two house guests. I'll let them fight it out over who gets which. The house only has a single bathroom, but I don't figure three guys will have that much trouble sharing.

I'd stopped at a Piggly Wiggly on my way to the safe house and picked up several bags of groceries and after dropping my travel bag, I go back to my car to unload the food. I have the trunk lid up and two arms full of sacks when I hear another car and turn to see David's Crown Vic pull in and park behind me. He steps out with a gym bag slung over his shoulder and helps me with the groceries.

I explain the living arrangements as I set the bags on the small counter in the kitchen. He nods and wanders towards the back of the house to lay claim to his sleeping area while I put the food away.

He comes back a short time later. "I'll take the sofa, it's fairly comfortable. Besides, I'm sure Alonso would whine if I left it for him."

I can't disagree with his assessment. For a big guy, he is prone to complain when his comfort is involved. I tell him as much and we share a laugh at the expense of our friend.

After the food is stored, David and I begin cleaning. I dust while he sweeps. We're almost finished when I hear another car pull in outside. It would've been almost impossible to miss as the volume of music coming from the lowered windows is nearly deafening. We go to the door to see what and who had just arrived.

I'm stunned as I open the door and see the vehicle that pulled into the drive. Sitting behind David's unmarked police car is the most god awful and gaudy car I've ever seen. A bright purple Lincoln Town Car with huge chrome rims and limo tint on the windows sits vibrating in the driveway. The music dies with the engine and the driver's door swings open. As we watch, Alonso levers his bulk from behind the wheel and waves at us, a huge smile plastered across his face.

Pulling an enormous suitcase from the rear seat of the pimp mobile, he makes his way across the grass. David stands beside me with a hand covering the lower portion of his face. His complexion has turned red and I can tell he's struggling not to laugh as Alonso lumbers up to us. "I'm here, let the slumber party begin!"

"Do you think you could have found a less conspicuous car?" I ask Alonso.

Without missing a beat, Alonso looks over his shoulder at the car and answers, "What, that thing? It's my cousin's, I had to borrow it because the Honda was destroyed by a demon, remember? Besides, I'm sure the neighbors here on KKK Lane will just love it."

I take in the size of his suitcase and ask, "Did you bring enough stuff?"

"This is the little one, the big one is in the trunk," he replies without sarcasm. David can't contain it any longer and bursts out laughing. Alonso glances evilly toward him and David starts sputtering, trying to get himself under control. Still red faced, but not laughing, David holds his hands up in surrender and Alonso continues, "Unlike you white boys, I don't wear jeans and T-shirts every day. Besides I believe in my comfort and I need all this stuff."

We leave David on the front porch as I show Alonso to his bedroom. I inform him that I'll have lunch ready in an hour and then we can discuss our plan while we eat. He'd already begun unpacking and waves his acknowledgement over his shoulder. I go back up front and find David still chuckling to himself. I pass on the information about lunch and walk back inside to the kitchen.

While I prepare our lunch, I think about the make-up of our unlikely group. Three very different individuals who've somehow meshed into an effective team. This invariably makes me think of Mrs. Betty and what happened to her. I push the thoughts from my mind so I can buckle down and finish making our lunch. Before I focus completely on the task at hand, I have one final though about revenge. I silently promise Mrs. Betty that the ones responsible for her horrible death will pay and pay dearly.

*****

I prepare a light lunch, having long grown accustomed to the American habit of the evening meal being the large meal of the day, of a garden salad and a fresh fruit salad. As I complete setting the small dinette table in an alcove attached to kitchen, David comes in and I can tell he is about as close to exploding with laughter as he was the last time I'd seen him.

"Have you been to the bathroom recently?" he asks. I shake my head. "He's unloaded an Avon display in there. I mean, there are bottles and tubes of stuff everywhere and I'm afraid to ask about some of the apparatus he has hanging in the shower. Oh, and you should see his bedroom. Looks like Wild Kingdom in there."

I chuckle and say, "Go easy on him. He can be a little sensitive." Which I've always found strange from someone as big and obviously not opposed to getting his hands dirty, but to each his own.

David nods his understanding and says, "I know and I like the guy, it's just funny."

"What's funny?" We both turn to see Alonso standing in the door from the living room. Without waiting for an answer, he walks over to the table and pulls one of the stainless steel framed cafe chairs out and lowers his ample backside down onto it. Once he seems satisfied that it will indeed hold him, he relaxes. "Where's the food?"

David takes his chair as I indicate the green salad and bowl of fresh sliced fruit. David helps himself to the greens while I go back to the counter and bring over a couple of bottles of Newman's Own dressing and a pitcher of iced tea. I notice that Alonso hasn't moved or attempted to put anything on his plate.

When I ask what the problem is, he says, "I'm not used to all this rabbit food. It's not a meal if there ain't no meat."

"Try it," I reply. "It's good for you. Besides, there's a grill in the shed out back and I bought steak for dinner. You can have all the meat you want tonight. I even bought a nice bottle of Robert Mondovi merlot."

"I'll try it because I'm hungry, but I won't like it."

David coughs and quickly covers his mouth with a napkin as Alonso scoops a small portion of salad onto his plate.

I ask David if he is okay and he nods, squeaking out, "Crouton down the windpipe." I know it's a lie because I've been fighting hard not to laugh myself. Alonso sits across from him giving him the evil eye again. He knows it's a lie, too.

David drains his tea in an attempt to wash down the offending bread crumb and pours another glass while I finally put some of the salad on my plate. We eat in silence for a few minutes. David and I sample the greens and fruit, while Alonso stares at the three lonely spinach leaves and a tomato wedge covered in half a bottle of ranch dressing.

After a couple of helpings of salad and a good portion of fruit, David pushes his plate away from him. "Good salad, Tony. I loved the feta cheese."

I poke at a few pineapple chunks on my plate and reply, "Yeah, it's my favorite."

We both look at Alonso as he grumbles, "Feta my ass." Neither of us can handle it any longer and both of us bust out in laughter. Alonso cries indignantly, "I'm glad you two are enjoying yourselves." His plight only serves to make us laugh harder.

Alonso eventually joins us in laughter. Several minutes later I wipe the tears from my eyes and try to catch my breath. David takes a sip of tea and sets his glass back on the table. "Okay, what are we going to do?"

Alonso answers short and to the point, "Find them and kill them both."

"Yes, but how?" the detective presses.

"We start at the bakery," I answer.

TWENTY-THREE

At eight a.m., the three of us are parked along Williams Street in downtown Atlanta watching the front door of the Pannier Bakery Company's corporate headquarters. We're waiting for James Kenison to arrive. He acts as the office manager and had been the one to provide us with the information that Erin and Brunelle Pannier were siblings. During our last conversation with him, David had warned Kenison that we'd be back if we suspected he'd tipped off Erin. The fact she had a trap waiting for us at the Druid Hills estate seemed to indicate that he might have ignored our warning. We intend to find out and whatever else he might know.

Last evening, we fixed the steaks I'd promised Alonso and had a pleasant dinner. Afterward, we sat in the back yard drinking a few beers and finalized our plan. To avoid easy identification, David had called a rental agency and reserved a full size cargo van for the morning. The van would also make it easier to execute our plan, which involved waiting for Kenison to arrive at the office. As he neared the door, Alonso would open the sliding side door, grab the office manager and pull him into the van. I'd help Alonso zip tie and hood our target while David drove away. It was a simple snatch operation. We'd bring him back to the safe house where we could question him at our leisure.

Each of us has a ski mask pushed up on top of our heads. We plan on lowering them when we see Kenison walking down the sidewalk. Unsure of which direction he'll come from, David watches in front and I adjust the mirror on my door to watch behind us.

The back of the van doesn't contain any seats, so Alonso sits on the floor directly behind my seat, ready to jerk the sliding door open when we give him the word. We'd gone over the plan several times last night and we all know our parts. Conversation seems unnecessary, so we sit in silence, each deep in his own thoughts. I know Alonso is thinking about revenge and I'm sure David has thoughts about losing his job as a policeman if word of our kidnapping ever comes to light and, for some strange reason, I find myself thinking about Lilith, the witch that cursed me so long ago.

She had been such a sweet and lovely girl. Being raised by her busy father had made her desperate for attention and I had provided it. I should've seen that she was falling in love with me, but being young myself and not interested in forever, I was happy with things the way they were. If she had waited and perhaps talked to me about what she had planned I might have even drank the potion voluntarily. I had no real concept of time or immortality. The idea of being young and able to enjoy the pleasure of each other's bodies forever had a certain appeal.

However, being murdered by her father, dumped in Rome's sewers, and then the terror of waking up to find I had, in effect, been poisoned did not. It destroyed any chance for me to see what I had become as anything other than a curse and it drove me half-mad. The chance meeting and subsequent murder of Lilith after I returned to Rome only drove me closer to the edge because I was now racked with guilt.

Why couldn't she have been just a normal girl? I would have grown old, maybe with her and been long dead now. I possibly could have had children, who knows?

I sigh and I sense David glance at me. He probably thinks it due to my being impatient, but it isn't. Just a melancholy moment for what my life could have been. Instead, I hunt monsters for the Catholic Church and this morning, I plan to kidnap someone to get information about two witches that had been making my life hell. Just another day in paradise.

*****

The first words spoken by any of us since parking come from David. "Heads up. Kenison is coming our way."

My eyes shift from the mirror to the windshield and I watch as James Kenison strolls toward the entrance of the Caughorn Building. Dressed in an immaculate charcoal gray suit, the office manager walks as if he doesn't have a care in the world. All of that will change in about fifteen seconds.

I hear Alonso grunt behind me and then the click as he unlatches the sliding door in preparation for grabbing our target.

"Masks down," David orders quietly.

I reach up and pull the dark blue ski mask down over my face as I continue to watch Kenison approach. He walks in the center of the sidewalk until just before reaching the entrance where he angles slightly toward the doors. Pulling a set of keys from his right front pocket, he pauses trying to find the right key and David gives Alonso the order to grab him.

Alonso flings the door back with such force I worry he might have broken it and I feel the van shake as his bulk slides out. I watch for just a second as my friend charges across the short expanse of concrete and grabs Kenison in a bear hug. I swivel toward the center of the van and slide between the seats into the back, ready to help secure our captive.

The few seconds between when Alonso leaves and when he returns feel like an eternity. He literally pitches the struggling man into the cargo area. I catch him just as he lands on the metal floor and pull him into a sitting position as Alonso slides back in and yells, "Go!" The engine was already running and the transmission is in drive, the only thing holding the van back had been David's foot on the brake. He releases it and hits the accelerator at the same time. Alonso slams the door closed and we're away.

As David turns the corner and races for the safe house, Alonso pulls the roll of duct tape from the bag and rips off a strip. Wild eyed and still struggling, Kenison begins to speak in a language that I know neither of my friends will understand, but I do. He's a freaking witch, too. I scream at Alonso to hit him. Our only hope is that the punch will land before he can finish whatever incantation he's reciting. True to form, Alonso doesn't hesitate and lashes out with a right cross that could've killed a moose. Kenison slumps unconscious back against me.

Without turning, David asks, "We okay?"

"I think so."

I take a closer look at the unconscious witch to ensure he isn't dead and see his chest rise and fall. A large lump begins to form on the side of his face and is already turning purple. He'll be sore and have a hell of a bruise for a few weeks, but he's alive. I nod to Alonso and he winds a long strip of the tape around Kenison's head to gag him. Then he pulls a laundry bag over the unconscious office manager's head and secures the draw strings around his neck. Rummaging in the kit bag one last time, Alonso comes out with several zip ties to secure the hands and feet of our captive.

With Kenison finally secure, I relax a bit and lower him to the floor. I tell Alonso to watch him carefully and if it looks like he is regaining consciousness to knock him out again.

"Gladly," he growls with a hint of undisguised malice.

I warn him to go a little easier next time. Kenison still needs to answer some questions before we dispose of him. Alonso nods and I slip back into the front passenger seat, pulling the ski mask off as I go. David already has his off and drives sedately through the Atlanta morning traffic on our way back to the safe house as if nothing odd had happened.

As I settle in my seat, David looks over and asks, "Problem?"

"You might say that," I respond.

"What happened?"

I shake my head for a second, still having a hard time grasping the new information and answer his latest question, "He's a damn witch, too."

David drives in silence for a few minutes and I can see he is processing the information. I take the time to look in the back and ask Alonso if he's still out. "Like a baby," he replies happily.

We cross Ponce De Leon on our way to the far northeast of the city and David asks, "What does this mean

208 LA MISERIA di BIANCO

for us?"

"Well, it increases the difficulty exponentially."

"How so?"

I look over at him as I relate the problem, "To be able to answer our questions, he needs to be able to talk. If he can speak, he can recite an incantation and cast a spell that could kill us all. If we don't keep him unconscious, he could kill us and that means he's worth shit as a source of information. The best thing we can do now is kill him."

I hear Alonso from the back, "No problem, just say the word and I'll see if this bird can fly."

"Hold on, give me some time to think. There may be a way around this," David says.

"I don't see how. He's far more dangerous to us, even as a captive, than we are to him. When he wakes up, he's going to try and kill us," I respond, trying to get David to understand our predicament.

"I get that, but there has to be a way." After a few seconds, he asks, "How does it work? Do they have to speak the incantation or can they just think it?"

"It must be spoken," I answer.

David nods his understanding and then asks, "Out loud or can it be mumbled, like if he had a gag in his mouth?"

I can see where he is going with this and he might be right. There might be a way to do this after all. "It has to be spoken plainly in their ancient tongue. It's got something to do with the power of the words themselves. It's part of the way the power of the spell is generated. I don't understand all of it."

David nods and activates the turn signal indicating a left at the next intersection. The way to the safe house lay straight ahead so, not left. "Where are we going now?" I ask.

"Adult bookstore," is all he says as he makes the turn.

Momentarily speechless, I think *well, this trip has taken a bizarre turn.* Alonso sticks his face up between the seats. "Hey, I know a good one. It's up on Parsons, called the Lion's Den."

David smiles and says, "That's the one."

*****

It takes around twenty-five minutes for us to make the drive to Parsons Road in the north along the beltway that surrounds Atlanta. None of us speak during that time, all deep in our own thoughts. Mine are mostly of the trying to figure out why we were taking a side trip to an adult bookstore, but David has a plan in mind and I'm curious to see exactly what it will be.

I see the building coming up and David swings the van into the parking lot, pulling straight up to the door. The plain, concrete block building has a sign that proclaims 'The Lion's Den, for all your adult book, movie, and novelty item needs'. There aren't many cars in the parking lot at this time of the morning and we have our choice of parking spaces.

As soon as David stops the van, he pushes the shift lever into park and says, "Back in a minute." Then he jumps out and hurries through the door.

I look back at Alonso, hoping maybe he can shed some light on why we are sitting in an adult book store parking lot at nine-fifteen a.m. with a kidnapping victim—and witch—in the back of the van.

Alonso shrugs his shoulders, saying, "Hey, don't look at me. You're the one that found him. Personally, I've always thought he was a freak. Too quiet, too cerebral, those kinda guys are always kinky."

Before I can respond, the door opens and David walks out of the store. He has a small sack in one hand and I ask, "Find what you needed?"

"Yep," he replies as he sits down in the driver's seat. He tosses the bag into the back and says to Alonso, "Try that."

I watch Alonso open the bag and peer inside. After a second, he reaches in and pulls out a leather harness contraption with a big red ball attached to it. Holding it up so I can get a good look at it, he says, "Huh, a ball gag. Why didn't I think of that?"

David laughs, "Yeah, great place to pick up those last minute abduction supplies you might need. That should work as far as keeping him from being able to speak. We just have to work out a way now for him to be able to answer our questions and we're home free."

I'm impressed, and a little afraid to ask how he knows about such things. Alonso figures out how the thing works and pulls the hood off of the unconscious Kenison. Then he rips the tape from his mouth and fits the gag into place. It takes less than a minute before he has the hood back over the witch's head.

As soon as he finishes tying the bow knot with the draw string under Kenison's chin, Alonso throws both hands in the air yelling, "Done! A new ball gag world record."

He looks up at me with a silly grin on his face and it reminds me why I like him so much. No matter what happens or how much shit we're in, I can always count on Alonso. I'm well on my way to feeling the same about David, but Alonso and I have history. For two years, he's been the only friend I've had and that counts for a lot in my book.

Back on the road, it takes almost forty-five minutes to reach the safe house. David's portable police radio that has remained silent. It appears our abduction might have gone unnoticed because no calls had gone out and there had been no 'Be on the lookout' issued for our van. We are only a mile or so from the house, safe for the moment, and I feel a little more confident that we might pull this off. What I didn't think about was this is usually the time when the black helicopters show up and haul you off to someplace like Guantanamo Bay.

Our particular 'Black Helicopter' turns out to be a silver Ford Explorer. As David pulls into the drive way I hear him say, "Trouble!"

I whip around, trying to see why and ask, "What is it?"

He doesn't immediately respond. Instead, he pulls all the way forward and puts the van in park. I notice his right hand pull the pistol from the waistband of his jeans and point it toward the driver's window, low across his lap. His attention seems to be focused on his side mirror, so I lean over to get a look at what he sees.

A vehicle I've never seen before, a Ford SUV stops a

few yards behind us and the driver's door opens. A woman steps out and as she comes around the door and starts toward the van, I see she's wearing a badge clipped to her belt. She also has a gun holstered to her right hip and I know we are in real trouble.

"David, you can't…" I start to protest, but he looks at me and the expression on his face freezes the blood in my veins.

"I got this," is all he says.

Alonso starts to ask what's happening and I hold my hand up to silence him. Everything, all of our futures, depends on what happens in the next thirty seconds. If David shoots this lady cop, there will be no way for him or Alonso to come back from it. Their lives will be ruined and they will spend the rest of their time running or in prison, if they aren't dead. I'll be okay, I'm mostly invisible anyway and will be able to disappear like I've done so many times before, but it will be over for them.

This is as bad as it can get and my brain runs at warp speed trying to find a solution to our predicament, nothing comes to mind. I know David isn't a hothead and hope he has something up his sleeve other than simply shooting her when she steps up to the window. His expression tells me that he'd made a decision and I have no choice but to sit back and wait for the outcome.

The gravel crunches close by as she steps up to the van. David slides the Glock under his leg and rests his right hand in his lap to conceal the grip. I breathe a short sigh of relief that he doesn't intend to shoot her immediately.

I can't see her, but I hear her voice when she says, "Good morning. Could I see your license please?"

David leans out the window slightly and says, "Hi, Debbie." I should have realized that he probably knew her and would count on their cop to cop relationship to get us out of this. It's still too early to know for sure, but I think we might actually survive.

"David?" she asks in surprise and steps around to the window so I can see her. "What are you doing here?"

He has his left arm resting on the window frame and

uses his hand to point in my direction saying, "Just helping a friend move some stuff into his house." She looks over at me and I try to smile. Then David asks, "What are you doing here?"

"Drug complaint, some of the neighbors thought someone might be setting up a drug house and called it in. I took the call and happened to be doing a drive by when I saw the van pulling in the drive. Figured I'd find out who it was if nothing else."

He laughs, "Yeah, I can see how that might happen. House has been empty for a while. He just moved in and I'm sure his other friend's car didn't help." Alonso and I both know that he means the Lincoln. I can't see him, but I'm sure the big man is burning holes in the back of David's skull with his glare.

"Yeah, it's a little colorful for this neighborhood," she agrees with a soft chuckle. "Well, I'll get out of here and let you two get to it. Don't work too hard."

"Thanks, Debbie. There won't be much work, but we intend to drink a lot of beer doing it." They both laugh and she takes a step in the direction of her vehicle. I inhale for the first time in several minutes and think *thank God, we made it*. That's when all hell breaks loose.

Kenison picks that moment to regain consciousness and begin thrashing around in the back, his feet kicking against the metal floor and screaming around the gag in his mouth. My heart instantly drops as I hear a meaty smack and know Alonso hit him again. He stops thrashing, but the damage had already been done.

Debbie steps back saying, "What the hell?" As she leans into the window to see what had made all the noise, I see the gun in David's right hand come up.

He presses the muzzle just below her left ear. "Don't, Debbie. Please don't do it."

TWENTY-FOUR

Agent Deborah Anderson, Debbie, works for GBI, the Georgia Bureau of Investigation. She'd been in the office that morning for the first time in two weeks. Just coming back from a vacation where she spent her time camping, hiking, and mountain biking on the Appalachian Trail that ran along Tennessee Valley Divide in north Georgia, near Dahlonega.

Temporarily assigned to the DEA Drug Task Force, she was catching up on email and just trying to get back in the swing of things. As it happened that morning, all the other agents were out and she found herself alone in the office. That's when the call about a possible crack house on the northeast side of the city on Nathan Bedford Forrest Avenue came in. Debbie figured, *What the hell* and decided to drive by the place. It was better than sitting in the office alone and she could get outside for a little while. She really liked being outside. If nothing else, she'd be able to pinpoint the address and get a few pictures of the place.

Sitting in her vehicle in the parking lot of the US Federal Building in downtown Atlanta, Debbie checked the batteries in her camera then drove northeast on Ponce De Leon Boulevard. Weaving her way through the increasingly smaller streets, she finally made it to the street where the suspected drug house was located. Watching the mail boxes and looking for number 1503, she noticed white van in front of her slowing. As she passed 1501, the left turn signal on the van came on and she watched it pull into the drive of the house she wanted.

The overgrown yard and ratty little house, along with the several vehicles sitting in the drive—especially the bright purple Lincoln—told her the caller could have been right. This place definitely had the potential to be a new crack distribution house. Drugs were a constant problem for Atlanta. Latino gangs had moved in and made the city a distribution hub for cheap Mexican methamphetamine. The inner city had always had a problem with crack cocaine and there were always the good ol' boys that liked to grow their own marijuana. A new drug house in a neighborhood like this wouldn't surprise anyone.

She knew she shouldn't do it, procedure dictated that she should wait until she had a partner with her before approaching a suspected drug house, but it was such a beautiful morning and she felt especially good after just returning from her vacation.

I'll just check them out and get their names. Nothing dangerous, she thought as she reached for the hand microphone of her vehicle's radio. Debbie called in the plate for the van to dispatch and told them she would be out of her vehicle and gave the address. She pulled her portable radio out of the console and clipped it to the back of her belt as she stepped out of the vehicle.

Debbie approached the van carefully, staying behind the driver's window. She peeked inside to see if the driver had anything in his hands. She could tell the driver was male and skinny, but nothing else. She was able to see his left hand that rested on the window frame of his door. His right hand rested in his lap, but didn't appear to be holding anything.

When she asked for the man's driver's license, it surprised her when a familiar face poked out of the window and said, 'Hi.' She immediately recognized Detective David George of the Atlanta PD, she'd worked with him on a couple of cases. He'd always impressed her as being thorough and dedicated, a real professional at investigations. She knew he worked for the Homicide Division and wondered what he could be doing in a neighborhood like this.

He explained that he'd been helping a friend move. She looked at the young man sitting in the passenger seat and immediately liked his smile, he was cute. Everything made more sense now. The guy was young and probably just starting out on his own. A fixer upper like this was probably all he could afford. Detective George was just lending him a hand moving. Satisfied with the explanation, they said goodbye to each other. Just as she started back for her vehicle, a commotion began in the back of the van. She heard the thrashing around and a muffled scream.

Immediately on alert, she stepped back and made what she knew was a fatal mistake. She leaned into the window to see what had happened in the back of the windowless van. That's when she felt the muzzle of a gun pressed into her flesh.

Detective George said, "Don't, Debbie. Please don't do it."

Debbie knew she was about to die and several emotions flashed through her mind. The strongest of which was anger. Anger at herself for getting into this mess when she knew better and anger at the man she'd called friend, another cop.

Knowing there was no way for her to draw and fire her weapon before George could send a forty caliber bullet screaming through her brain, she decided she could stall him until maybe she'd get a chance. At the moment, she had no chance and she knew it. She raised both her hands high so George could see she had nothing in them and said, "Okay, David, I'll do what you say."

George kept the muzzle of his weapon pressed to against her and reached out the window with his left hand, sliding down until he touched her gun in its holster. Unsnapping the thumb break, he pulled a Glock, identical to his, out of her holster and pulled his arm back in the window.

"Reach down with your right hand and open the door. Slowly, so we all move together."

She did as he instructed and, with the gun still pressed to the base of her skull, she backed up as the door came open and George stepped out. Moving the gun long enough to close the door, George stepped around and Debbie took the chance to back up a step. George now had the gun pointed at her, instead of pressed against her and he said, "Stop, that's far enough."

Debbie stopped. Staring into the face of a man that until a few moments ago had always stayed on the right side of the law, she asked, "What now?"

*****

Of course I didn't know any of Debbie's part of the story at this point. I only knew that David stood outside the van holding another cop at gun point. I didn't find out what had led up to this very tense moment until much later that night. What I *do* know is that we need to get this circus inside. If the neighbors already thought we could be running a drug house, what would they think if they saw this?

I step out of the van and come around the front saying, "David, we need to get inside."

"Just a minute," he says, never taking his eyes off Debbie. An instant later, I hear the garble of a radio. Then I notice that she has a portable clipped to her belt behind her left hip.

The voice on the radio says, "954, I have the information on that van when you're ready."

"There it is," David smiles. "Go on, answer, slowly." The woman reaches back, unclips the radio and brings it up toward her mouth, David speaks, "Remember, I know the duress codes, so don't try to be clever."

She nods once, then speaks into the radio, "954 here, just hold onto it. Turned out to be nothing, I'm back in service." The voice on the radio acknowledges her and signs off.

"Good, now hand the radio to him," David directs her, indicating me. The woman holds the radio out to me and I take it. "Tony, go open the door." David motions to the woman to walk to the door and she slowly turns and walks toward me where I wait at the door. I step out of the way and she goes in, followed by David.

Once inside, he tells her to stand still and calls me into the kitchen. As soon as I step in, he says, "Search her."

I look at her and she turns her head so she can see me. This is the first time I've actually taken a good look at her. A very attractive woman in her late twenties, slim, and fit. Auburn hair, blue eyes, and a wholesome complexion that gives her a girl next door kind of look. She isn't wearing makeup and is dressed in a pair of dark gray slacks with sensible shoes and a light gray top. Her clothes, while not tight, do conform to her figure nicely and I can tell she doesn't have anything hidden underneath.

When I point this out to David, he looks a bit annoyed and says, "Humor me and do it anyway."

I step over to her and apologize, "I'm sorry for this."

She continues to stare at David saying, "Sure you are. Just get it over with." I move in behind her and start running my hands first across the top of her shoulders and down each arm, then her back. As I kneel behind her and prepare to slide my hands across her buttocks, she interrupts me with, "It's not that I don't like having a guy's hand's on my ass, I just don't want *your* hands on my ass. What you're looking for is taped to the underside of my belt." I glance around at David and he nods, so I stand up and move until I can unfasten the belt and slide it out of the loops. On the underside of the belt, covered with a piece of medical tape, I find a handcuff key.

I hold it up for David to see, a questioning look on my face. "In case we ever get our own cuffs used on us," he explains. I nod and he says, "Here," pitching a set of cuffs pulled from his back pocket. "Cuff her to the table."

I do as instructed, placing one bracelet on her right wrist and the other on a stainless steel cross support of the table. When I finish, I move a chair out so she can sit.

She had just sat down when Alonso steps in the door carrying Kenison. "Where do you want this?"

She reacts well for someone in her position. The only indication of surprise I can see are her eyes widening as she watches the four hundred pound black man carry an obviously unconscious white man with his hands and feet zip tied and a bag over his head into the house.

"Put him on one of the chairs and tape him to it good." David instructs. I move the chair out and Alonso unceremoniously drops him onto it. I hold him while Alonso runs loops of tape around his torso and the chair back. While we work on Kenison, David talks to the woman. "Debbie, please believe me, I didn't want this to happen and I'm going to try and explain everything if you'll just listen."

"I'm listening," Debbie replies calmly.

David takes a deep breath and I know how he feels. Trying to explain all of this to a normal person isn't the easiest thing to do. He looks at me for direction and I answer his unspoken question out loud, "Tell her all of it. If we have any chance of her believing us, it will be because we told her all of it."

He nods and begins. "The guy they're tying up is a witch and we've brought him here to get information about two other witches who've been killing people in Atlanta." He looks at her to see her reaction. It's about what I expected.

"Oh well, in that case, you can turn me loose and I'll just go about my way and you guys can just carry on then. I won't say a word, promise."

Alonso glances at her then back to me and says, "You know, I don't believe her." We need to get her to believe us soon. We can't keep her hostage forever and I sure as hell don't want to kill her.

David tries again, "Debbie, it's the truth. Tony there works for the Vatican destroying things like witches and demons and other nasty stuff. I've been helping him for about a week and you wouldn't believe the things I've seen. On top of that, Tony is immortal, can't die." I cringe when he says that, thinking I'd have probably waited before I dropped that on her. At least until she was halfway buying the other stuff.

She looks at me and I nod then she turns back to David and screams, "You are nuts! Certifiable! I swear, if you don't let me go this instant, I'll see that you go down for every violation I can dream up!" When none of us budge, she takes a deep calming breath. Then in a quieter voice, she says, "Look, you've obviously had a mental breakdown. It happens, but you have to let me go and turn yourselves in."

Alonso finishes taping Kenison and stands up, I step out from behind and stand a little apart between David and Alonso. David tries again, "Debbie, I swear I'm telling the truth."

She looks at him for a second and then starts to scream. We all jump at the volume as she recites, "Let me go!" over and over at the top of her lungs.

David looks at her with near panic in his eyes and I have no idea what to do at this point. He glances at me and then at the pistol in his right hand and then back at me. Before I can say anything, he raises it until the muzzle points squarely between my eyes. I know what is coming and have just a split second to think, *Oh, not in the face!* before he pulls the trigger.

*****

My eyes pop open and I become aware of an intense pain in my forehead right between my eyes. A corresponding pain makes itself known on the back of my head. I rub both spots with my hands as I sit up and say, "Ouch, son of a bitch that hurts." I look around and see three sets of eyes staring at me. I don't know how long I've been out, but long enough to heal from an entrance and exit wound made by a forty caliber round scrambling my brain.

I look at David and say, "That's the second time you've shot me." I struggle to get to my feet. Alonso helps me up. "Thanks, big guy." One thing is for sure, Debbie had quit screaming and she watched me now with disbelief in her eyes. I look around at all of them and ask, "What did I miss?"

David speaks first, "Sorry about that. Couldn't be helped. I had to do something to convince her we weren't nuts…"

"Yeah, but did you have to shoot me in the face?" I continue to rub the sore spots as I move over and sit down at the table.

He nods. "Yes. It's the only way to be sure she could tell you were really dead. If I shot you in the chest, she might have thought we were faking it and, technically, the first time I shot you wasn't my fault. Besides, this made less mess."

I look over where I had fallen and he is right. There is

only a small puddle of blood and when I check, I don't have any on my clothes. I look up at him, "Didn't ruin my shirt this time, but let's not do that again." I look over at Debbie to see how she is handling all this. "Well, do you still think we're nuts?"

"I saw him shoot you in the head. I watched you die." Debbie says in a daze. "You guys weren't kidding."

I smile at her, "No we weren't kidding. I know it's a little tough to deal with all this." I turn my chin in David's direction and continue, "He got introduced about the same way, except, it was a piece of two-by-four stuck in my gut that time."

David adds, "And a werewolf instead of a witch."

"True," I agree. Debbie turns back and forth between us, not sure if we're joking or being serious. I look back at David, "I think we can take the cuffs off her now." I look at her for confirmation that she isn't going to run screaming from the house and call every law enforcement entity she could think of.

"Yeah, I'll cooperate. I want to know what the hell is going on."

I look around at Alonso, who is standing beside Kenison's chair again and hasn't said a word since I came back. I can tell by the look on his face that he's angry. "What's wrong?"

David answers for him, "He's pissed about me shooting you."

"I'm okay, buddy," I tell him. "He had to do it. Only way to prove it to Debbie and get her to stop screaming."

"It's a good thing he had that gun is all I got to say," Alonso growls.

When I look back at David, he shrugs. "I had to hold the gun on him. I thought he would tear me apart after I shot you. I kept telling him you'd come back in a minute, but he wouldn't listen."

"Just don't turn your back Mister Police-man." Alonso turns and leaves the room.

David and I look at each other and he shakes his head. I say, "I'll talk to him, he'll be alright. Give him some time."

Debbie sits, rubbing her wrist where David removed the handcuff and he reaches behind his back and withdraws her service weapon from where he had it tucked in his belt. He lays it on the table and slides it across in front of her. They look at each other as he removes his hand and everyone knows this is a test to see what she'll do now that she is armed again. Her right hand comes over and rests on the grip for a second before she picks the weapon up. Holding it in her hand, she looks from one to the other of us and with a practiced movement, slides the gun back into its holster and snaps the thumb break. David and I both start breathing again.

"Okay, who's going to tell me what the hell is going on?" she asks.

"David, why don't you bring Debbie up to speed and I'll go talk to Alonso," I suggest and he nods his agreement. As David explains the situation to Agent Anderson, I go to find my big friend.

TWENTY-FIVE

It took everything I had to get the big guy to calm down. He was determined to cause severe bodily injury to the detective and he described it to me in graphic detail. In the end, it came down to him being concerned about me and he thought David should have shown a little more care in his choice of tactics to get Debbie onto our side. It took me pointing out that I didn't want to see him go to jail, which he surely would have if she had gotten her way. That calmed him somewhat.

He finally gave in and said he wouldn't break David's neck or anything else after I told him I agreed with the way the detective had handled the situation. Which isn't exactly true, but I'll never tell Alonso that.

I think David's conversation with Debbie went about the same way. She halfway believed him, but still harbored some serious doubts about all of our sanity. She knew deep down what she saw when David shot me wasn't fake and that there was definitely something different about me. She just wasn't sure what it was or if it qualified as immortality.

She wasn't convinced about the part of our story involving the unnatural creatures we'd been doing battle with. Debbie would have to see them before she passed judgement. She told him, "What you're saying isn't possible. If there are as many deaths and they're as prevalent as you say, there's no way we wouldn't know about them." Of course, she meant normal people when she said 'we.' Shaking her head, she finishes with, "Nothing can stay hidden that well for that long. Nothing."

I hear her comments from the kitchen where Alonso and I stand after our conversation. Not waiting for David to answer her, I say, "You'd be surprised."

They both turn to look at me. "I exist and you'd never heard about me and if David hadn't shown you *by shooting me in the face*," I say it loudly with a pointed stare at David, who shrugs apologetically, "you wouldn't have believed it. All that he's told you is true and the creatures do exist.

Those, and a lot more. David and Alonso have only scratched the surface when it comes to the unnatural. I've been doing this for a hundred and thirty-one years and they're out there hunting and killing every day. The question now is, will you keep our secret and let us get on with what we need to do?"

Debbie looks thoughtful for a moment and then after looking each of us in the eye, me last, says, "No."

My heart sinks. What would we do now? The only thing I can think of would be to keep her hostage somewhere until we finish this cleansing and then David, Alonso, and I will have to leave Atlanta. Their lives here would be over, no way around it.

Then she continues sternly, "I want in. I want to be a part of whatever you're doing. If I see it for myself, then I'll believe and keep the secret, besides I'm good in a fight. From the way it sounds, you guys have been getting your asses kicked lately and could use my help," she adds with a smirk.

David looks at me. "I don't think it's a good idea." I state. "The last woman who helped us ended up in two body bags."

"And I've been pushing it being away from the office so much, my boss is about to lose his mind over where I've been. How will you explain it?" David adds.

"You let me worry about that. If you don't let me come and play, I'll tell," she says the last part with a smile, but I know she really means it.

Alonso surprises all of us by saying, "Let her come along." We all turn and look at him with our mouths hanging open. "She's right. We haven't been doing that great. If she can help us kill these things and get back to a little normalcy, I'm all for it." He looks at me and I can tell he's serious, "I'm scared, Tony. The shit I helped you with before was spooky, but this has been bad. I think we need all the help we can get."

"Okay, big guy. If you think she can help us, I'll agree she can come along," I say, placing my hand on his shoulder. David nods in agreement and brief cloud of doubt passes in front of Debbie's eyes. She has to be thinking, *If that big guy is scared, what have I just volunteered for?* I smile because I felt the same way most of the time. "Welcome to the team, Agent Anderson."

I pause and then continue, "We need to get this place cleaned up. There are way too many vehicles parked outside and we're already attracting the attention of the neighbors—the gunshot doesn't help, either." I couldn't resist another jab at the detective. "Debbie, Alonso, why don't you two see what can be done about it. David, can you clean up the puddle of blood on the floor before someone slips and breaks their neck?"

They all start moving to their assigned tasks and I walk over to where Kenison sits. Conscious again, but still wearing the hood, I'd noticed him moving around as soon as I came back to the kitchen. Standing beside him I say, "Don't think I've forgotten about you, my friend. Very shortly, we are going to have a nice, long conversation." I untie the knotted draw string and pull the bag from over his head. He turns and looks up at me. I stare back into the eyes of one truly pissed off witch.

*****

"How are we going to do this?" I ask, frustrated. Debbie, David, and I sit in the living room of the small house discussing how we should proceed with the interrogation of Kenison. Alonso rests in the doorway of the kitchen so he can listen to us while keeping an eye on our captive. Kenison is still zip tied and taped to the cafe chair with the ball gag firmly in place.

After explaining the situation that if Kenison can speak he will be able to kill us with a spell, Debbie suggests we free one of his hands and let him write the answers to our questions. If he starts to write an incantation, we'll see it fast enough and can stop it. I don't know if the written words have power or not, but I don't want to risk it. So far, it's the best suggestion we have. We tried talking to him and even asked a few questions. The only response we received from the witch was for him to smile as best he could around the big red ball lodged in his mouth.

In short, we'd gotten nowhere. I consider letting Alonso work out some of his frustration on the guy, but Debbie won't allow it. I haven't told her yet exactly what eventually lay in store for Kenison. It's still a little early in our relationship for me and her to discuss cutting a person's heart out.

We'd been at this stalemate for over an hour and don't seem to be getting anywhere. I point out that he will never voluntarily give us anything and we have nothing with which to induce him. For the cops, it's much easier to get a suspect to talk. All they have to do is dangle freedom or a reduced sentence over their heads. Most bad guys jump at the opportunity. Some just want to get it all off their chest and confide in someone to lessen the guilt.

We have none of that with Kenison. He knows the score and he knows what I am. The only way he'll leave this house alive is if he manages to escape. To make him talk, pain will have to be applied.

I try pointing this out and while David and Alonso are in full agreement, Debbie is not. "I will walk out of here and go straight to the police if any of you start to torture that man!" I've begun to regret my decision to let her join us.

Then Alonso says, "Shame we don't have that little girl demon here. She'd make him talk right quick. Plus, Miss Human Rights there would be able to see for herself just what we been talking about."

I don't think Debbie likes the implication of Alonso's words, but I ignore her and think on what he said. I look at David and he looks back expectantly. I can tell he thinks it's a good idea. I'm not sure. I've dedicated my life to destroying all these monsters and now I'm considering actually bringing one into our world?

"Could we really do it?" David asks.

I nod slowly. "Theoretically, it's possible. I'm just not convinced we should."

"Why not? It would kill two birds with one stone," David tries.

226 LA MISERIA di BIANCO

"You haven't dealt with these things like I have. It never turns out good for the person who calls one of the beasts up. They usually get torn apart," I casually remind him. "Besides, I work for the Vatican. You know, the big Catholic Church in Rome. They'll probably be a little miffed if they find out that I summoned a demon."

"You'd have control, Pannier didn't and we'll be there to help in case anything does go wrong. Plus, you have something I bet she'll want more than you." When I look questioningly at him, he adds, "Kenison. Let her have him as payment for helping us."

He has something there. Bella does have a real hatred for the witches, she might consider him enough of a payment that she'll leave us alone. I can't believe I'm actually considering this. It goes against everything I've believed in since taking this job... Then the image of Mrs. Betty's skin held up in that stinking little witch's hand flashes into my mind and I teeter on the edge of a decision.

"What else you gonna do?" asks Alonso. I don't have an answer for that.

David can tell I'm about to fold, so he asks, "Could you do it? Do you know how?"

"There are some things I'd need, but yes, I know how."

David stands up and asks, "What do you need?"

"There's a book at my apartment that I need. The rest of it, I have here or we can make. The book is the big thing."

Excited now, David asks, "Where is it and what does it look like? I'll go get it while you get everything else ready."

"Old, leather bound, in the weapon cache at the back of my closet. It's the only book in there, you can't miss it. Take Debbie with you, none of us should be alone right now."

He nods and motions Debbie to follow him. Still unsure about what we're doing, she hesitates for a second before finally following him out of the house. I hear their vehicle start up and back out of the drive.

"You sure about this, big guy? I thought she scared you?"

"She does, but these freaking witches scare me more. Anyway, it's the quickest way for us to get what we need from this turd in here." Alonso points toward Kenison as he speaks.

"All right, we might as well get started. I'll need the bucket out of the cupboard over there."

"What's the bucket for?" my friend asks.

"Remember, the offering." When he looks confused, I say, "Remember what Pannier had you do in the bucket at Erin's house?" I can tell he does by the sour expression that comes over his face. "That was the offering that brought the demon up. That's why he made you do it."

"Why me? What does she like my flavor or something?"

I laugh and say, "I'll do it. I just asked you to get the bucket."

He turns and starts for the cupboard and says, "No, I'll do it." He comes back a minute later with the metal pail and stomps toward the back of the house and the bathroom saying, "Can't believe I gotta crap in a bucket again."

I walk into the kitchen and go to the cabinets. I glance at Kenison and he watches me with interest as I pull open a drawer and retrieve a small piece of sidewalk chalk that had been left by the previous owners. He continues to follow me with his eyes as I walk toward him and kneel about a foot away from his chair. As I draw a Thaumaturgic triangle on the vinyl floor, I look up at him. He isn't angry anymore. Now his eyes reflect sheer terror.

*****

It takes less than an hour for David and Debbie to make the round trip to my apartment and back. During that time, Alonso and I had the rest of the needed items gathered and ready. When David walks back through the kitchen door, the first face to greet him belongs to Kenison, who sits, eyes bulging, grunting around the gag, and struggling to get free of the tape that holds him to the chair.

I stand leaning against the counter watching him and as David hands me the book, he asks, "What's up with him?"

"I don't think he's as excited about what we're about to do as you are."

He turns and looks at the twisting and jerking man. "You had your chance, Ace. Now we do it our way." Kenison only struggles harder.

I notice Debbie for the first time as she stands just inside the doorway. I look from her to David and ask, "Any problems?"

David answers, "No."

I can see Debbie has something she wants to say and I already know what it will be. As she opens her mouth, I hold up a hand to stop her. "I know what you're going to say, so don't. You asked to be part of this and said you wanted to learn about what I do. I agreed—reluctantly. So you're part of it now, but I call the shots when it comes to the monsters. I don't arrest and there is no court that will hear this case. This ends with his death."

I point at Kenison for emphasis before continuing, "He knows it because he knows that I'm a Cleanser. And Cleansers cleanse the world of their vile taint, so if you intend to run to the police, go on and do it, don't threaten. Or you can help us and learn exactly what we're up against, the choice is yours. Either way, get on with it so I can do my job."

She looks back at me a little astonished at the strength of my words and after a few seconds says, "Okay, what you want me to do?"

"Stay beside David and Alonso and follow their lead. If anything goes wrong, I'll need the three of you to distract the demon until I can destroy it. Other than that, watch and learn."

She nods and moves over beside the two men at the far end of the small kitchen. David has his pistol out, checking it and she does the same. Alonso has one of the weapons taken from the cache I keep here. It's an Italian Navy cutlass blessed by Pope Pius IX many years ago that I'd applied a thin layer of Oleum Infirmorum to the blade, just in case.

I flip through the book until I find the page I wanted. The book was old even before it came into my possession. I took it from a man during a cleansing in New York City back in the 1920s. He'd been using it to call up one demon after another in an attempt to amass a personal fortune. He would never tell me how he came to possess it and showed no remorse about what he'd done. I cleansed him and took the book. By all rights, I should have sent it to the Vatican, but I didn't. I kept it and now I was about to do the very same thing that I'd killed him for.

The ritual itself is fairly simple, requiring very few ingredients and a spoken incantation. The most important aspects are the offering, grudgingly provided by Alonso, and the calling of the demon's name. I set the bucket in the center of the Thaumaturgic triangle and begin to add the other ingredients while I recite the words. At the appropriate spot, I speak the name Belphegor and strike a wooden match. It flares to life and I drop it into the bucket. As I had witnessed when Brunelle Pannier had summoned the demon, the match ignited the ingredients. After a brief flash, a pillar of black smoke rises from the bucket all the way to the ceiling. I hear a sharp intake of breath and look back to see Debbie standing in awe of what is happening.

I back up so I'll be out of arm's reach when Belphegor makes its appearance and watch as the pillar of smoke roils and solidifies into the form of the demon. Within seconds, the smoke disappears and in its place stands the eight foot tall, horned and clawed beast from Hell, slightly hunched because of the low ceiling. No sooner had Belphegor's form appeared than a shimmer over it sent the beast's image out of focus and Bella appears in its place.

There hasn't been much noise since I quit speaking. Just the hiss of the flame and a slight pop when the demon's form appeared. The room is eerily silent as Bella looks around, her gaze falling on each of us until finally coming to rest on the bound and gagged witch.

Looking back at me, her first words send a chill racing down my spine. "It's a good thing I'm hungry!"

I glance behind me at my three friends and notice that Debbie's mouth is hanging open and her eyes are wide with shock, but the other two are ready. I turn back to the demon, saying, "Bella, I called you here…"

"Yeah, yeah, I know what you want," she interrupts, looking down at Kenison. "Only one problem. I'm still under the control of my previous master and I suspect that's who you want to find. Am I right?"

"If it's the female witches that Alonso saw at the bar on Euclid, you're right," I answer.

"Hmm, decisions, decisions. What should I do," she says, standing with her hip cocked to the side with her arms crossed under her breasts and a perplexed expression on her face. I know she's just being dramatic. She'd already made her decision. After a moment she says, "Okay, I'll help you. It took a lot of balls for you to summon me. I'll make you a deal. I'll make our little witch here tell you everything he knows if you promise to do me a favor."

"What kind of favor?" I ask, knowing I won't like the answer no matter what it is.

She smiles as she says, "Oh, don't worry about that right now. You just promise to do me a favor sometime when I ask and I'll turn old James here into my own personal hand puppet." Turning serious, she asks, "Do I have your word?"

"Do I have a choice?"

"Sure, you have a choice. You can say no and I'll pop back to Hell lickety split. Of course, I'll have to be paid first."

I dread where this is going. "I intended to give you Kenison as payment."

"That will work if you take the deal, but if you don't…" she trails off, licking her lips as she glances around the kitchen. "Who I take will be my choice and the sweet little piece in gray looks simply delicious. Is she new?"

I glance at Debbie and am surprised to not see the frightened expression I expected, but an angry and determined one. Her stock just went up a couple of notches in value, so I turn back to the demon. "Bella, meet Debbie, she's new to the group, but I think you'll find her a bit tough and gristly. Probably wouldn't taste too good."

Bella laughs at my poor attempt at humor and then asks again, "Do we have a deal?"

"Yes, we have a deal," I acknowledge, already regretting it.

"Great! Then let's get to it, shall we?"

She turns back to Kenison, changing both of her hands back to the huge, scaly claws of her true form. She slips the razor-sharp nail of the index finger of her right hand under the tape and slices up, parting the tape like it is tissue paper. Next, she slips the nail under the harness holding the gag in place and parts the tough leather just as easily. Kenison spits the gag out and immediately starts to recite an incantation, which Bella silences by digging all five nails of her right hand into the flesh of his neck and shoulder.

The only sounds issuing from the witch's mouth now are screams as she raises him effortlessly to a standing position. With the index finger of her left hand, she uses the nail to quickly slice away the tailored suit coat and shirt, leaving him naked to the waist. His screams have died down to a pitiful mewling sound, but start up again in earnest as she draws intricate patterns on his chest and stomach with the same hooked and hideously sharp talon. It only takes a few seconds of this before he pleads with her to stop.

She raises the claw from his raw, bleeding flesh. "Will you tell them what they want to know?"

"Yes, yes, just please stop," he cries. She looks at me and, with her bloody claw, indicates I should ask my questions.

I take a single step forward and ask, "Do you know who's responsible for what's been happening to me?"

A little of his former arrogance returns as he answers, "Yes, but you aren't going to like it."

TWENTY-SIX

"What do you mean, I won't like it?"

"Because nearly every terrible thing that's ever happened to you is her doing," he says quietly, the pain making it difficult for him to concentrate. "She's followed you around since you became immortal, well almost, and she arranges for these little accidents. Influences events and the people around you so that anything you touch sours. Starting with your family."

I still at his words, remembering back to that day so long ago when my dreams of returning home had been dashed. "What does this have to do with them?"

"She killed them all and razed their home to the ground just to watch you in agony. She hates you and wants to see you suffer eternally," explains Kenison.

My mind whirls at his words. If true, it explains a great deal and as I think about it, anger floods my thoughts. My family was killed simply to torture me. Everyone that I'd ever cared about, every relationship destroyed, just to cause me pain. I have to end this. "Why? Who is she?"

"Lilith's mother," he states flatly.

It hits me like the bullet from David's gun. I reel and lean against the counter for support. My vision blurs and a throbbing begins behind my eyes. It isn't enough that I carry the guilt of killing Lilith. Her mother, obviously a witch, has been making my life hell for over one hundred and sixty years. It all makes sense now and all of the questions I had were answered by those two words.

I stay leaning against the counter for support, unable to speak. David picks up the interrogation and asks, "Where are they now?"

Kenison doesn't immediately answer and Bella digs her claws into his neck a little deeper, eliciting a groan from him. "At an estate northwest of Atlanta, about seventy miles," he gasps. "It's outside of Calhoun. The estate is called La Miseria di Bianco."

"What's it mean?" asks Debbie.

I speak before Kenison can. "The Misery of White." Kenison smiles at my obvious understanding of the Italian name and her intention in naming the estate after me and the game she played. "What's her name, Lillith's mother?"

"Rionach O'Gormely, she goes by Reena now," the doomed witch answers.

I nod my understanding and look at Bella. "He's all yours."

She smiles and just like with Pannier, she shoves her left arm down Kenison's throat up to her elbow before he has time to protest and with a heave, brings everything that had been inside the man, outside. A deflated James Kenison hangs from her right hand as again she swallows the entire steaming and stinking mass in one giant gulp.

Finished with her meal, she looks at me and says, "It's been fun, Tony. I look forward to our next meeting. Remember, you owe me a favor and I always collect." She glances at Debbie, "I hope to see you again also. Toodles." With a pop, she vanishes, taking what was left of Kenison with her.

"We needed more information, Tony!" yells David.

I haven't moved, don't want to move, but I reply softly, "We have all we need."

David throws his hands up in frustration and walks into the living room. Alonso remains silent, standing as still as a statue with the sword clutched in his hand as if he's afraid Bella might come back.

Debbie comes over to where I lean against the counter and quietly asks, "Tony, what do we need to do now?"

I shrug, but don't speak, lost in my own troubled thoughts. I wish uselessly that I could go back and change all of it. Debbie gives up trying to get an answer from me and leaves to join David in the front part of the house. Alonso comes over and places the cutlass on the counter.

I look up into his face as he says, "It's gonna be alright." He pats my shoulder and goes to the cupboard where I stored the cleaning supplies.

He pulls a mop and another bucket out and I pick up a towel from the sink. I wet it, then go to the demon door I'd drawn on the floor. Kneeling down, I use the sopping wet cloth to erase the triangle, closing the door forever. Alonso joins me and together we remove the last remnants of James Kenison. The more I clean, the better I feel. I guess simply moving, doing something, helps to take my mind off of what I'd just learned.

I hear Debbie ask about garbage bags, I point to the cabinet underneath the sink and go back to wiping the blood and other unrecognizable bits off the floor. As I go to the sink to rinse the bloody towel, David joins us. Together, we have the kitchen cleaned and straightened in only a few minutes. Alonso carries the large garbage bag to the curb while I carry the old spell book to my bedroom and temporarily hide it underneath the mattress. Feeling exhausted, I decide to lie down for a few minutes and instantly fall asleep.

My body lies in the small house I'd bought, but never used until now, while my mind wanders to all the places I've ever been.

*****

In my dream, I was once again in Rome with Lilith. In an instant, I stood on the rocky hillside of my family home searching for my lost parents, brothers, and sister. Next, in Austria, I stood and listened to Baroness Schaller as she laughed at one of my stories. Then an inn somewhere that I didn't quite recognize, but I was with Elspeth and I stood looking at her beauty as she reclined on our bed naked, a smile on her lips.

Dozens of others flashed across my memories until finally I sat on the porch of The Magnolia House with Mrs. Betty and listened as she told me to end this.

In her cigarette smoke coarsened voice, I heard her say, "You're a good boy, Tony, but you need to get off your ass and kill this bitch once and for all. Now, get your friends and get it done."

*****

My eyes pop open to the darkened room. I sit up to see that night had fallen. After visiting the bathroom to splash some water on my face, I walk into the living room where my three friends sit. They turn to look at me as I come in and without any preliminaries, I say, "We need to come up with a plan to attack La Miseria di Bianco."

As I sit down in one of the chairs scattered around the front room, Debbie smiles at me. It is the first time I've seen her really smile. I think to myself that she's very pretty in a fresh, country girl sort of way.

"I'm familiar with that area," she says. "Calhoun's about an hour and a half north, right off I-75. I love the area and have spent a lot of time up there."

"Good," I answer, "Do you know where this estate is?"

"No, but it shouldn't be too difficult to find. Calhoun's in Gordon County and its quite rural. Like every other small town in the South, everyone knows everyone else. Somebody will know where it is."

"Is Calhoun a very big place?"

"Not at all, I think the population in town is around fifteen thousand."

David asks, "Do you know any law enforcement up there?"

"I know where the Sheriff's office is. It's on North Wall Street. Runs right through the middle of town," she responds.

"That's good. We can find out where the estate is through the tax records or the 911 system. That should be our first stop."

"Will they tell us with no problems?" I inquire.

Debbie answers, "Sure, I'll flash my badge if I have to, but it shouldn't be a problem. Tax records are public information anyway."

David nods and adds, "Debbie and I will go in, that way it'll be cop to cop. We'll tell them we're working a case and the name of the place came up. Atlanta PD has a pretty good relationship with the agencies around the state." He pointed at Debbie, "And remember, she's a Fed. It won't be any trouble."

Alonso speaks for the first time since I'd come in the room, "I'm hungry."

I suddenly realize that none of us had eaten since early

this morning. Quite a bit had happened since I crawled out of bed at five-thirty. Including Debbie, we'd committed two kidnappings, summoned a demon, and interrogated a witch. Not to mention the fact that said witch was dead at the hands of the demon who I now owed a favor to and that my life is a complete wreck because of a vengeful witch. In short, it had been a hell of a day.

I ask Alonso if he wants me to fix dinner and he says, "I'd rather not eat at that table in there just yet. It's still a little soon after seeing Kenison's guts splashed all over it."

The other two not in agreement, so I say, "That's okay. We can make sandwiches and eat in here. That way, we can keep discussing our plans for tomorrow."

They all like the idea and we spend the next several minutes in the kitchen, each of us preparing our own meal. Conversation turns lighter and there is even some laughing and joking. Moving back into the living room, we take a few more minutes to eat before we get back down to the business of planning our trip north.

By the time we have a tentative plan ready, it had gotten late and we all decide to turn in. I bring some more bedding into the living room for Debbie. David gives the sofa up to her and he sleeps on the floor. She thanks me as I head back to my room. I wave and tell her no problem. Alonso has the door to his room shut and I can hear soft music coming from inside. I knock and after he answers, I open the door.

He's sitting on the edge of the bed, a bible in his hand. I ask him if he's ready for tomorrow and he says, "Absolutely, it's about time we put an end to this shit." I couldn't agree more. I bid him goodnight and go back to my bed.

Still feeling drained, even after the earlier nap, I fall asleep as soon as I crawl into bed. Once again, the faces of ghosts haunt me all night. When my alarm sounds at six a.m., I'm groggy and weak from an unrestful night. I know the others will be up soon, so I take a quick shower, dress, and go to the kitchen to start the coffee brewing. By six-thirty, everyone is awake and are either getting ready or are in the kitchen with me drinking coffee.

Alonso comes in and pours a large bowl of cereal and without thinking, sits at the table and starts eating. When I remind him of what he said the night before about the table, he looks at me for a second. "What the hell," he says and goes back to eating.

David catches the tail end of the conversation. Looking at me, he says, "I guess the old Alonso is back." I nod in agreement and look up in time to see Debbie come into the kitchen.

She'd changed clothes from the dress slacks and top of yesterday to a pair of cargo pants and T-shirt with hiking boots. The holstered Glock is back in its place on her right hip, but the clip-on badge isn't. When I ask about the clothes, she explains, "I always keep at least on spare set in the vehicle. You never know when you might need them."

As she steps past me to get a cup for coffee, I notice her hair smells really good, something tropical. When I ask, she tells me it belongs to Alonso and, turning to him, thanks him for letting her use it. His mouth full of sugar-frosted goodness, he raises his spoon in a salute and goes back to eating. Turning back to me, she laughs and I can't describe how wonderful it sounds. I spend the next few moments looking at her and think she's a very beautiful woman

While not as curvy as Erin had been, her trim body, wholesome face with just a few freckles scattered across the bridge of her nose, and bright blue eyes are striking. She has her long auburn hair pulled back in a simple ponytail instead of the knot she'd worn yesterday. Her whole appearance speaks of good health and outdoor living. She catches me staring at her and smiles back as she sips her coffee.

The moment passes and David interrupts, "We'd better get on the road."

We all agree and after a quick cleaning of dishes, we go out to the cars. It had been decided last night that we'd take Debbie's SUV and after loading several gear bags into the back, we pile inside. I ride in the front passenger seat, with

Alonso and David in the back. Debbie backs out of the drive and speeds toward the beltway. By seven-thirty, we are on I-75 driving north toward Calhoun.

*****

The hour and a half drive passes quickly and we reach Calhoun before I know it. Pleasant weather and the change in scenery from the urban sprawl of Atlanta to the rolling country side of northern Georgia helps to make me feel better. We kept the conversation light purposefully in order to relax a little before the real hard and dangerous work begins. Debbie takes the Calhoun exit off the interstate and I soon find myself on quiet, tree-lined streets with quaint shops in older buildings and clean, well-manicured lawns holding beautiful old southern homes. Calhoun, as Debbie said, really is a beautiful place.

Turning onto North Wall Street, we pull up to the Gordon County Sheriff's Office. After parking, David and Debbie step out of the SUV and go inside. Several newer model black and white police interceptors sit in the parking lot and by all appearances, the Sheriff's office must be well funded. Surprising for a town this size, I figure it must come from drug interdiction operations along the stretch of interstate that runs through Gordon County.

Our two cops return after a few minutes and climb back into the vehicle. Debbie turns to me and flashes a brilliant smile. "Piece of cake."

"Yeah, they didn't even ask who we were or why we wanted to know. Debbie asked if they had ever heard of La Miseria di Bianco and the lady behind the counter said, 'Sure,' and then gave us directions," David adds.

"It must be my winning smile," Debbie says, flashing an even more brilliant toothy smile. I have to agree, it did make my heart flutter looking at her.

Alonso brings me back to the present by asking, "So, where is it?"

Debbie answers as she back out onto the street and turns north, "Only about six or seven miles from here. We take Highway 136 up to Dobson Road and head over toward Baugh Mountain. I've been up there before, it's really beautiful."

We have to drive much slower on the narrow, winding roads leading toward the mountain, so it is close to eleven by the time we drive past the entrance to the estate. Easy to find, it turns north off of Dobson Road between two large, tree-covered hills. An asphalt drive passes through a stone archway with a wrought iron double gate and disappears into more trees as it follows a fast running stream. A stone block built into one leg of the archway has the name La Miseria di Bianco chiseled into its surface.

Debbie slows as we rolled past, but doesn't stop. The gate appears to be electronically controlled, but I don't want to announce our presence just yet. About a mile past the entrance, we find an old, overgrown logging road off to the left and Debbie steers the SUV onto it. David turns around so he can see out the back window as Debbie continues forward. She only has to drive about a hundred yards before David informs her he can no longer see the road.

She parks and shuts off the engine as we all climb out. There hadn't been any traffic on this old road in a long time and the vehicle should be okay until we return to it sometime tomorrow and after we have attacked the estate. Each of us grabs a gear bag and commences the process of pulling equipment and weapons out. Fifteen minutes later, we are prepared and after Debbie locks the SUV, we make our way back toward Dobson Road.

With very little traffic traveling the small country road, crossing to the north side undetected is a relatively easy task. We climb up into the hilly terrain surrounding the estate, giving ourselves plenty of time to find it. We keep conversation to a minimum not only because we're trying to be quiet, but also because the three men are using all our breath to keep us going on the steep wooded terrain. Debbie seems in her element and every time I look at her, she has a smile across her face and doesn't seem to be sweating or breathing hard.

After about an hour, we stop for a rest and water break. While Alonso, David and I lean against trees, swallowing water and trying to get our breathing under control, Debbie walks further up the hill until she vanishes in the trees. She's gone about ten minutes and I begin to get worried when I see her silently slipping back down the hill toward us.

When she gets closer, she puts a finger up to her lips to quiet us until she makes it back to our position. We gather around her and, in a voice just above a whisper, she explains, "The hill goes up about another three hundred yards or so and ends at a cliff. The cliff is about two hundred feet high with that stream we saw running along its base. Out beyond that is a flat meadow that looks to be around fifty, maybe sixty acres. The estate sits in the middle of the meadow."

"Is there good observation?" David asks.

"Yeah, all along the cliff face, there's plenty of concealment and an unobstructed view all the way to the house. And boy, let me tell you, it's some house. Three stories, has to have twenty or thirty rooms, it's huge."

"Did you see anyone around it?" I ask.

"Nope, it's quiet right now and I didn't see anyone moving around. No cars visible, but the back side of the house is a huge garage so they could all be parked inside."

"Okay," I say. "Debbie and I will go further up the hill to the left. Alonso, you and David watch from over on the right." Neither of them look pleased with my choice of his partner, but that is the reason I paired them together. "We observe until six a.m. tomorrow, just like we planned and then meet back here to finalize how we're going to attack them."

Everyone acknowledges their assignments and we pick up our gear so we can move off to find locations to observe from. We have radios to stay in touch, so if either team gets into any trouble, they can call the other for help. It will be a long night and I'm glad I'll be spending it with Debbie. Not that Alonso or David aren't good company, I just want to get to know her a little better.

So much for not chasing skirts for a few hundred years...

TWENTY-SEVEN

I ease forward underneath the low hanging boughs of a pine tree until I reach the edge of the cliff overlooking the meadow. Another half-step and I would be exposed for anybody down there to see. A full step and I would splash into the shallow, rushing stream two hundred feet below. The low hanging branches and several large rocks right at the cliff edge make this a perfect spot from which to observe the comings and goings of La Miseria di Bianco and its residents.

I look down at the large, three-story mansion. Calling it a mansion is like calling a Ferrari a car. La Miseria di Bianco had been built from huge granite blocks at least two feet thick. The roof is slate tile and the copper gutters and roof reflect the rays of the dying afternoon sun. A round tower built on one end gives the place a medieval look and more closely resembles a castle in Bavaria than a southern plantation estate.

Debbie kneels a few paces behind me after directing me to the observation point. I kneel and glance back at her, giving her thumbs up to indicate I can see the estate and am ready to take my turn at watch. As the afternoon wears on into evening, the sun begins its slow slide to the west and as our observation point faces to the east, long shadows are beginning to grow along the meadow. It won't be long until the small valley becomes completely obscured by the dark.

David equipped us well. In addition to our portable radios and binoculars, Debbie and I also have a night vision device that amplifies the ambient light given off by the stars and moon. Commonly called a Starlight scope, we can sit on the top of the cliff and watch the goings on below just as well on the darkest night as we could in daylight. The only thing that takes a little getting used to is everything that shows up in the lens has a pale green tint to it. It won't be long before we will need the device and Debbie sits back away from the cliff about fifty feet and works on getting it ready to use.

We've already been here several hours and have seen no movement at all coming from the house or any of the many outbuildings scattered around the estate. We still have no idea if anyone is at home or not. If we can't verify by morning that our targets are there, we will have to call off the attack and come back another time.

We'd brought only a limited amount of supplies and can't stay here indefinitely. Besides, someone is bound to find Debbie's vehicle eventually. When they do, the police would most likely be called and then word would go out about a missing GBI agent and the woods would be crawling with cops and rescue personnel. That would end any chance we have of sneaking into the estate and catching Reena and the other witch by surprise.

As I watch, I silently will something to happen, someone to move down there so we can at least verify the place is inhabited. I can only imagine that the same thoughts are passing through the minds of the other three that are sitting watch with me.

Time creep by and I can't help but be amazed as the sky turned first an orange then to purple before becoming the black of night. You never see sunsets like this in the city. Most usually, you weren't even aware of the transition between night and day. It would be daylight one minute and the next time you looked, it would be dark. This was the first time I'd enjoyed a sunset in a very long time.

As soon as the cliff face and valley are covered by the darkness, Debbie moves up to where I'm watching the mansion. It will be impossible for any human below to see us now, so I had no fear that her presence would compromise us. Besides, I enjoyed her company, that's why I chose to be with her.

She kneels first, then twists her legs around until she sits cross-legged beside me. Looking over at me, she whispers, "Anything?"

I shake my head and then realize that she probably can't see me, so I whisper, "No." After a few seconds, I lean toward her. "It's really beautiful up here."

Even in the dark, I can see her smile as she leans into me and whispers back, "I know, that's why I love coming up here so much. I've rented cabins up on Baugh Mountain for years and you can't beat the views."

I raise the Starlight scope to my eyes and pan it across the valley floor, hoping for movement and seeing none. As I lower the scope back to my lap, I ask, "Do you come up here by yourself or is there someone?"

Again, she graces me with her smile and answers, "I usually come by myself or with a girlfriend and to answer your other question, no, there isn't anyone special." I nod again, more to myself than to her.

I lean toward her again and as I open my mouth, I hear a quiet rustle of leaves. An instant later, I notice for the first time that the night insects had suddenly gone quiet. My senses go on high alert and I freeze trying to hear anything that might be out there. Debbie sees the look on my face and stills. After a few seconds, she silently mouths, "What is it?"

I shake my head that I don't know and just as I prepare to tell her I'd heard a noise, I hear it again. This time it sounds like it came from an elevated position, maybe up in one of the trees surrounding us. I quickly turn to face in the direction I thought the sound came from. The light evening wind washes against my face and brings the telltale scent that I'd feared. The ammonia and copper scent of bloody urine. Somewhere out in the woods, a vampire is stalking us.

I snatch my crossbow off the ground where I'd laid it and bring it up to my shoulder. I hear Debbie quietly ask, "What do you hear?"

Without turning, I say, "Vampire, at least one, maybe more. They're in the trees."

I hear a sharp intake of breath and the sound of her pistol sliding out of its holster. Another slight rustle sounds to my left and as I swing the crossbow in that direction, I see a fleeting image of a pale creature as it drops silently onto the carpet of leaves a few feet from Debbie.

I shout, "Debbie, behind you," and let fly one of my

remaining arrows. As I pull the trigger, something strikes the crossbow, knocking it up and the arrow flies harmlessly out into the trees. Before I have time to react, I'm struck in the chest hard and stumble backward.

I put my foot down behind me in order to regain my balance, but instead of the firmness of solid ground that I expected, I step onto nothing but air. My body continues its backward motion and I curse as I realize what is going to happen. Standing so close to the cliff edge when I stepped back, I step completely off and fall two hundred feet to the rock-strewn stream below. I feel the splash as I hit the water and then a sharp impact to the back of my skull as it hits one of the numerous rocks, then blackness envelops me.

*****

My eyes pop open and I awake in panic calling Debbie's name. Only then do I feel the pain in my head. Gingerly feeling of the back of my skull, I find the hair is still matted with blood and the skin tender. A painful ache pounds behind my eyes and I have trouble focusing. It takes three attempts before I finally make it into a sitting position and can look around at my surroundings.

I'm sitting on a cold concrete floor in a windowless room. The lights aren't on, so I can't tell very much about the size or construction, but my instincts tell me the room isn't large. The headache has begun to ease a bit and I attempt to stand. It only takes two tries before I raise myself to my full height, so I'm improving. Holding my hands out in front of me, I take a few steps to my right until I make contact with the wall. Same construction as the floor. I slide my hands along the wall until I come to a corner and proceed to trace the outline of the room.

In the third wall I inspect I come to a door, metal with no knob or fixtures of any kind on my side and it becomes apparent that I'm in some kind of cell. I still have one wall to inspect and I move beyond the door, looking for the next corner. Finding it, I move my hands along the uninspected wall, looking for anything that might give an indication of where I am. I assume this is part of the estate, either the basement or one of the numerous outbuildings Debbie and I had observed. That I'm a prisoner of Reena's is also a safe assumption. I guess we haven't been as sneaky as I hoped.

I'd taken maybe four or five short, shuffling steps when my foot comes in contact with something on the floor. I know right away that it is a body and as I kneel down, I think *Please don't let her be dead or worse.* I bring my hands down and feel my fingers touch soft hair. It still smells of the shampoo she'd used and I confirm it is Debbie... I quickly move to her neck and checked for a pulse. She has a strong one so at least she still lives. With my hands still at her neck, I check for any wounds that might indicate she'd been bitten during our capture.

I find nothing and proceed down her body, searching for any injuries. Even with the dire situation, the feel of her warm, firm flesh beneath her clothes begins to arouse me. Forcing my mind back to trying to determine if she is hurt, I run my hands along her legs and find no injuries. Moving back to her head, my fingertips probe at her scalp until, just below her right ear, toward the back I find a lump. It's about the size of a goose egg and puffed up, indicating that she had either fallen or been struck.

Debbie will have a headache when she finally wakes up, but she'll be okay otherwise. Sliding my hands underneath her arms, I raise her into a sitting position and lean her back against the wall. After insuring she won't fall over, I sit down next to her and pull her toward me. The dampness and heat-sapping nature of the concrete room has begun to make me feel chilled. I feel sure she will be cold when she regains consciousness, so I wrap my arms around her and pull her close so we can share our warmth.

Her head rests on my chest and I lean forward to smell her hair. Now the smell of dirt and dried leaves covers the tropical smell I noticed this morning, but it still lingers. I lean my head back against the cold concrete and surprisingly, fall asleep.

I couldn't have been out for more than a few seconds when Debbie regains consciousness. As I start to wake up,

I hear a groan and then a shriek and she starts fighting, trying to get away from me. Instead of trying to hold onto her, I let go and she scrambles back away from me. I call her name and after a few seconds, she says, "Tony?"

"It's me. Are you okay?"

"I thought you were one of those things," she whispers, her voice shaky.

"We're by ourselves," I assure her. She slowly crawls back over to where I sit and snuggles back up to my side.

"Sorry about that."

"Not a problem, I have women run screaming from me all the time. I'm used to it," I say lightly.

She laughs quietly. "Would you put your arm back around me?"

I raise my arm and Debbie curls up against my side. Once she is comfortable, I ask, "Do you remember anything about being taken?"

"Yes," she pauses for a second before continuing, "I saw you go over the edge of the cliff and then one of those things grabbed me. They're so damn fast. I don't remember much until we got to the house. There was another of them carrying you and they stopped outside a door in the side of the house." She stops talking for a moment and then, "I saw her, the woman you told me about, Reena. She came out of the door and spoke to the things carrying us and then she went over to you. She raised your head and I could see a lot of blood, you looked dead."

"It's okay, it happens a lot," I mutter, trying not to remember just how many times I'd died in the past two weeks alone.

"She came over to me and looked at me for a long time and then motioned to one of the creatures. Then something hit me and I don't remember anything until I woke up here with you."

"Debbie, we need to talk about what's going to happen next." I feel her head nod in the darkness and snuggles tighter against me. I hate to spoil the moment, but she needs to know. "Reena will come for me eventually. She won't be able to resist torturing me, it's her nature. I don't have any idea what she has planned, but whatever it is, it won't be good. If I had to guess, she will probably make one of the vampires turn you and then have you feed on me." I feel her shiver when I say this and I go on, "Once you're bitten, there is no coming back, so you need to think about what that means."

After a couple of minutes she asks, "Do I need to kill myself?"

That question tears at my heart. She's here because of me and now she will die because of me. This horrible game that Reena is playing with me is going to claim another life and it will be my fault. The more I think about it, the angrier I become.

That's when I say, "No, we are going to destroy every one of these stinking monsters and I'm going to get you out of here." The door opens, interrupting us.

Weak light floods the room and after the near total darkness, Debbie and I are momentarily blinded. As my eyes adjust, I look around the cell, seeing it is in fact as I had pictured it in my mind. We're in an empty concrete box, about ten by ten feet. As of yet, no one has appeared in the door. I start to stand up when a female voice says, "Bring them upstairs."

Two vampires, pale and stooped with large red rimmed eyes, enter through the door. Debbie scrambles backward in an attempt to get away from them, but I know it is useless. Where can we go? I have no weapons and I have plenty of experience to know that I can't hope to win against two of the beasts unarmed. I stand as one comes to me and gently takes me by an arm, guiding me toward the door. I pause out in a wide hall with other doors similar to ours along one wall and watch as the other vampire carries a kicking and swearing Debbie out of the cell.

"Calm down, there's no way to win here, but keep your eyes open for an opportunity," I tell her, afraid she'll get hurt.

I have no fear of speaking in front of Reena's creatures, it would be stupid to think that we won't attempt to escape and it serves to calm Debbie. That will keep her from getting hurt by an overzealous vampire ensuring she doesn't get away. She relaxes and the rest of the trip down the hall and up a long flight of stairs and then down another long, dimly lighted corridor goes with no trouble.

The two vampires deliver us to a large, ornately carved double wooden door. I can see light seeping around and between the two large wooden slabs, but nothing else. The creature that escorted me steps forward and knocks. The right hand door slowly opens and I become even more surprised when I see a very large and shaggy werewolf. The two vampires shove Debbie and I into the room, but don't follow.

As I look around, I know why. There are several large floor to ceiling windows in the room and sometime during our imprisonment, the sun had risen. Bright sunlight streams into the room and bathes it in a golden glow. The room itself is impressive. Deep, rich wood paneling covers the walls and a solid oak floor with a finish so deep it appears you can sink into it is below our feet. A large stone fireplace fills one wall and several chairs sit in a cozy arc in front of the hearth. There isn't a fire in the fireplace, but I do notice wood piled in it and a large cauldron hangs from a hinged bracket at one side. Typical.

A female voice calls from one of the chairs, "Otto, bring our guests over and have them take a seat."

A werewolf, Otto I assume, indicates with his hand that we should precede him and we walk toward the chairs. As we get closer, Otto steers us to one end of the arc and, as I take my seat, I see a woman sitting in the end chair of the other side of the arc.

She appears to be a well-kept forty year old woman who is very well dressed in a tailored pant suit and handmade heels. I can't see any jewelry, but she doesn't need it to be striking. Long, dark red hair frames one of the most classically beautiful faces I've ever seen. High cheek bones and a narrow nose above full, if a little pouty, lips, but it's the eyes that hold my attention. Those same poison-green eyes that her daughter Lilith and, now I realize her daughter Erin, had. I suspect that if I could get a second look at the little bitch that stabbed me at my apartment, I'd find that she is a daughter as well.

Debbie takes the chair next to me and once I'm comfortable, I say, "Hello Rionach." pronouncing her original Gaelic name.

She smiles and says, "I prefer Reena now. The name Rionach O'Gormely has no meaning any longer."

"Very well, Reena. I know this isn't a social call, so why don't you get on with whatever it is you've brought us here for."

The smile vanishes and she speaks, "There's no need to be rude. I've waited a long time to have you in front of me like this and I intend to savor every moment of it… but if you want to get down to business, I'll oblige. You are responsible for the death of my first born and I want revenge. The things I've done to you in the past were simply a warm up for what I have planned for your very long future." The smile returns as she delivers the last part.

I sigh, preparing myself for just how bad this day is going to get. "Yeah, I killed Lilith. I'm also responsible for Erin's death as well. Oh, and I watched your idiot son, Brunelle, die. Though I can't claim credit for him. I seem to remember there's another daughter, though I don't know her name. I owe her a little something and look forward to our next meeting." I end with a grin of my own, relishing in the fact that I had, with a bit of help, nearly wiped out this wicked witch's entire family.

I notice a slight twitch begin at one corner of her mouth. She maintains her composure, but I can tell I'd gotten to her. After a few seconds, she says, "As you seem to know my family so well, I'm going to tell you our story. It might add to the pain I intend to inflict on you later and that will bring me great pleasure."

I figure the longer she talks, the longer I can keep Debbie alive and look for a way out of this hell, so I nod and she commences.

"I was born in 1815 in Ireland to a very rich and powerful family, the O'Gormelys. We had Royalty in our ancestry and I grew up privileged. My mother was a witch, but she went to great pains to hide the fact. Of course, it would have meant her death if it had been known."

"Too bad it hadn't," I mutter without thinking, earning me an evil glare.

"I found out at an early age that I too had been born a witch and my mother took it upon herself to train me and to teach me discretion. I learned everything, but the discretion. Several rather spectacular and public displays in my early teens convinced all the locals that I was a witch in need of a good burning. Luckily for me, my father loved me despite what I was and packed the entire family off to Italy in 1829."

I let her drone on about the old family history, but my thoughts are elsewhere. One thing jumps out at me, Alonso and David. She hasn't said a word about them. Are they still out there? If they are, do they know what happened to Debbie and me? Both excellent questions and if they are out there, they had to know by now something had happened. What will they do about it? My hopes go up a notch because I know Alonso won't leave me here without trying to rescue me.

TWENTY-EIGHT

Debbie and I sit in the large, well-appointed room in the estate known as La Miseria di Bianco and listen as Reena tells her entire family history. That's the problem with immortals, no time management skills. As boring and uninteresting as her story has proven to be, it's giving me a chance to look for a way out of our predicament. Debbie sits in a chair beside me, pretending interest, but I know her thoughts were the same as mine.

"I gave birth to Lilith in 1833 when I was eighteen, but my parents wouldn't hear of me marrying a baker or keeping a child out of marriage. So the father took the child and I went back to see her when she turned thirteen." She referred to Alberto as the child's father, I bet she didn't even remember his name. "I taught her about her powers and visited her occasionally to see how she was coming along. The last time I saw her was shortly after you came to work for her father. She told me she loved you and wanted the two of you to be together forever, so I taught her the immortality potion. I told her to be careful with you, that you were no good. Of course, you proved me right by killing her."

Reena pauses and I take the opportunity to ask, "If you thought I was no good, why did you teach her how to make me immortal?"

She seems reluctant to answer at first, but finally she does. "Like me, she was a headstrong girl and determined to have you. To make sure you behaved, I also taught her several controlling spells that would have kept you tame, faithful, and obedient. Pity she wasn't able to use them before you murdered her," Reena snaps.

"For what it's worth, I didn't want to kill her. It just happened." I don't add that it had almost cost me my sanity and that I still felt guilty because of it. That admission might have given her too much pleasure.

"Your words are worth nothing to me, bastard. You killed my first child and I've sworn you will pay until the end of your days," she snarls in response.

"Even though it has cost you two other children?" I ask incredulously. "I'm sure they would love to have heard Mommy Dearest say that. That they were only good to sacrifice so you could get what you wanted."

Her voice rises to just below a scream as she spits, "They were not sacrificed! They were victims, just like Lilith! Victims of you!"

"Well, they wouldn't have been victims if it hadn't been for this insane vendetta of yours," I reply calmly. "Following me around for more than a century and half? I'd say that qualifies as insane. How did you know how to find me? I mean, you weren't hot on my trail or anything or else I would've seen you."

Her breathing slows as she calms down. After a minute or so, she answers, "I always know where you are. I'm connected to you by blood. No matter where you go I can follow."

Curious now, I ask, "By blood? What do you mean?"

She laughs and takes great enjoyment in her answer, "I have your blood and with a drop and a little spell, I can see you anywhere in the world and know right where you are. Lilith took a jar of it when you slept. I told her to take if it for the other spells that she would have used on you, if she'd gotten the chance. After her death, I recovered the jar and used it to track you everywhere you've been."

So that's how she knew where and who I'd been with. I should've known it would be witch magic, but I don't know what I could have done about it, short of killing her, which I now plan to do at my earliest convenience. "How did you know we were here or did your pets just happen on us?"

I'm not sure she'll answer that one, but after a slight pause she says, "I knew you were coming and simply had Otto watch for you." I glance over to where the hulking werewolf stands. "He has very good eyesight and saw you with no trouble at all. You probably don't remember it, but you met his brother once. You were with a young trollop in some little village in Germany. She killed Hans."

I know immediately she meant Elspeth and the encounter that changed my life forever because it led to my becoming a Cleanser. I turn to look at the werewolf again and this time, I can see the hatred in his yellow eyes. The menace is clear, if Reena allowed it, he would tear me to pieces. As I watch, his long tongue comes out and licks the side of his muzzle, the implication plain. He looks forward to eating me.

Reena speaks again and I turn back to her. "Since you brought up my other children, how did Brunelle and Erin die?"

As I explain how Brunelle Pannier had met his fate at the hands of the demon Belphegor, I see something through one of the large windows looking out over the front lawn of the estate that raises my spirits considerably. A black and white police car drives slowly down the long drive toward the mansion. I don't have a clear view of it, but it is obviously the police or Sheriff. I nudge Debbie and I sense her look to in the same direction. I know she saw it because she abruptly straightens in her chair.

I hope the move had gone unnoticed by our hostess, but I can hardly keep a smile from spreading across my face. The cavalry is about to arrive and I know I have my two friends, Alonso and David, to thank for it.

*****

"...and buried her in the backyard," I finish recounting the details of Brunelle and Erin's demise to their mother. I'd watched the black and white disappear past the window and now sit trembling with anticipation, waiting for the attack to commence. It has been several minutes since the police car had arrived and there still isn't a sign anybody knows. It further surprises me that Reena hadn't shown any emotion at the details of her children's deaths.

I keep thinking, *Something has to happen soon*, and I am a little shocked when it finally does. We sit looking at each other, deep in our own thoughts when the doorbell rings. Not at all what I expected. Reena looks to the werewolf, "Otto, we have another guest. Will you go see who it is, please?"

The shaggy beast turns without a word and leaves the room. Again, I anticipate a burst of gun fire or at the very least some shouting as they join in battle, but I hear nothing. I do become a little concerned when I glance at Reena and she is watching me with a smile on her face. That smile causes my confidence to slip some, but what happens next totally destroys it.

The same doors we entered through open and I watch as a man in a dark brown uniform, complete with pistol belt and badge comes into the room, followed by the werewolf. He doesn't seem the least bit concerned about the creature two paces behind him and Otto isn't dragging or pushing the man. No one seems to be concerned and that scares the crap out of me.

As the uniformed man steps around to face Reena, she says, "Ah, Sheriff Richards, so nice of you to drop by. Is this a social call or do we have business?"

As the Sheriff responds, my optimism vanishes, "Business, Mrs. Reena, I just wanted to make sure you'd found the two folks that came to my office looking for your place."

She turns from Richards to look in our direction and with her hand held out toward us, said, "There they sit Sheriff, safe as little bugs."

Richards looks first at Debbie, then at me, lingering on me for what seems a long time. He then turns back to Reena and says, "I don't understand. Are you saying there were three of them?"

It is Reena's turn to look confused as she asks, "What do you mean? You told me there were two of them, a man and a woman. There they are, a man and a woman."

Richards looks a little frightened as he answers, "Yes, ma'am, I can see that, but that's not the man I saw. It's the woman for sure. I'd remember her anywhere, but it ain't the guy."

"What do you mean, it isn't the man? You'd better be sure or do I have to remind you what happened to your predecessor?" Reena asks, agitated now.

"No, ma'am. You don't, and I mean it. That's not the

guy that came to my office asking about you. There must be another one out there."

Reena looks at me with rage glowing in her eyes and I have to smile at her discomfort. "Otto, find him and bring his head to me!" she snarls.

I can't help it, this is too funny, so I say, "Yeah, Otto, go on, run out there and see what happens to you. Better get ready for the reunion with your dearly departed brother because it's right around the corner." I laugh, unable to control myself anymore.

My laughter only infuriates Reena more and she screams, "Otto, get out there and find him and take this idiot with you," indicating Sheriff Richards, who doesn't look at all happy about going outside or the idiot comment.

Once again, I can't resist poking the hornets' nest just a little. "Run along, Sheriff. Do as your mistress tells you. She doesn't care if you get killed. Look how she sacrificed her own children."

"Shut up!" Reena screams. Her face is a blotchy red mask as she loses all control. She turns back to the sheriff and the werewolf. "Get out now or I will destroy you both! Find him and kill him, NOW!" The wolf and Richards slink like beaten dogs from the room. Debbie and I both begin to laugh at Reena's discomfort.

It doesn't take Debbie long to figure out that when a witch is in control, they're one of the most diabolical creatures on the face of the Earth. But when they sense they're losing control, they react poorly and that only makes the situation worse. It is laughable watching this woman who was so self-assured a few moments ago slip completely over the edge because of a little hiccup in her plan. Debbie starts laughing and not a little quiet laugh, but a side splitting laugh from her gut.

More and more, the rage grows inside Reena. I can see in her eyes that it won't be long before she reacts to Debbie's insult and I know that reaction will mean death to Debbie. My eyes roam around the room, frantically searching for anything I can use as a weapon. I know there won't be anything like a ward or blessed item that would be fatal to a witch. Not in this house, but maybe there is something that I can injure Reena with long enough to destroy her.

As I search, my eyes keep coming back to the cauldron hanging beside the fireplace. A long leap will bring it into my reach and the cast iron will definitely do some damage if I can swing it and connect with her head. Debbie keeps laughing and Reena continues to become enraged. I slowly, and hopefully without being detected, slide forward to the edge of my chair and gather my legs underneath me in order to spring for the cauldron once I see that Reena's focus was solely on Debbie.

That's when I hear my old Browning double barrel speak just outside on the lawn. I had given it to Alonso, so I know he is close. Its thunderous double boom is quickly followed by the almost as loud single barrel pump that I'm sure belongs to David. The battle I'd hoped for had begun.

*****

I listen to the sounds of the battle raging outside and can now hear the lighter, almost laughable pops of an automatic pistol. The shotguns continue to blast away and over all of the noise, I hear the enraged howls of the werewolf. I'd given David and Alonso the last of my silver double aught and I'm sure they are using them to good effect. I worry there won't be enough.

A shotgun blast sounds again and then a scream, human not werewolf and I know that someone has connected with a shot. I can only guess that the person shot was Sheriff Richards. In the time it takes me to think these thoughts, I hear several rounds fired from the lighter caliber pistol, one of which whizzes through the plate glass of the window directly behind Reena, shattering it. Pieces of glass tinkle to the floor and a solid whack sounds as the errant round buries itself into the wood paneling across the room.

My prayers are answered as Reena turns to look at the window. I shoot to my feet and lunge for the hanging cauldron. As my hand grasps the bail and lifts it from the hook on which it hangs, Reena turns back toward us.

Seeing me and realizing my intent, she jumps to her feet and speaks in that ancient language known only to the witches. I step toward her as I bring the cauldron behind me, preparing to swing it with all my might into her demented face and, with a little luck, disabling her until I can cleanse her.

As my arm comes up into the swing and the cauldron reaches about the level of my head, a vicious pain grabs me in the chest. It feels as if my heart is being squeezed in a molten fist. So intense is the pain that I immediately stumble and my arm holding the cauldron drops as my left hand comes up to grip my chest, searching for relief. I know Reena is responsible and that if something doesn't happen quickly, she'll kill me. If I die now, Debbie is as good as dead. I look toward where she's sitting and she sees the pain reflected in my face.

Acting on instinct, she jumps to her feet and picks up the sturdy Victorian chair she'd been sitting in, and hurls it at Reena. The weight of the chair and her relatively small stature don't allow her to put much power behind the throw, but it does save me. The chair hits the floor in front of Reena and manages to carry enough force that it slides the rest of the way into her, striking her in the knees. The impact send her reeling backward, the spell momentarily forgotten. As her legs come into contact with the chair she'd been sitting in, it serves to trip her and she sits back down with such force that the momentum carries the chair over onto its back.

If this hadn't been a life and death struggle, I might laugh. There she lay, flat on her back, both feet sticking up in the air, struggling like a turtle on its back trying to right itself. Recovering somewhat from her attempt to kill me, I move forward with all the speed I can muster until I stand beside her. Reena looks up at me and as I bring the cauldron behind me, preparing to swing it again, she recites the spell. Just as I feel the twinge in my chest, the cauldron reaches the apex of the swing and arches down. The pain swells around my heart, but I know I can't give into it and fight to stay on my feet.

"You pathetic man," she says as I drop the cauldron, unable to hold onto it any longer. "You think you can come into my house and defeat me? With that?"

I try to stay standing, but my vision is blurring from the pain and it drives me to my knees. Reena regains her feet and stands over me, her hand held out in front as she pushed down on me with her magic. I had to stop her, had to keep Debbie alive, but the force of the spell was too much.

"You will die now and then when you come back to life, you'll watch as I give your friend over there to Belphegor," she says madly. "You'll watch as the demon tortures her and eats her guts one by one!" She mutters another spell and with her other hand, shoots it toward me. My face slams into the hardwood floor and I am paralyzed.

"Hey, bitch," I hear Debbie yell.

I manage to turn just enough to see Debbie holding a broken chair leg like a bat. She swings for Reena's head, but the witch is too fast. She yells another spell and it lifts Debbie off her feet and pins her to the wall, helpless.

"You've got guts, girl. Too bad you weren't one of my own. I might have let you live—"

With her efforts now focused on Debbie, I struggle back to my feet and heft the cauldron back up. Using what remains of my strength, I charge forward, swinging. Reena turns just in time to catch a face full of cauldron.

The heavy cast iron pot weighs around twenty-five pounds and the force of my swing means it is traveling at considerable speed when it makes contact. The thin bones that form the structure of the human face could in no way stand up to that much force. Reena's face shatters and allows the pot to sink further into her skull, causing the thicker and heavier bones of the cranium to first split, then splinter. All of this, the heavy pot and all the bone fragments, are driven into Reena's brain. The gelatinous organ shreds under the onslaught and she crashes to the floor. I collapse beside her, breathing heavy and rubbing my chest, knowing she is already dead. Debbie slides down the wall and lands on her front with an audible, "*Oof!*"

"Are you insane," I gasp, trying to catch my breath as the last of the pain subsides.

She gets to her feet and grins a bit madly. "What? Who said you get to have all the fun?"

"Don't do that again, ever," I say as she helps me to my feet and we stare down at the dead Reena. "She won't stay dead for long," I mutter. Why can't they just be easy to kill? "I need to remove her head and heart."

Her face screws up a bit at that and she pats my shoulder. "I'll let you handle that part."

"You could at least find me a knife," I say through clenched teeth.

Debbie runs from the room in search of a knife and I fight to stay on my feet. I go to Reena and, grasping her hands, drag her away from the chair out onto the floor. Lifting the cauldron from her ruined face, I toss it aside and inspect the damage. Her entire face has been pushed into the back of her skull and without the bones to support the shape, her face splayed out until it looked three sizes too big. As I watch, some of the splintered bone moves, sliding back into the proper place. She will be healed soon.

"Anytime, Debbie," I yell. Just then, Alonso rushes into the room. He's carrying my Browning double barrel in one hand and the Navy cutlass in the other.

As he hurries toward me, he asks, "That's not Debbie is it?"

"No, she went to find a knife. You didn't see her as you came in?" He shakes his head no and I reach for the sword, saying, "I need that."

He hands the old sword to me and I raise it high. Hesitating only long enough to ensure my aim, I bring the heavy blade down onto the fragile neck of the witch. Unlike other times, her head does not roll away from her body and it takes two more cuts to insure that the two were properly separated. I grasp the dark red hair and fling it into the fireplace. Rushing to one of the bookcases that line one wall of the room, I pull a book at random and go back to the fireplace.

Ripping pages and crumpling them and pulling a long

match from the supply handily sitting on the mantle, I quickly build a fire and watch as the flames devour Reena's head. In truth, it brings me little satisfaction. I should feel more for all the pain she's caused, but all I can see in the middle of the flames was Lilith's head burning once again.

Turning to Alonso, I say, "That will have to do for now. Let's go find Debbie." Without another word, I turn for the double doors and Alonso falls in right beside me.

TWENTY-NINE

Going through the big double doors at full stride, I wonder where David is. I expected to see him shortly after Alonso came in, but as I look up and down the dimly lighted L-shaped corridor, I don't see him anywhere. Retracing my earlier steps, I hurry back the way Debbie and I had come from the basement. Searching the short leg of the L seems a waste of time, for that's the direction Alonso had so recently come from and he hadn't seen her.

Still moving fast, I ask Alonso, "Where's David?"

"Outside, that son of a bitch sheriff shot him," he snaps. I slide to a halt on the highly waxed floor and look at Alonso with my mouth hanging open. Alonso stops also and, seeing what I'm thinking from the look on my face, continues, "He's not dead. He took one of those pussy-ass nine millimeters to his left thigh. Didn't look like it hit anything important, he's just having trouble walking."

I start back down the hallway as I ask, "You left him outside?"

"Yeah, we got it bandaged up and he's watching the furry thing and the cop to make sure they don't get up again."

Makes sense, but I have to ask, "The werewolf?"

Alonso raises the cutlass and says, "I took care of him good. You'll have to do your thing, but he ain't getting back up." And to answer what he anticipates my next question to be, "Don't know if the sheriff was a monster or not and I didn't cut his head off, cause there ain't much of one left. David caught him up close with a full blast from his pump, right in the face."

Hmm, David seems to have a habit of shooting people in the face. Wonder if I need to talk to him about that...

I nod to him as we move toward the stairs leading down under the estate. There are no doorways off this section of hall and if Debbie had come this way, her only choice would have been straight ahead. I stop briefly at the top of the stairs, looking down into the even more dimly lit basement. I remember what is down there.

Alonso sees my hesitation and asked, "What is it?"

"There are at least two vampires down there. Debbie wouldn't have gone down these steps willingly." He doesn't look happy about my latest revelation, but I don't have time to deal with that, I need to find Debbie fast before the blood suckers have a chance to bite her.

From the top of the steps, I shout her name down into the basement three times, pausing after each to listen for a reply. I hear nothing and, looking at my friend, I shrug and start down the steps. Moving cautiously, I try to peer into the half-light for anything that might lie in wait for us. I make it two steps from the bottom when I hear a noise that freezes my blood. From somewhere far down the hall, I hear Debbie scream my name.

Without thought, I break into a run, forgetting that I don't have a weapon. I'd given the cutlass back to Alonso while I built the fire in the study and he's still carrying both my double barrel and the sword. As I've said in the past, Alonso is pretty agile for a guy weighing four hundred pounds and it really doesn't surprise me when I look over my shoulder and see him right behind me. I hold my hand out and ask for the sword and he passes it to me the same as a relay runner passing a baton.

Armed now, I put on a little more speed and yell, "Debbie, I'm coming! Let me know where you are!"

Closer this time, but still sounding as if it comes from the far end of this long corridor, I once again hear her call my name. Tapping the last of my reserves, I speed up even more and close the distance rapidly to where I think she is being held. As I draw closer to the end of the hall, I see her pushed against the gritty, concrete block wall. The filthy hand of a vampire is wrapped around her throat.

The vampire stand in front of her, its left arm extended out straight, pushing her against the wall and half-turned so it can watch my approach. I never slow, advancing at full speed, with a practice developed over years and years, I know the precise distance from which I need to strike. I bring the sword up and over my left shoulder. When I hit the imaginary mark in my mind, I let fly with a powerful backhand swing aimed at shoulder height, screaming, "Get your hand off of her, you bastard!"

The vampire sees what is about to happen and raises its other arm in a feeble attempt to ward off the blow. The honed blade slices through skin, muscle, and bone like a hot knife through butter. The arm and head of the vampire topple to the floor, the body remains standing for a second before it follows. I brake hard, trying to stop before colliding with the wall or Debbie and have to hop over the fallen body of the almost-dead vampire.

I come to a halt a half pace from where Debbie stands and we look each other in the eye for a second before she throws herself into my arms. Burying her face in my shoulder, she says, "I knew you'd find me." I hold her, softly stroking her hair, trying to calm her.

We stand like that for no more than a couple of seconds before a thunderous boom almost shatters my hearing. Debbie and I both look in time to see the second vampire flop, mangled, to the ground and begin to writhe in pain.

Alonso stands back from us a few feet, the double barrel Browning still leveled at the open doorway behind where I stand, twin columns of smoke curling from the barrels and says, "You're welcome!"

*****

"They were waiting in the corridor when I went to find a knife. When I came through the doors, they grabbed me. One put its hand over my mouth so I couldn't scream and dragged me down here. I guess they expected you'd come looking for me," Debbie explains to my question of what happened.

When I ask if they'd bitten her, she indicates no. *Thank God,* I think as I lead her back toward the steps. I'm not sure how I would've taken it if I'd gotten another woman killed, especially one that I'm developing feelings for.

I ask her if she saw any other vampires or if it was just the two and she answers back, "I only saw the two." I walk alongside her, my arm around her shoulders, holding her close as we ascend the stairs.

Back in the L-shaped corridor, we move toward the front door, bright sunlight, and fresh air. Alonso covers our backs with the shotgun and in no time, we step out of La Miseria di Bianco and onto the wide, stone front walk bordered on both sides by a rich carpet of green grass. David is leaning against a stone planter, his trusty Remington pump lying across his lap. I can see the blood-soaked bandage wrapped around his left thigh a few inches above the knee.

When I ask about the wound, he shrugs and says, "I've had worse."

We both laugh and I help Debbie sit beside him while I inspect the carnage they caused during the short, violent fire fight. Sheriff Richards lays face down in the grass, a few yards from the window that his bullet had shattered. Just as Alonso had described, most of the Sheriff's cranium is a red mist painted on the granite stones of the estate.

The hulking werewolf Otto lays not far from the door on his back, a pool of blood forming on the walkway where it leaked from the stump of his neck. The terrible head is a few feet away, eyes and mouth open, the sharp teeth bared in a final snarl. I told him a reunion with his dead brother was imminent. He should've listened.

I go back to David and see that Debbie has begun to reassess his injury and bandage it a little better. She'd retrieved a first aid kit from the trunk of the Sheriff's car and David grits his teeth as she works on his leg. I look around for Alonso and find him sitting on a stone bench, on the opposite side of the entryway from where the bodies lay. He looks deep in thought and I hate to disturb him, but we still have work to do.

I come up and sit beside him on the cold marble. "Whatcha thinking about?"

"I was wondering where that little witch got off too," he answers. A very good question, I had been so busy, I'd forgotten all about her. Reena's last living child and a vicious little bitch in her own right.

"Hopefully, she's around here somewhere," I say.

"Come on, we have to search everything and finish the cleansing. Debbie's doctoring David and I need your help."

He stands without speaking and follows along behind me as I turn back for the front door. I go to David and ask for his shotgun, which he reluctantly turns over after I tell him Alonso and I are going to finish clearing the property. Debbie asks me to wait a moment and comes back with another Remington 870 riot gun from the Sheriff's cruiser. When I realize she means to accompany us, I tell her I want her to stay with David. He can't move and I don't want anyone alone until we are positive all the unnaturals on the estate have been dealt with. I can tell she isn't pleased with the assignment, but she relents, which is the sign of a true professional. Professionals do everything to the best of their ability, even the jobs they don't like.

She does surprise me, though. As I turn and prepare to enter the house once again, she leans up and kisses me on the cheek, lingering for just a second and whispers, "Be careful."

A goofy grin spreads across my face and promise I will.

Alonso had already gone inside and as I pass through the door, I hear him say, "Here he goes again."

I point out to him that there are several spots on my anatomy he can kiss if he wishes, all of them were much further south than where Debbie kissed me, of course. I hear David laugh out on the walkway as we move deeper into La Miseria di Bianco, hunting the last of the unnaturals. One item in particular tops my list of must-find items is the jar containing the remainder of my blood. I want it back.

I suggest to Alonso that we start in the basement and clear upward, one floor at a time. He agrees and we jog back down the stairs at the end of the long corridor. At the bottom of the steps, we immediately began clearing rooms by pushing the door open and moving inside fast, me to the right, him to the left.

If the room is empty, we move back into the hall and hit the next door. We flow down the hallway, searching one room at a time. One advantage we have this time that we've not had before is light. I find the switch that controls the overhead lights and turn it on. Now we can see and, if a vampire happens to be hiding in one of the rooms, his nocturnal eyes will leave him at a disadvantage.

*****

It takes nearly four hours to thoroughly search the mansion and its outbuildings. During all that time, we never find another creature, living or dead, anywhere on the property. Reena's daughter isn't there and we have no idea where she might be or how to go about looking for her. I don't even know her name. It's a question I meant to ask, but circumstances didn't allow it.

After finishing the search, Alonso and I go back to the main house and carry out the final cleansing tasks. Except for Reena and Sheriff Richards, I anoint each head with holy oil and carry them to the fire place in the big study where I burn them to ash. The bodies we carry to a small outbuilding about a hundred yards behind the main house and pile them inside.

The building appears to have been built as a garden shed and had been constructed of all wood. With the help of five gallons of diesel fuel taken from the shed holding the lawn tractor, the garden shed makes a nice crematorium. I know the bodies won't be completely consumed, but they will be reduced down to the point where positive identification of the unnatural characteristics of the werewolf and the two vampires will be hidden. Anything odd will be blamed on fire damage and the investigators that will surely descend on La Miseria di Bianco won't have cause to be asking about the bodies of weird creatures.

I do make one fascinating discovery. Reena's casting room in the basement contains an assortment of witch-related artifacts. A great find is a book of spells and incantations written in both the ancient language of the witches and modern English. I keep the book in hopes that it might serve to teach me the language and help me more readily identify what a spell is designed to do when I see them in the future. And I find my jar of blood.

She had it sitting on a shelf, in a place of prominence and it even had a label, *White's Blood*. It goes into the fireplace and is destroyed with the heads. The rest of the items in the casting room are either destroyed, if they present an immediate danger or left alone, if they don't. That room, of course, would cause a lot of questions from the investigators I mentioned, but I figure it will be put down as satanic or as some crackpot, rich bitch playing with witchcraft.

We spend a long time wiping down any surface that we might have touched. I don't want Debbie's, David's, or Alonso's prints to be found anywhere in the place. Mine have never been taken, so I don't worry about it since they will have nothing to match them to. Debbie points out that we probably left DNA in several areas. I agree, but there isn't much we can do about it. The nearly all stone construction of the house makes it unsuitable to burn down and that would be the only sure way of destroying any evidence of our presence.

It had been dark several hours by the time we are completely finished with the cleansing and David still isn't in any shape to hike back to Debbie's SUV. She decides to jog back to it and then bring it onto the estate grounds to pick up David. Alonso volunteers to stay with David, looking at me with a sly grin, so I go with Debbie to retrieve the truck

On the jog to her vehicle, I decide to ask about the kiss. She smiles and says, "I knew you were working up the courage to ask me out and with all that seems to happen to you, I figured I'd better let you know I was okay with it, sooner rather than later. Who knows, you might get yourself killed again before you could ask me out."

I reach out and pull her to a stop, "Well, at least you know I always come back for more." I slide my hand up into her hair and lean in for a more thorough kiss for the both of us. When we finally break apart, she grins and suggests that I stay the night at her place, just in case she has nightmares from today. She winks then continues jogging toward the truck, leaving me giddy as a school boy… and praying to God she isn't a damn witch, too.

*****

It's been two weeks since the ordeal at La Miseria di Bianco and the death of Reena. In that time and as I predicted, the entire state has been spell bound by the happenings in Gordon County. It even made it onto the national news and several law enforcement agencies are involved with the investigation. I think Homeland Security even tried to get a little piece of it. The FBI had definitely made their presence known and were quickly told, "Thank you, but no thank you," by the Georgia Bureau of Investigation. GBI has now taken the lead in the task of trying to unravel what the hell happened in Gordon County.

Debbie went back to work at the DEA Task Force and immediately asked to be reassigned to the Homicide Division of GBI. Her request was approved, she was due anyway, and she is now one of the investigators assigned to the case trying to determine who's responsible for killing the sheriff and a prominent woman in the county, along with three unidentified males believed to be workers on the estate. For her part, she's spending time investigating a possible tie in between the prominent woman, Mrs. Reena Pannier, the Chief Executive of Pannier Bakeries, home office in Atlanta and matriarch of the Pannier Family and anything illegal that might have been going on with the Gordon County Sheriff's Office.

So far, all of the other Pannier family members have been unavailable for comment to the press or to answer questions by law enforcement. I'm sure the little witch will turn up eventually and the fact that she'll be a pain in my ass is a foregone conclusion, but I'll worry about that when the time comes.

Right now, I'm enjoying a new lease on life. I feel like a giant weight has been lifted from my shoulders by the death of Reena. I know she won't be sitting in the background waiting to screw with my life any longer.

David went back to work after Alonso hooked him up with a doctor friend of his. A little minor surgery on the down low and a bottle of Percocet and David was able to play off the gun shot as a bicycling accident that would keep him on crutches for a couple of weeks. His boss bought it and David is sitting in the office doing paperwork for the other detectives until he comes off of light duty and can go back on the street. Thankfully, the bullet didn't hit anything, but meat. A neat through and through that required a few stitches and nothing else. Alonso and he are actually friends now and get together to enjoy barbeque a couple times a week.

Alonso's back at the morgue with only minor problems. I think they wanted to fire him for his unexplained absence, but I guess it's hard to find people willing to work all night, by themselves, in a building full of dead people. So, at least for now, I still have my friend ready to help if I should come in as a paying customer.

Debbie and I are seeing each other and it's great. I don't have to worry about trying to hide what I am or what I do. I think we have a great shot at a real relationship and I'm excited. And, for the record, she is not a witch. She about slapped me when I asked before she tackled me back to the bed. As a matter of fact, I'm on my way to meet her at her at my favorite coffee place now. Turns out she's a coffee snob also. I have to park a couple of blocks away and I'm strolling down the sidewalk feeling fantastic.

As I turn the corner onto the street where I'm supposed to meet Debbie, I'm suddenly confronted by an individual that I'm not at all surprised to see. Standing in the middle of the sidewalk, obviously expecting me, is my little demented Christmas elf. She's dressed identical to the way she was the last time I saw her, right down to the large butcher knife in her right hand. The only difference is she isn't holding what's left of my landlady in her other.

The maniacal grin on her face tells me she has a plan to fix that, though.

Before I can even begin to respond to the threat, she takes half a step forward and drives the knife to the hilt into my chest. I feel my ribs crack and separate from the force of the blow. As the point of the blade punctures my heart, I feel the organ stutter and then seize up from the damage.

My eyesight fades as if a black veil is lowered over my face and my knees buckle, I grimace to myself and mutter, "Here we go again…"

ABOUT THE AUTHOR

Stephen Woods is from Scottsville, KY. He graduated from Allen County Scottsville High in 1979 and went to Marine Corps boot camp at Parris Island, South Carolina shortly after graduation. He reached the rank of Sergeant, then transferred to the US Army in 1987, volunteering for Special Forces in 1988.

He served with the 5th Special Forces Group at Ft. Campbell, Kentucky until he retired from the Army in 1995. Stephen became a police officer with the Scottsville Police Dept. in 1995 and transferred to the Allen County Sheriff's Department in 1999. Promoted to Detective in 2000, he served in general investigations and as a member of the Allen County Drug Task Force and the Kentucky State Police Drug Task Force. In 2008, Stephen began working as an advisor to the US Military in both Afghanistan and Iraq.

An avid zombie fan, *We Go On* is his first book, which can be found on Amazon.

FOLLOW STEPHEN ON SOCIAL MEDIA
Facebook: www.facebook.com/TheDell.Zombies
Twitter: www.twitter.com/TheDellZombies

www.ingramcontent.com/pod-product-compliance
Lightning Source LLC
Chambersburg PA
CBHW072225190626
46809CB00017B/552